CHARITY CASE

What Reviewers Say About
Jean Copeland's Work

Poison Pen

"Such an exciting story with a lot of relatable moments for authors in this genre and reviewers alike. I couldn't help but chuckle at the premise of the story and just knew it was going to be exciting and filled with such scandal. …A very eye-opening read and emotional romance with lots of moral lessons explored and to learn from."—*LESBIreviewed*

Spellbound—*Co-authored with Jackie D*

"The story is a mixture of history and present day, fantasy and real life, and is really well done. I especially liked the biting humor that pops up occasionally. The characters are vibrant and likable (except the bad guys who are really nasty). There is a good deal of angst with both romances, but a lot of 'aww' moments as well."
—*Rainbow Reflections*

"*Spellbound* is a very exciting read, fast-paced, thrilling, funny too. …The authors mix politics and the fight against patriarchy with time travel and witch fights with brilliant results."—*Jude in the Stars*

"[T]he themes and contextual events in this book were very poignant in relation to the current political climate in the United States. The fashion in which existing prejudices related to race, socioeconomic status, and gender were manipulated to cause discord were staggering, but also a reflection of the current state of things here in the USA. I really enjoyed this aspect of the book and I am so glad that I read it when I did."—*Mermaid Reviews*

The Ashford Place

"[A] charming story that I can recommend to anyone who likes a well-written mystery with a good dose of romance."
—*Rainbow Reflections*

"Another enjoyable story from Jean Copeland with a bit of a difference. I think this book is definitely one to enjoy with a glass of wine near the warm fire."—*Les Rêveur*

The Revelation of Beatrice Darby

"*The Revelation of Beatrice Darby* at its epicentre is a story…of discovering oneself and learning to not only live with it but to also love it. This book is definitely worth a read."—*Lesbian Review*

"Debut author Jean Copeland has come out with a novel that is abnormally superb. The pace whirls like a hula-hoop; the plot is as textured as the fabric in a touch-and-feel board book. And, with more dimension than a stereoscopic flick, the girls in 3-D incite much pulp friction as they defy the torrid, florid, horrid outcomes to which they were formerly fated."—*Curve*

"This story of Bea and her struggle to accept her homosexuality and find a place in the world is absolutely wonderful. …Bea was such an interesting character and her life was that of many gay people of the time—hiding, shame, rejection. In the end though it was uplifting and an amazing first novel for Jean Copeland."
—*Inked Rainbow Reads*

One Woman's Treasure

"Copeland seems to have found her writing groove and it makes me excited to see what she will write next."—*LezReview Books*

"*One Woman's Treasure* is a very aptly named book and not a light reading. It is about pursuing what you love in life, and I highly recommend this romance."—*Hsinju's Lit Log*

The Second Wave

"This is a must-read for anyone who enjoys romances and for those who like stories with a bit of a nostalgic or historic theme."
—*Lesbian Review*

"Copeland shines a light on characters rarely depicted in romance, or in pop culture in general."—*The Lesbrary*

"The characters felt so real and I just couldn't stop reading. This is one of those books that will stay with me a long time."
—*2017 Rainbow Awards Honorable Mention*

Summer Fling

"The love story between Kate and Jordan was one they make movies about, it was complex but you knew from the beginning these women had found their soul mates in each other."
—*Les Rêveur*

"Copeland shines a light on characters rarely depicted in romance, or in pop culture in general. *The Second Wave* is a sweet story that's worthy of your time."—*The Lesbrary*

Visit us at www.boldstrokesbooks.com

By the Author

The Revelation of Beatrice Darby

The Second Wave

Summer Fling

The Ashford Place

One Woman's Treasure

Poison Pen

Pantheon Girls

Charity Case

Co-authored:

Spellbound

Swift Vengeance

CHARITY CASE

by

Jean Copeland

2025

CHARITY CASE

ISBN 13: 978-1-63679-593-5

This Trade Paperback Original Is Published By
Bold Strokes Books, Inc.
P.O. Box 249
Valley Falls, NY 12185

First Edition: June 2025

Credits
Editor: Shelley Thrasher
Production Design: Susan Ramundo
Cover Design By Tammy Seidick

Acknowledgments

Endless thank yous to the readers, my friends and family, Sandy and Rad and the whole Bold Strokes Books crew for your support and enthusiasm over the last ten novels! It's been an amazing ride!

In Loving Memory of Susan Gilman
1965–2024

CHAPTER ONE

As Lindsay Chase emerged from the airport terminal, Connecticut's unpredictable April weather slapped her with its raw, blustery palm. A rude welcome home after twenty plus years in Southern California. She stood on her toes, checking the line of vehicles for her brother Kyle's pickup, then sat on the largest of her suitcases. Tanned faces of parents and children returning home from a school vacation spent at a beach or amusement park flashed by her in various shades of tired and disappointed. Lindsay related, but on such a different level. With a sigh, she dropped her head into her hands, trying to mentally prepare for what lay ahead.

This sucked. Her former life of free-wheeling self-indulgence had drawn to a dramatic close, and like it or not, she was going to have to do a major reset. She'd dwelled in the darkness of rock bottom since her arrest, but now that she was back in Connecticut, it was time to climb out into the light. The bright side of a blank slate was that she could create any future she could imagine from scratch—as long as she could keep her demons at bay.

Finally, the Chase Landscaping and Design pickup rolled up. Was it too late to run back into the terminal and fly home to LA?

"The prodigal daughter returns," Kyle said as he hopped out and hugged her.

After absorbing the warmth of his embrace, she gave him a fierce eye roll. "All hail the queen," she said as he helped her toss her bags in the back.

"Where to, Sis?" he said as he drove out of the terminal. "The Four Seasons or your probation officer?"

Lindsay studied his profile. "I'm not sure what's happening here, but this level of snark at my lowest moment is a bit harsh even for you. Not exactly a sign of personal growth."

"Come on. I'm entitled to a couple of zingers after all the crap I've gone through with you and your shit."

"A gambling addiction is a disease, not some *shit* I decided to dump on everyone for kicks. And trust me. I'll be dealing with the consequences of it for a long time."

"Interesting that you chose to rehab in the state with two of the biggest, best casinos in the free world."

"Where should I have gone? To stay with Mom and Ernie in their retirement double-wide in South Carolina? I don't think so. My family is here."

"The offer to stay with us is still good. You really don't need to stay with Dad."

"Hmm. Two cranky kids under four or one cranky man in his early seventies? I prefer my odds with Dad."

"We'll see how long you can stand the musty furniture smell and war documentaries on max volume every night."

Lindsay shifted in her seat. "You know what? He can't wait to see me in spite of my temporary setback. He's gonna be delighted to have me around, and that kind of unconditional acceptance is exactly what I need right now during my retooling phase."

"Hey, I'm happy to see you, too," he said.

"Thank you. A little sincerity goes a long way."

"Anyway, how does one retool their life when one has lost it all and is on probation?"

"Maybe start by avoiding sarcastic younger siblings until one is mentally and financially fit to be on their feet again."

Kyle laughed. "You know I'm just messing with you. This is what we do." He leaned over and elbowed her in the meat of her upper arm. "You're still my favorite person in the whole world. But please don't tell my wife and children that."

"I'm totally adding it to the vault of blackmail I have saved up on you."

"Seriously, though. I am happy you're back, despite the circumstances. Gretchen and I are here for you, whatever you need."

"Oh, Kyle, you've already done more than I can repay you for. Like literally financially repay."

He turned to her with an arched eyebrow. "You are gonna try though, right?"

Lindsay giggled at his retort, and suddenly the tension in the truck dissipated. "You know I'm good for it. But man, did you have to hire me the most expensive attorney in New Haven?"

"Blair Maddox is the best defense lawyer around. She negotiated the transference of your probation, didn't she? I mean grand larceny, and you were still able to leave California to serve it out in Connecticut. That kind of legal wheeling and dealing doesn't come cheap. And besides, I think she plays for your team."

"Oh, well, if she plays for my team, then let me just throw more money at her." She let her head fall against the headrest with a sigh. "I really fucked up my life…like to a cataclysmic level."

"Well, you never did do anything halfway."

After another giggle, Lindsay patted Kyle's knee, so glad to have him by her side again. "Just take me to my musty quarters. I need a nap."

"Then I'll let you borrow my noise-cancelling headphones."

Despite so much still to say, they sat in silence for much of the ride home from the airport. Lindsay rested her head against the passenger window, watching the budding trees lining the highway whip by in a blur. She was completely spent and appreciated that Kyle seemed to sense her fragile state.

Tomorrow could be the first day of the rest of her new life.

❖

Ellie Tuttle stood outside the courtroom with her client, Lola Middleton, a trans exotic dancer, who might or might not have followed Ellie's imperative to appear in court sober. At least she'd remembered to wear the pressed blazer she'd given her yesterday.

"Ms. Middleton, did you have anything for breakfast this morning?"

The young woman stood still for a moment, then nodded. "Something with berries. Or meatballs. I don't really remember."

"It's okay. I don't think full sobriety is necessary at this stage in the proceedings anyway." Ellie forced a smile, but inside she was worried about her client. She needed help and compassion, but she would probably get thirty days in jail with little to no medical care for her withdrawal from alcohol.

She offered her a paper cup of water. "You better drink this. Your PD needs you coherent while we're before the judge. Speaking of your attorney," she mumbled to herself, "where the hell is he?"

Lola drank all the water. "Don't worry, Miss Tuttle. I won't let you down." She offered Ellie her jack-o'-lantern grin.

As Ellie scanned the hallway for the public defender and his wrinkled suit, she spotted a gorgeous blonde walking closely beside attorney Blair Maddox, the chic white-collar criminal lawyer whose record was as flawless as her fashion sense. She was sporting her game face before court was even in session. Whoever her hot client was, she surely would receive tailor-made justice.

The two of them walked past her and Lola, neither giving them even a first glance. Naturally. But Ellie couldn't stop staring at the duo. With their sizzling synergy, they'd make a striking couple if they were anywhere but in a courthouse. As she attempted to adjust the ill-fitting blazer around Lola's bony shoulders, she stared at the blonde. Not only was she beautiful, but she also looked rather familiar.

Before she could figure out from where she might have known her, they moved on to a different section of the court. She sneered. It must be nice to be able to afford the best lawyer in Connecticut and saunter down the halls of justice radiating carefree confidence.

When Lola's case was finally called, Ellie rubbed her clammy hands together, ready to do her best to support her client.

The public defender shuffled his papers as he spoke. "Your Honor, I'd like to call a character witness for Ms. Middleton—Ellie Tuttle from the Department of Social Services."

Ellie stepped up into the witness box.

"Ms. Tuttle, how long have you been Ms. Middleton's case worker?"

"About seven months, but I've known her since she was in the foster-care system. During that time I've tried numerous times to get her to—"

"Objection, your Honor," the prosecutor said robotically.

The judge lowered his glasses at her. "Ms. Tuttle, you've been in my courtroom before, and you know well enough that you need only answer the questions that have been asked."

"I'm sorry, your Honor. I just want to help—" Ellie saw the public defender's glare.

"Ms. Tuttle," the public defender said. "In the time you've been acquainted with Lola Middleton, have you known her to be a violent woman?"

"Absolutely not," Ellie said. "If she hit someone in the mouth with a stiletto, I'm sure it was entirely in self-defense."

"Objection. Conjecture."

Ellie looked at the judge and conveyed her expertly contrived contrition.

"Sustained," said the judge. "Ms. Tuttle. These are yes-or-no questions. If I have to admonish you about editorializing again, I will cite you."

"I'm sorry, your Honor." Ellie looked down at her bouncing knees rattling the entire witness box.

"Your Honor," the public defender said. "My client has no documented history of violence or unstable behavior other than what she's been accused of during this incident. The alleged victim, on the other hand, is quite familiar to this court. There are no other witnesses other than the defendant and the alleged victim. Therefore, I move for a dismissal."

"Quite succinct. I like that." The judge looked at the prosecutor. "Mr. Charlton, where is the alleged victim?"

"I, uh, was just notified that he was seen boarding a Greyhound bus this morning."

"Vacation?" the judge asked.

The prosecutor lowered his head. "I don't think so, your Honor."

"I'm going to dismiss this case due to lack of evidence and on the condition that I never see your face in here again, Ms. Middleton. Is that clear?"

Lola perked up. "Oh, hell yes."

Ellie smiled and clapped lightly.

Outside, on the steps of the courthouse, she tugged Lola's sleeve before she could wander off. "Lola, can I give you a ride back to the shelter?"

"No, thank you, Miss Ellie. I'm gonna appreciate my freedom on this beautiful day and walk." She turned her head toward the corner intersecting the street where her favorite dive bar was located.

Ellie forced a smile. "Okay. If you ever decide you want to try out a meeting at the church again, I'll gladly accompany you."

"You do enough for me, Miss. I wouldn't ask you to put yourself out like that."

"It wouldn't be an imposition. I love free doughnuts and coffee."

Lola offered a gravelly laugh that mixed with a cough. "You're a class act, Miss Ellie. God bless you."

Ellie watched Lola saunter off toward her own undoing and scolded herself to stop thinking about all the things she wished she could do to help her.

CHAPTER TWO

After appearing in court, Lindsay and her attorney, Blair Maddox, moseyed over to a trendy cocktail lounge a mere block away from the courthouse. Surrounded by an array of business suits of muted colors, they sat at a sunny corner of the bar on velvet-lined swivel stools and assessed each other on a personal level. Lindsay watched her attorney sip expensive red wine from a fat, round glass. She was sexy in a domineering sort of way. The tailored suits, slicked-back hair, and direct way of speaking made Lindsay want to melt into her capable hands. Kyle's earlier speculation about Blair's "team" affiliation was all but affirmed, and if the evening ended the way Lindsay hoped, she'd be melting into Blair Maddox by sunset.

"Today's proceedings went well." Blair smiled as she swirled the wine around in the glass.

"What a relief that part is over," Lindsay replied. "Now I can truly focus on moving forward and getting my shit together."

Blair cocked her head slightly and tossed a few pieces of Asian snack mix into her mouth. "That's indeed a cause for celebration."

"Do you always celebrate a win for your clients like this?"

Blair grinned as she casually glanced around the bar area. "Of course not. I'd be out buying cocktails every other day."

Lindsay assumed a strategic pose, so into this unexpected, flirty side of Blair. "That must mean I'm special."

Blair slowly turned her head toward Lindsay and favored her with a riveting gaze. "All my clients are special. But you're special and incredibly good-looking."

Lindsay sucked at her lip. "Is this a billable hour?"

Blair replied with a slight giggle. "I never mix business with pleasure. But our next office appointment will be. We have thirty days to get you into a treatment plan for the gambling and arrange your community-service hours."

Ugh. Perfect way to extinguish a round of promising flirtation. "I don't need a gambling treatment plan. I'll go to a few of those Gamblers Anonymous meetings to make everyone happy, but the stipulation in my probation is motivation enough. Gamble again, go to jail. It's pretty simple."

"It's anything but. You should get into therapy and ferret out the root cause of your addiction. The effects of punitive consequences usually last only as long as the punishment."

Lindsay smirked. "Oh yeah. The mystery trauma that caused my pathological need to use success for validation." She punctuated the statement with a click of her tongue and the okay sign.

"Don't laugh. It was a mitigating circumstance that allowed the judge to go easy on you. That and this being your first offense."

"Great. Who's gonna pay for a shrink? I'm unemployed, and I've used the last of my 401K to repay my brother for you."

Blair grinned and tapped Lindsay's forearm. "By the way, dinner's on me tonight."

"Thanks. Otherwise, I'd have to go find a game of dice in an alley somewhere to cover my half."

"That's exactly the kind of joke you shouldn't be making."

"Come on. It really was a joke. Look. I know what I need to do going forward. I get how badly I screwed up. I'm gonna be paying for it long after my probation ends. But we don't have to talk about all this tonight, do we? Tonight is for celebrating." Lindsay flashed a smile that had yet to fail her.

"Jesus, you're charming," Blair said. "Are you sure you don't have a woman waiting for you back in LA?"

"Not that I'm aware of." Lindsay thought briefly of her ex, Marcella Hughes, and the less-than-subtle innuendo that accompanied her "gift" of restitution money. "Anyway, I'm back in Connecticut to stay. That's all that matters now."

"At least until you fulfill your legal obligations."

Lindsay shrugged. "I'm a take-things-as-they-come kinda woman, but too many temptations are waiting for me back in WeHo."

"West Hollywood isn't the only locale where temptation resides." The hungry look in Blair's eyes clearly indicated she was off the clock. "I'm looking forward to seeing where this night takes us."

Lindsay leaned back in her chair to savor the titillating moment. All indeed had not been lost. At least her ability to win over any woman of her choosing was as robust as ever.

❖

The next morning, Ellie returned to the shelter to commiserate with the director, Rosa Ortiz, a tough yet tender social-services veteran who had been Ellie's mentor since she began her work with the young, unhoused citizens of New Haven many years ago. And whose hugs were epic, bar none.

She plopped down in the chair at the desk beside Rosa's that she occasionally used in Rosa's tiny office.

Rosa lifted her head from a pile of paperwork. "Hey, mama. Why do you look like that? You saved your client from the slammer yesterday, didn't you?"

"I did, but I couldn't convince her to come back with me so I can get her into treatment. What's the point of saving people from jail time if I can't talk them into a program that might turn their lives around?"

"Come on, Ell. You've been doing this long enough to know how it goes. You helped her have a successful defense, and now she's free. Take the win."

"Free to do what? Drink herself to death? Fall victim to street violence?" She leaned back in the rickety chair. "Ugh. I wish I could just turn off my feelings when the clients walk away."

Rosa chuckled. "I wish you could, too, for your own sake. But we know that'll never happen. Here's an idea. Try to focus on any of the other cases screaming for your attention. You've helped set so many on the path to a better life."

Ellie nodded. Rosa was right, but she had also lost a few along the way, and they were the ones who haunted her. She just didn't want Lola to become the next name added to her loss column. She expelled the thought with a sigh. "How are things here? Have you heard about the grant yet?"

"Not yet, but I know we'll get it. The problem, as usual, is it won't be enough."

"You really think they're gonna close Hope House down?"

She shrugged. "Operating costs are through the roof, and the grant funds just don't keep up with them. Worst-case scenario, they move us into the city shelter uptown."

"No! Rosa, most of my clients are from this district." Ellie sprang up and paced the cramped office.

"You'll move. Most of them will follow you."

"But they're from this neighborhood. This is where they're comfortable."

"You don't say? It's a never-ending story. We do the best we can…"

"With what we have. I know, I know." Ellie caught herself, not wanting to take her frustration out on Rosa. "Can't we do anything about it? Have a fund-raiser? Anything? God. I just hate sitting around waiting for the ax to fall."

"Can you please sit down?" Rosa asked in calm tone as she indicated the chair by her desk. "Look. You know we're at the mercy of the state. We always do fund-raiser events, but they barely raise enough money to supplement the grant. We're just not sexy enough to score ourselves an endowment from a wealthy, dying widow."

"Speak for yourself." Ellie jumped up again and playfully flung back her wavy brown hair.

"Seriously, though, if we can get more volunteers, that would help lower our bottom line."

Ellie rubbed her chin with two fingers. "Maybe if we threw in a few puppies, we could wrangle up more enthusiasm."

"Now you're thinking like someone dedicated to their work in social services."

Ellie grabbed a few files from the desk and headed toward the door. "Well, I'll keep my ear to the ground."

"Be careful. You can catch hepatitis that way."

She stopped in the doorway and glared at her. "You're hilarious, Ro."

"A sense of humor is the only way to survive this job. You should look into getting one."

"Ooh. Sick burn." She grinned with a nod of approval and headed out.

By early afternoon she'd decided to grab a salad and take a break outside in the beautiful weather on the New Haven green. As she watched the eclectic flow of people pass, she wondered if her increasingly dour mood would ever lift.

Since she'd begun college, she couldn't imagine herself being anything but a social worker. She'd thrived on the philosophy of working to help people find the tools to lift themselves up when they were at their lowest, but lately she hadn't had much return on her emotional investment. Ellie had witnessed plenty of raising up, but far too much cascading back down for her to feel like she was truly making a difference.

Maybe a career change was the answer. Or pursuing more outside interests, so she wouldn't be so hyper-focused on saving the world. She glanced at a young couple strolling by drinking bubble tea. A relationship would be nice. She hadn't had anything significant since right after college. Wouldn't it be lovely to meet a down-to-earth, professional woman who liked hiking or pickle ball or dinners at restaurants along the shore? A woman who would introduce her to new and exciting things, someone with whom to share her good days and bad, and help her stay grounded when her worries threatened to sweep her away.

Yes, that all sounded wonderful, but in the meantime, she had more clients to attend to this afternoon.

❖

The morning after her night at Blair's lavish beachfront home, reality hit Lindsay like a rogue wave. Here she was doing the walk of shame out of her lawyer's house and having to concern herself with things like probation, community service, and eventually finding a job again. At forty-one. Even when her record was expunged, as per the plea agreement, who would ever trust her as a financial planner again? Her name in Los Angeles was dead for sure.

She breathed in the briny air and watched a heron take flight from the marsh as she stood beside her father's aged car. For the first time since her arrest for embezzlement, she felt completely lost, like space junk stuck floating in an aimless orbit. She was beginning to understand why so many addicts relapsed. Obviously, it must happen when they were overcome by the bleak reality of being responsible for rebuilding their entire world. And not having a clue where to begin.

She headed home to her dad's senior-housing complex for a shower and a cup of coffee. To her surprise he was sitting at the kitchen table when she came out from the bathroom in her fluffy robe.

"Oh, hi. I thought you were working the morning shift." She grabbed a mug and carried the coffee pot to the table.

"That's tomorrow," he said. "You and I have been ships passing in the night since you got back."

Lindsay looked away in embarrassment, the kind that had made her a ship intentionally steering away from him. "Well, you know. I've had some matters to take care of upon my return."

"Yes," he said as he glanced out the window. "How are those matters? Are you all set?"

She nodded, starting to feel suffocated from the tension.

As if feeling it too, he kept his gaze toward the window. "If, uh, if you need any help with anything, let me know. I have some money saved…" His voice grew softer as it trailed off.

"Thanks." She sipped her coffee and tried to force out the words at the edge of her lips. Why was it so hard to open up to him? He was her father, and they'd managed a reasonably healthy relationship while she was growing up. If anyone, he was the person she should feel safe being vulnerable with. "That's, um, that's nice of you to offer."

"I mean it." After he cleared his throat, he turned to her and sounded more certain. "You could've gone down to stay with your mother, but you came here. I'm glad."

"Dad. I'm an out lesbian with a fairly decent amount of self-respect. I'd rather stay under a bridge than with Mom and her redneck husband in rebel country."

Her father chuckled. "Eh. Ernie's not that bad. If he can handle your mother's tantrums without shipping her back up here, then he's okay in my book."

Lindsay conjured a wicked grin. "She's so much easier to love from a different state."

"It's done wonders for our relationship."

She raised her coffee mug to his, and they shared a moment before her conscience gave her back her voice. "Dad…I'm sorry."

"What for? Moving so far away for so long?"

Lindsay recoiled a bit. That wasn't even remotely close to what she was apologizing for. She hadn't known that was still an issue, but the slight tone of indictment in the question stated it loud and clear. "No, Dad. For screwing up so bad. I'm a compulsive gambler. I let a bad habit get a grip on me, and I destroyed everything that was good in my life."

He shrugged. "It happens."

Lindsay frowned at his unusual response. "Yeah, well, I never thought it would happen to me. Aren't you ashamed of me? Of what I've done?"

He scratched at his forehead, seeming to want to downplay the severity of her situation. "I'm glad you're safe. A lot of addicts don't fare so well. And I'm proud you're doing something about it now."

"It was either that or do jail time, so…"

"Look. You're here, and you're gonna get your life back. That's why you came home, isn't it?" He added a few pats to the top of her hand for emphasis.

After a sip of warm coffee, she smiled, slightly reassured. "It's good to be home."

❖

With the pressure on to start taking measurable steps toward redemption, Lindsay knew of only one person she could lean on. She rolled up at Kyle's house one evening as he was hosing the soap off his landscaping pickup in the driveway.

He stopped spraying as she parked in front of the mailbox. "Hey." He smiled and twirled the hose around as she approached. "How's life at Dad's bachelor pad?"

"If you love me, you'll wrap that hose around my neck and pull it as tight as you can."

"It can't be that bad. We joke about him, but Dad's a mellow dude."

"It's not him," she said as she got out of the car. "It's my entire life. I feel like I'm sixteen again…no job, driving my father's jalopy, depending on everyone else for everything. You can't imagine what it's like to lose one's autonomy."

He raised an eyebrow. "I also can't imagine the fun of underground poker games with celebrities in West Hollywood."

Lindsay smiled in fond recollection. "Ah. Those were legendary. That Sarah Paulson is such a peach. Not the sharpest player in the bunch, but watch out for Holland Taylor. She's a shark."

He blinked several times before responding. "What can I do for you, Linds?"

"What do you think?" she asked curtly. "I need a loan."

"For what?" He didn't even try to hide his suspicion.

"To buy a car, Kyle. I have to start community service soon, so I'll need reliable transportation."

"Where are you going to do it?"

"I have no idea. I think my lawyer is going to set it up."

"Go inside and see Gretchen. Her friend, Ellie, is over. She's a social worker. Maybe she can hook you up with some volunteer work."

"Social worker?" Lindsay grimaced. "Don't they work with the homeless and the downtrodden?"

"Yeah." He nodded profusely. "A perfect match since you, yourself, are homeless and downtrodden."

"There is no way in hell I'm gonna do that kind of volunteering." She shivered in the warm air. "Ick."

"Then just go inside and say hi to Gretchen and the kids. I'm rapidly losing compassion for you out here."

Lindsay followed the stone sidewalk up to the front door, mumbling to herself. "That'll be the day I spend three hundred hours of my life working with the dregs of society."

"Lindsay." Her sister-in-law squealed as she rushed her from the massive island counter in the kitchen. "It's so good to see you."

"Same here, Gretch," Lindsay said, rubbing her neck where Gretchen had latched on. "You've never looked better."

As they spoke, Lindsay couldn't help staring at the woman sitting quietly at the counter with what looked like a large cup of iced coffee in front of her. What was her name? Erin? Ellen?

"Lindsay, this is my very dear friend, Ellie Tuttle."

"Nice to meet you, Ellie." Lindsay extended her hand.

"Nice meeting you, too." Her reply was aloof in that way that suggested a whiff of rudeness. Or crippling shyness. It could've gone either way.

But she was adorable. Her dark, shaggy hair framed her blue eyes like artwork, and even with her being so hard to read, an allure emanated from her. When she did finally offer a smile, Lindsay was taken aback. Her aura suddenly filled the room.

"I understand you're in social work," Lindsay said. "What an honorable profession." She felt her mouth curling upward. Her effusive charm blossomed without warning whenever she was around a beautiful woman.

"Thanks," Ellie said. "Most days it feels like shoveling shit against the tide, but I couldn't imagine doing anything else for a living."

"She's being modest," Gretchen said. "Yes, I may be biased because she's my bestie and former co-worker, but I've never met a more caring, giving soul in my life."

Lindsay adjusted her posture and picked a speck of lint from her shirt. "I'm gearing up to do some serious giving myself."

Ellie perked up. "Oh. Do you like to do volunteer work?"

Gretchen and Lindsay exchanged looks.

"Uh, sure, sure." Lindsay suddenly felt awkward, a feeling foreign to her in the presence of women she'd sooner woo.

Gretchen widened her eyes and gave Lindsay a covert nod to elaborate.

"But, um…in this particular case, it's court-ordered."

Ellie seemed to deflate. "Oh."

"I didn't murder anyone," Lindsay blurted.

"Listen," Gretchen said to Ellie. "I'd trust her with my babies any day. Her crime was white-collar."

This conversation was beginning to spiral. "Uh, speaking of babies, where are they? I'm dying to see them."

"I just got them down for the night. I can wake them if you'd—"

"Oh, no, no. I'll see them another time." Lindsay scooped up her keys and cell phone from the counter. "I've intruded on your gals' night long enough."

"Linds, you don't have to go," Gretchen said. "Stay and have a drink with us. I'm about to open a bottle of wine."

She glanced at Ellie and her impossible-to-read countenance. "Next time. I promise." And with that, she scurried out the door and back into the driveway with Kyle.

"That was quick," he said. "No deal on the community service at the shelter?"

"Kyle." Lindsay needed a second to regroup. "I just made a fool of myself in front of a woman I just met. I'm not gonna ask her to take me on as her charity case."

"You didn't hit on her, did you?"

"What? No. She's not my type," she said, still jittery. "It was fucking humiliating talking to your wife's friend about my white-collar crime."

He stared at her for a minute. "You liked her, didn't you?"

"That nerd? Please. I don't think so." But the more Lindsay protested, the more transparent she felt she sounded.

"Well, it's probably for the best you don't do your community service with her anyway. She's a sweet girl. You'll only end up soiling her."

Lindsay chuckled. "I'm not the girl you knew when I left here twenty years ago."

"That's for damn sure. The question is who is Lindsay Chase now?"

She looked at her watch. "I'd love to answer that, but I must be on my way to do the responsible thing and attend a Gamblers Anonymous meeting. So can I count on you for a loan?"

"Let me talk to Gretchen, and I'll transfer it to you later."

"Thank you, brotha." She kissed him on the cheek and sped off.

She drove to the meeting smirking to herself as she replayed his ridiculous comment about her liking Ellie.

As if. He must have springs in his legs to be able to jump to that conclusion.

❖

After Lindsay left, Ellie took a big sip of her iced coffee and fanned herself with a paper plate. It all came together why that hot woman she'd glimpsed in court the other day looked familiar. She was Gretchen's sister-in-law.

When she looked up, Gretchen was grinning at her. "Lindsay has that effect on a lot of women. At times I've wondered if I married the right Chase sibling."

She appreciated the quip. "I think I need something stronger."

"I think so, too." Gretchen grabbed two stemless wineglasses and filled them.

"She's stunning," she said wistfully. "I saw her and her lawyer walk by in court the other day."

"Then it must be kismet."

"What, me running into a defendant I saw in court? That's happened before."

"No. Her catching your eye in court and then you meeting her here in my kitchen."

Ellie scrunched up her face. "That's called a coincidence. Besides, she looked pretty cozied up to her hot lawyer when I saw her."

"Nevertheless, I'll put in a good word for you."

"I'm sure it'll be a waste of your time." Ellie stacked pepperoni and cheese on a cracker from the mini charcuterie board between them.

"Why? She's not your type?"

"Don't be ridic. She's everyone's type. My God. Look at her. But I know I'm not hers. She clearly likes living on the wild side. And to be quite honest, I don't think I'd want to get involved with someone so closely involved with what I do for a living."

"Because she's an addict."

Ellie shrugged, ashamed to admit that was a factor.

"You might be great at dating a recovering addict," Gretchen said with a grin. "It's a role you've been preparing for your entire adult life."

"Meh. I should probably take a pass on that."

When Kyle came into the kitchen for a bottle of water, Gretchen wasted no time. "Ellie wanted to know why we were keeping your hot, sexy sister a secret from her."

Ellie almost sprayed out her wine. "I did not say that."

Gretchen giggled. "No, but I know you were thinking it."

He leaned against the counter and looked at Ellie as he sipped his water. "She's kind of a train wreck right now. I wouldn't get any ideas." He glared directly at Gretchen.

She frowned. "Kyle. She's your sister. She has a lot of amazing qualities."

"And some not-so-great ones. She needs time to get her shit together."

"I'm not looking to be set up with anyone," Ellie said. "Especially my best friend's relative. That could get really problematic really quick."

"Or it could lead to the love affair of a lifetime."

Ellie pursed her lips. "What exactly did she do to get community service anyway? I know she had a gambling problem."

"She also had an embezzlement problem," Kyle said.

"I see." Ellie tried to sound cool, but inside she cringed at the trust issues she'd have to contend with dating a woman with that in her past.

"But she's finally dealing with all her demons," Gretchen added. "She's a strong, brilliant woman, and I know she'll become an even better version of herself after she's done the work."

Ellie smiled, the advocate in her emerging. "That's wonderful. And she's lucky she has a loving, supportive family by her side. That makes all the difference."

"I'm sure she could use some friends, too." Gretchen glanced at Kyle, who was shaking his head in apparent resignation. "Kyle,

Lindsay could use a friendly influence like Ellie in her life right now."

Ellie gently clutched her friend's hand. "You know, Gretch. I do have a life, even if I'm not in a relationship."

"Oh, Ellie, of course you do," she replied. "It's just rather consumed with work. Depressing work."

Ellie shrank in the glare of the spotlight. "That's not true. I'm here with you having a fabulous time with wine and these lovely snacks."

"And I spent most of it wrangling up the babies for bed. I'm an exhausted mom. I've got nothing to offer you."

They both shot Kyle a reproaching glare.

"I gotta do the lawn before the sun goes down." And with that he vanished into the yard.

"Look, Gretchen. I appreciate what you're trying to do for both Lindsay and me, but if we were to strike up a friendship, I'd rather it happen organically, not because we were guests at a pity party."

"Ell, I would never throw you a pity party. You know that. You're my best friend and such an incredible woman. I figured you might have fun hanging out with my crazy sister-in-law. She may be somewhat untamed, but her firecracker spirit is hard to resist. I think you two would balance each other perfectly—as friends, of course."

Ellie's nerves tingled at the possibility of becoming friends with Lindsay. As attracted as Ellie was to her, Lindsay would never be interested in someone like her. No one had ever accused Ellie of having a "firecracker" personality. She just didn't have what it would take to make Lindsay sizzle.

"Well, if we happen to cross paths down the road and hit it off, as friends, that would be very cool."

Gretchen's eyes lit up as though she'd found a new reason to live. "We're having a cookout next weekend, so that will be your chance to chat and get to know each other. Unless you want me to set up something else before then."

"Nope. Nope. No setting anything up. Next weekend is fine." Ellie placed her hand on her chest to see if she could actually feel her heart beating out of it.

Gretchen grinned as she sipped her wine. "You're so into her."

Ellie tried to conceal her excitement as she flipped her friend the double birds.

CHAPTER THREE

L indsay reluctantly descended the steps to the church basement for her first Gamblers Anonymous meeting. If something like the rapture were to exist, she'd have given anything for it to strike at that precise moment. The smell of percolator coffee and doughnuts hit her nostrils like a cliché as she slowly opened the door. Of all the ways she could amuse herself on a Sunday night...

"Hi. Good evening." A smiling, wiry, red-headed man waved her over before she could change her mind. "Hey. Hi there. I'm Justin." He extended a pink, freckly hand and firmly gripped hers. "I'm leading tonight's session. Have a seat. Thanks for coming."

"Thank you." After she sat in a small chair and turned off the volume on her phone, she stared at the door to see if any other unfortunate, wayward gamblers would make their way in. She consulted her watch. Seven on the dot. "Do you usually get a lot of people?"

"Not so much anymore. Now that the Department of Mental Health offers virtual meetings, the young ones prefer those. But a few older regulars still like to come in person. I'm glad you decided to join us."

Lindsay smiled politely. He appeared to be pandering to her, but then she checked her ego and realized he was just trying to be warm and welcoming. "Not that I'm some old war horse, but I feel like I need the reality of an in-person meeting, especially for the first one."

Justin had opened his mouth to reply when the door swung open, and two well-coiffed, seventyish women stormed in gabbing at each other. "Ah, Barb, Angie, better late than never." His impish grin revealed their familiarity.

"Sorry, sorry," Angie said as she rearranged the small circle of chairs to her liking. "We stopped at the diner for a bite, and the service was *tarr-ible*."

"It didn't help that this one has to make a special order out of everything," Barb said, her honey-blond hair not moving as she tilted her head toward Angie.

"Okay, ladies," Justin said in his soothing tone. "You're here now, and that's all that matters. As you can see, we have a new member tonight."

Lindsay looked up from her phone and saw three unfamiliar faces staring back at her. Suddenly, all the cool, all the polished audacity that had fueled her personal and professional success for years in LA abandoned her. She felt sucked into a vast, black hole of unfamiliarity.

Justin leaned across the empty seat and touched her hand. "If you're not comfortable participating yet, please feel free to just listen." He began with the prayer inviting participants to thank their higher powers and then launched right in. "I'm Justin, and I'm addicted to gambling. Who would like to share first tonight?"

"My name is Angie, and I'm addicted to gambling." The woman's eyes were wide as she sat literally at the edge of her chair. "My thick-headed husband keeps sneaking our overweight dog food from the table, and I should be retired now, but I can't afford it, and I really want to go to bingo this week. That's all I got." She sat back, flipped a hair off her shoulders, and folded her arms.

"Thank you, Angie," Justin said.

The other woman casually waved her hand. "I'll go. My name is Barb, and I'm addicted to gambling. I miss my husband, and

I'm sick of working, too, but if I stop, I'll wind up in subsidized senior housing. Today I'm feeling mad that I put myself in this position."

As Justin nodded and observed the ensuing silence, Lindsay squirmed. Ugh. Something about this scene was making her predicament feel more real and awful than court dates and lawyers and unemployment combined. It was like these women were coming to her as the ghosts of her gambling future. Restarting her life at forty-one was one thing, but if she continued her reckless ways, she would end up like them, starting again in their seventies.

When she returned her attention to the present, three sets of eyes were trained on her.

"Oh, okay. Uh, apparently, it's my turn."

"Only if you're comfortable," Justin said. "We can continue with the topic of the night if you'd like."

"Uh, okay. I think I'm comfortable enough," she said, rubbing her palms on her thighs. "No time like the present, right?" An uneasy chuckle took its own agency. "Um, my name is Lindsay, and I'm addicted to gambling."

"Hi, Lindsay." The three friendly voices in unison helped release some of her tension.

"I love poker, and I fucked up big-time." She exhaled deeply in relief to have it out there.

Angie's eyes glimmered. "Well, dive right in there, honey."

Lindsay sat up erectly and went for it. "When my townhouse in West Hollywood was being foreclosed on, I embezzled from the investment firm I worked for and got arrested. Lost my job, lost my home, and maxed out my credit cards. Now I have a shit-ton of debt that I'll never be able to pay off unless I file for bankruptcy."

"Bankruptcy's a given for us," Angie said. "Don't sweat it."

"Don't sweat it? How can you be so chill about having lost everything you've ever worked for?"

"That's Step One," Barb replied. "Admitting that we are powerless over our gambling and that our lives have become unmanageable."

"Once you work through that step," Justin said, "you won't keep beating yourself up over your past decisions. Doing that will only prevent you from progressing in your recovery."

"And how do I stop doing that when my past decisions have thoroughly ruined my present life?"

"Sounds like now is a great time for us to explore Step Two."

"*Gawd,*" Angie said in her north-Jersey accent as she fingered a gold crucifix that hung on a delicate chain around her neck.

"I'm not religious, certainly not Christian." Lindsay waved her Pride bracelet at Angie.

"It's not necessarily God," Justin said. "It's a higher power, as you understand Him…or Her. Something greater than yourself you can turn to that'll help restore you to a healthy way of thinking and living."

Lindsay rolled her eyes. "Oh yeah. A higher power that just stood by and watched as I spiraled down the drain is now suddenly gonna make me normal again?"

"Not suddenly," Justin said. "One day at a time."

"There it is, the catchphrase," Lindsay said. "You guys give out T-shirts with that saying on it?"

"This one's a piece of work," Barb mumbled to Angie, who seemed to be giving Lindsay a death-ray stare.

"Aren't we all, Barb," Justin said. "All it takes is one scratch-off ticket or one ride past the casino on a sunny day, and we can all be back to square one. This may be Lindsay's first meeting ever, but we're all not that far removed from where she's starting."

Lindsay was satisfied with their contrite expressions after Justin slapped them down, but how was a woman who didn't believe in God supposed to whip up a higher power?

The rest of the hour flew by with the conversation more geared toward philosophy and theology than gambling. That was quite fine by Lindsay, since the last several months of her life that was all she'd been forced to talk about.

When she got in the car, she gripped the steering wheel with both hands and allowed her eyes to well with tears. After a few escaped down her cheeks, she shook off her feelings with a breathy, "Ah, shit."

What a bitter dose of reality. How she missed the days of being able to just let loose and be careless and naughty after a stressful day. With no more secret celebrity poker games or Hollywood parties in the Hills to crash with Marcella, she landed on her lawyer's doorstep.

Blair opened the inside door but not the screen door. "Why didn't you text first? It's after nine."

"I had my first GA meeting tonight. I didn't feel like going back to my father's."

"So this is your new flophouse?"

While Lindsay wasn't digging the attitude, Blair looked awfully cute, relaxed and informal with no makeup and wearing a New York Giants hoodie. "I'm sorry. I should've called first. I'll go."

"No. Wait." Blair clicked open the lock on the screen door. "You're here. You may as well come in."

"Gee. Thanks." Lindsay walked in and kissed her, but Blair's face was hot with hesitation. "I can tell this is a bad time. We can meet up later this week for dinner if you want. Or not." Lindsay turned toward the door, but Blair's tone stopped her.

"Did you come because you wanted to see me, or because you just didn't want to go home to your father's?"

"Of course I wanted to see you. I could've gone to my brother's place if I just wanted an escape. Blair, is everything okay?"

"Can we just go to bed?" Blair's eyelids looked heavy.

Lindsay looked at her watch. "I'm not tired."

Blair shot her a glint of a smile. "Neither am I." She grabbed Lindsay by the hand and led her up to that master suite with the stunning view—both inside and out.

If anything would help dissipate the distaste of her new reality in group therapy, it would be a night of Blair's strong, skillful lovemaking. Not that Lindsay was a pillow queen, but the idea of being topped by a power-thirsty Scorpio after a long, shitty day strongly appealed to her.

❖

After an hour of doom-scrolling her social-media account in bed, Ellie still wasn't tired enough for sleep. She turned the light on again and grabbed her phone, opening her Google app. She typed in *Lindsay Chase* and waited the second or two for the hits to fill her screen. The first was a link to an article in the *Los Angeles Tribune*. She clicked on the article entitled "Popular Money Manager to the Stars Arrested."

Ellie devoured the story like she'd discovered new Dead Sea scrolls. With an opening line like "Disgraced celebrity financial planner and serial actress-dater, Lindsay Chase, has fled California," how could she not?

"What the fuck," Ellie whispered. While working at the prestigious Los Angeles Group, Lindsay had embezzled over a hundred thousand dollars from the firm. How was she not sitting in jail? She read on. Blair Maddox, that's how. Maddox was able to get her probation and community service, and through an interstate compact, she was able to negotiate a transfer of probation to Connecticut. That would explain why they seemed so cozy walking together in the hall at the courthouse.

"What the fuck," Ellie whispered again, her voice squeaking in disbelief. "Ah, the perks of being rich and white with no priors—a trifecta none of my clients ever had the luxury of cashing in on."

As she continued reading, she wondered if this story might end up as a Netflix docuseries one day. It certainly had all elements for one.

And then the plot twist.

Lindsay had been able to make full restitution to the Los Angeles Group, allegedly by way of her ex-lover, 80s sex siren and movie star Marcella Hughes.

"Oh, what the fuck." Ellie pitched her phone across her bed. Seriously? Lindsay had an affair with Marcella Hughes? She'd been every lesbian's dream in the 1980s. Though Marcella's prime was before Ellie's time, Ellie had an enduring crush on her, as any devoted 80s movie aficionado had. And Lindsay knew her? Had an affair with her? Was saved from prison by her?

She started to call Gretchen to find out how none of this information had been provided the night she'd met Lindsay, but the thought of waking her and her sleeping babies at that hour implored her to have patience. She opted for a less-intrusive text, but that showed that Gretchen had her phone on Do Not Disturb.

From there, Ellie knew sleep was out of the question. With so many links available to click on, she would be occupied till dawn.

CHAPTER FOUR

Her laptop perched on her thighs, Blair was working from home, in her bed to be precise, as Lindsay lay beside her, flipping through the morning TV news shows. The idea of being a kept woman had never entered Lindsay's mind, but not having to wake up at four every morning to patrol stock activity before the market opened felt pretty damn good.

"What do you think of a food pantry for your community service?"

"What's a food pantry?" Lindsay asked, her attention still glued to the TV.

"Are you serious?" Blair asked.

"I know what a food pantry is. We had one in the house growing up. What does that have to do with community service?"

"Lindsay, a food pantry is an organization that provides for people with food insecurities." She could tell Blair was trying not to sound impatient. "You could work at a warehouse packing meals and essentials for clients in need."

Lindsay's hair made a sweeping noise across her pillow. "A warehouse? Eww. Who wants to spend their summer days inside a dark warehouse? Pass."

"You can't keep saying 'pass' to everything I suggest. You have exactly six business days left to begin your community service before a marshal comes knocking on your father's door."

"He won't find me if I'm hiding out here." She shot Blair her signature grin.

Blair glared at her. "One of these days you're going to meet someone who won't fall so easily for that Lindsay Chase charm. Then where will you be?"

Lindsay giggled at Blair's deadpan. "I'm not kidding, though. Can't you come up with something slightly less unappealing than warehouses and shoveling poop at an equine rescue sanctuary?"

"I suggested the rescue because you said you love animals. Here's an idea. How about you start investing some of your own time finding a suitable place? You need to get yourself into a humbler headspace, Linds. I've run out of ideas for you. And patience."

"No kidding," Lindsay mumbled. Just then her daily random thought about Ellie and her aloofness and heavenly blue eyes made its appearance.

"What about a homeless shelter?"

"I suggested that to you the first week you got here. You acted like I wanted to send you to clean up a toxic-waste dump."

"Well, I've recently learned of a shelter that caters to LGBTQ kids and young adults. Seems decent enough."

"Perfect. Where is it? I'll contact them right now."

"It's in New Haven. Hope House, I think is the name."

"I'll make the call." Blair motioned to get out of bed, but Lindsay grabbed her arm.

"Not so fast. Can we check it out first to make sure it's not gross?"

"You're through making demands, lady. This needs to get done today. And by the way, you aren't supposed to like court-ordered community service."

"I know that. It's just that it all sounds so depressing."

"It *is* depressing, so thank the universe that you'll only have to be there for three hundred hours."

"Maybe I should look around for other opportunities," Lindsay said as she played with the fine hairs on Blair's forearm. "How about the local animal shelter? But instead of cleaning cages, I can socialize the kittens and puppies all day."

Blair gently flung her hand off her. "You sound like an idiot. Look. The sooner we get you set up in something, the sooner it'll be over."

Lindsay smiled and rolled over, facing the window that overlooked Long Island Sound. "Speaking of setups, you have quite the view here."

Blair spooned her, lacing her arm around Lindsay's naked waist, and kissed the back of her neck. "I like waking up with you as part of it. You can leave a few things here if you'd like."

Lindsay rolled onto her back to face Blair. "We just met in person three weeks ago."

"And yet here you are lying naked in my bed."

"A crime of opportunity."

Blair grinned and crawled on top of her. "You know, I can just stash you here with me to keep you out of trouble."

"I've turned over a new leaf. No more gambling, no more risk-taking. I'm a good girl now."

"You were very good last night."

"It wasn't difficult. I happen to be exceptionally attracted to powerful women."

"You have quite a flair for getting what you want. It makes sense you were so successful in the financial world."

"*Were*. Unfortunately, success and excess were words too closely related for me. I definitely need to make changes."

"How are your meetings?"

"Well, um, I've only attended the one so far but—"

"One?" Blair shouted and rolled off her. "Lindsay, you should be well established in a group by now."

"I'm going to another one tonight." She spoke with such conviction, she almost believed her words herself.

"Where is it? Do you want me to come with you?"

"As what? My lover or my lawyer? Because I can't afford either one right now."

Blair huffed. "How about as your friend? We can just call it that for now."

For now? Lindsay suddenly felt trapped under Blair's weighted blanket. Was Blair expecting this to turn into something more than a fun, casual hookup after the legal stuff ended? She rolled over toward the spectacular view. "It's nice of you to offer, but I need to go at this on my own."

"You really don't." Blair tugged at her shoulder. "The support of people who care about you is paramount to a successful recovery."

Lindsay glanced over her shoulder and smiled softly at the obvious concern on Blair's face. "Thank you, Attorney Maddox. I'll take your words under advisement."

❖

Lindsay drove away from Blair's not knowing where she was going—the new metaphor for her life. It was ten a.m., and she had the whole day ahead of her. Most people would kill for the luxury of downtime, but it made Lindsay restless after years living in the LA fast lane.

She could hit a drive-thru for another, fancier dose of caffeine, or she could pop in at Gretchen and Kyle's, something that had become a regular habit.

Or...in about an hour she could be sitting at a poker table at the casino playing a few hands. Just a few.

That itch. It just kept getting itchier. And harder to resist scratching.

This was probably a good time to find a meeting.

Meh.

Instead, she opted to hit a bagel shop and head to Gretchen's. She was enjoying getting to know her sister-in-law on a more personal level. While she was in California, family had been rather abstract and, aside from Kyle, something she hadn't emotionally invested too much in.

Now her family had become a lifeline.

"And how are things going with your hot lawyer?" Gretchen was heavily involved in spreading cream cheese on her bagel.

"The woman is a towering example of success. I'm not quite sure what she's doing with me unless she's really into fixer-uppers."

Gretchen covered her mouth to keep the bagel inside as she laughed. "You are so much more than the pickle you've gotten yourself into. Anyone who meets you for five minutes can figure that out."

"That's debatable, but I don't think it matters. Our relationship seems to be based solely on sex."

"Gee. That must be dreadful." Gretchen's face matched the sarcasm in her quip.

"What must be dreadful?" Kyle came in and stuck a bagel in his mouth as he made a cup of coffee.

"Lindsay's physical relationship with her sexy lawyer."

He pulled the bagel out of his mouth and pointed at Lindsay with it. "You're not supposed to shit where you eat." He then headed into the family room and turned on the TV.

Gretchen called out after him. "I thought we could invite them both over for dinner some night."

"It's a little soon for that." Lindsay said it loud enough for Kyle to hear her in the other room.

"Yeah. You're right," Gretchen said. "If anything, I'd love for you and Ellie to hit it off."

"Lawyers, social workers…don't you guys know anyone I'd be more compatible with, like a felon?"

"I'm sure I can find one for you," Kyle said from the other room. And then he belched loudly.

Gretchen sneered. "On second thought, just stay single. Be a beacon of hope for the rest of us."

"This is fun coffee talk, but in reality, I have too much on my plate to even consider a romantic entanglement. Blair is a nice…" She paused and then smiled. "Diversion."

"I understand," Gretchen said. "You have other priorities these days. It's great that you're reconnecting with family. I know your dad loves having you stay with him."

"That's been the only positive in this whole nightmare. When I left for college eons ago, family meant something entirely different for me. My parents were on the verge of divorce, and Kyle was just a kid. Hell, I was still a kid, too, but I found something so magical about the idea of flying across the country and embarking on something so new."

"Do you talk to your mom?"

"Occasionally. Another benefit of probation is the excuse for why I can't go down for a visit."

"Atta girl. Never stop searching for those silver linings."

As they laughed together, Lindsay felt the meaning in Gretchen's words about reconnecting with family. She treasured the safety and warmth in being around her father, brother, and nephews. And she especially appreciated the friend she'd found in her sister-in-law.

"Do you think the boys will be up soon?"

Gretchen glanced at the kitchen clock. "Any minute. And they'll be very excited to see their Auntie Lindsay."

"Auntie," Lindsay repeated with a grin. After a month of thinking of herself as a gambler, addict, and felon, that new moniker made her feel human again.

The weekend finally arrived and so did the highly anticipated family cookout at Gretchen and Kyle's. After getting word a few days earlier that Lindsay would be completing her community service at Hope House and likely under her wing, Ellie was eager to get to know her a little better before she was locked into her mentorship. In this setting, perhaps Lindsay might come across a little less self-centered than during her first impression.

Or not.

Ellie sat in a lawn chair nibbling a charred hot dog loaded with relish. Despite the fun atmosphere of toddlers laughing and adults drinking spiked seltzers in the sun, she hyper-focused on the side of the house as party stragglers arrived in a steady stream. Where was Lindsay? She was already over an hour late.

Gretchen and the baby plopped down next to her, the baby clutching a stub of corn on the cob.

"You're letting him eat corn on the cob?" Ellie asked.

"I know I'm going to regret it when I change him later, but he loves it."

Ellie grimaced and dropped the remainder of her hot dog onto her plate. "I'm just saying that he has two teeth."

"He has four, and it keeps him busy for a while. Anyway, you're gonna be on my team for cornhole later, so finish eating."

"I thought your sister-in-law was coming."

"She said she was." Gretchen scrunched up her nose. "That's what makes Lindsay so dynamic. You never know what to expect from her."

"That's not dynamic. That's annoying," Ellie said. "You don't tell someone you'll attend a party, then roll in hours late."

"It's a cookout, not an inaugural ball. Disappointed?"

"No. I just appreciate promptness, especially if she's doing her community service at my shelter."

"Your shelter? You pop in a few times a week."

"I consider it sort of mine. Rosa and I are a team, and I happen to be looking out for her."

"I see. Well, I'm sure she'll take that obligation seriously. Don't you go to jail if you blow off your community service?"

"Not if you're sleeping with your lawyer."

Gretchen glanced around. "Shhh. I told you that in confidence."

Ellie replied with a who-cares jerk of her shoulder. "Do you really think Lucas cares that his aunt is a hoe?" She gently flicked a piece of corn from the baby's cheek.

Gretchen laughed as she shook her head. "That Lindsay. Leave it to her."

"Is that supposed to be something to envy? Sleeping around?"

"I don't know if she sleeps around. I just know she gets any woman she wants. I think that's kind of cool."

"The grass is always greener, my friend. You have a loyal husband and a beautiful family life. That's what most people can only dream of. I don't know why you look up to Lindsay like she's some goddess."

"I don't know why either." Gretchen absently bounced the baby on her knee. "I guess it's the freedom. She once lived a life most people can only dream of. She had loads of money, traveled, partied with celebrities. When you're catering to the needs of a leaky infant and toddler twenty-four-seven, living vicariously through others is a survival tactic."

"She's not so free anymore, but I get the point you're trying to make." Ellie picked up her hot-dog stub and stuffed it into her mouth, then licked the excess mustard and relish from her fingers. "Never having been one of the cool chicks myself, I can sort of see why Lindsay makes a splash wherever she goes."

Gretchen nodded as she attempted to clean her son's buttery face.

"Anyway," Ellie said. "She's sure to be a big hit in Niantic women's prison when she fails to complete her community service."

Before Gretchen had a chance to respond, Lindsay sailed around the corner wielding a twelve-pack of flavored seltzer.

"Hey, hey," she said with a beaming smile and breezed right by them.

This time Ellie couldn't stop her eyes from rolling if she tried. How rude. She looked at Gretchen. "Would you like me to hold your baby while you rush toward your knight in shining armor?"

Gretchen chuckled. "Eleanor Tuttle. Where is that meek little young woman I met when we were just starting out?"

"I stayed in social work. You got out."

"Oh yeah." Gretchen chuckled. "Wanna trade places?" She pretended to hand off her gooey-faced child.

"That's a hard pass," Ellie replied.

"Come on. Let's go set up for cornhole. You and me against Lindsay and Kyle."

Ellie followed, and before she knew it, she was standing side by side with Lindsay on opposing teams. While Kyle and Gretchen took turns tossing their bean bags, the three of them hooting and hollering in the spirit of competition, Lindsay stared at her phone, giggling. She typed a reply that made her giggle even more.

Ellie scooped up her bags and began tossing them as if Lindsay weren't there. When it was finally Lindsay's turn to toss, Ellie folded her arms across her chest and glared at her.

"Let's go, Linds," Kyle shouted from his side, and Gretchen added an equally aggressive "Yeah."

"I think they want you to go," Ellie said calmly.

"Oh, yeah. Huh." Lindsay shoved her phone into her back pocket and began tossing. Naturally, two bags landed on the board, and she sank the other two. She turned to Ellie and obviously noticed the look on her face. "What? I did other things in California besides gamble."

"Good to know." Ellie shrugged and refocused on the game.

After their stunning shutout defeat by Kyle and Lindsay, Ellie retreated to the cooler next to the booze table. As she pulled out a White Claw, poured it into a Solo cup, and added fresh berries, she glowered at the way Lindsay and Kyle were still peacocking around the yard acting like they'd medaled in an Olympic event.

She took a hefty swig of her drink and closed one eye, pretending to squeeze Lindsay's head between her thumb and forefinger.

"What in God's name are you doing?" Gretchen said from behind her.

"Gah." Ellie clutched at her heart. "Put your flip-flops back on so a person can hear you roll up on them."

"Don't be so bitter. We'll get them back later tonight at Jenga. My hands are as steady as a brain surgeon's. Better yet, let's switch up the teams—me and Kyle against you and Lindsay."

"Don't you dare."

"You're going to be working with her starting Monday. Don't you think it might be helpful to establish a rapport or at least get on good terms?"

"Who said we're not? Just because I privately find her irritating doesn't mean she has to know it."

"But that's the thing," Gretchen said. "She's not. Once you get to know her, you'll really enjoy being in her presence."

"Look, Gretch. You know me. I never have a problem with anyone, so you don't need to force us into some obligatory team-building activities here."

"Fine. Let me go get my flip-flops before I give someone else a heart attack."

Ellie smiled as Gretchen traipsed off.

❖

Later on, at dusk, as Kyle fired up the grill again for full meal number two, Lindsay was feeling herself after an afternoon of adding a splash of vodka to each can of White Claw.

Even though Ellie was a top-shelf tight ass, she was undeniably attractive. It was refreshing to meet a woman who didn't release a blast of "come hither" pheromones when all Lindsay did was smile at her. Ellie was different.

Leaning against the kitchen counter observing Gretchen and Ellie gather side dishes to take outside, Lindsay tickled her own bottom lip with the rim of the drink can. She imagined how erotic it would be to seduce a woman like Ellie. To tempt her out of that hard shell and into some soft, flowy bed sheets with a little flirting, a little teasing…

Ellie, on the other hand, was quite centered in the present moment as she helped Gretchen and tried to ignore Lindsay. Why was the woman just standing there like she was quality control or something? Had living in Hollywood for so long make her consider a family picnic beneath her? And why wasn't Gretchen putting her to work?

And her smoldering hotness only made her more annoying.

Ellie picked up a large bowl of macaroni salad in one arm and another 12-pack of White Claws to add to the cooler outside and headed to the door.

"Here. Let me help you with that." Lindsay pulled the heavy bowl from Ellie's one-arm grip and opened the door for her.

"Thanks."

"Any time," Lindsay said with a wink.

Ellie felt her face reshape into a goofy smile as Lindsay held her in a second of eye contact in the doorway.

"Let's move it along," Gretchen said behind them. "These baked beans are hot."

Snapped out of her momentary daze, she followed Lindsay out to the food table and dropped the cans into the cooler.

After they filled their plates with grilled chicken and steak kebabs, Ellie sat in a lawn chair, and Lindsay claimed the suspiciously unoccupied chair beside her.

"My brother is some grill master, huh?"

"He sure is," Ellie said, detecting a slight slur in her own voice. "You Chases seem to have a multitude of talent."

"Is that the word on the street?" Lindsay said.

Ellie shrugged.

"So Gretchen keeps trash-talking me about giant Jenga later. I don't know if it's the wine spritzers talking or she's really out for cornhole revenge. Would you do me a solid and be on my team?"

Ellie bit her lip to preempt a smile. She looked at her cup of alcohol and placed it on the table next to her chair. "Did she put you up to this?"

"No. She just kept going on about how good you two are at it, something about being undefeated champs at the company picnic. I just want to even the playing field."

"You seem pretty competitive."

"Not really. I just made a bet with her. If I lose, I owe her two weekend nights of babysitting, and who wants that?"

"You made a bet?"

"Oh, yeah. Just a stupid little one. For fun. No money involved."

"What do you get if you win?"

"She does my community service for me."

Ellie's mouth dropped open.

"That's a joke. Just a joke. I'm fully committed to giving my all to your shelter."

Ellie stared at her, trying to focus on Lindsay's face after losing count of the pudding shots and seltzers she'd consumed throughout the day.

"She's getting me a mani and pedi if I win. You know, these days, I don't have much in the way of disposable income for the luxuries in life."

Ellie followed Lindsay's long, athletic legs down to her toenails sporting a hot-pink hue.

"I did those myself," Lindsay said. "Can't you tell how awful they came out?"

She played along with an "uh-huh" and a smirk.

"Hey, if you don't want to be Jenga partners, that's fine with—"

"I didn't say no," Ellie replied.

Lindsay was about to say something clever, no doubt, when her phone started to buzz on the table between them with a call from Blair. "My lawyer. I better grab this." She got up and walked a few paces away.

Her lawyer. Ellie silently jeered. *Nice try, player.*

Lindsay came back and plopped into her chair. "Sorry about that."

"Your lawyer keeps interesting hours."

Lindsay smirked as she pulled pieces of chicken and pineapple from the skewer and nibbled them. "Her clients are in good hands."

Ellie smirked back. "She must get time and a half on a Saturday night."

"You're something," Lindsay said as she chewed. "Gretchen should've warned me about you."

"Ha! Well, I guess I have the advantage. Your brother warned me about you."

"He did? That rotten little snitch. He was always jealous that I used to get more girls than him." Lindsay winked and sipped her drink.

Ellie got a kick out of their banter, but she found it rather cheesy that a woman in her early forties was still bragging about her body count. Speaking of bodies, Ellie was still staring at Lindsay's long legs. She grabbed her Solo cup and poured out the remaining contents.

"Should we go kick some ass in Jenga?" Ellie said.

"And then some," Lindsay replied.

When the party had finally fizzled by around midnight, and the thank yous and goodbyes said, Lindsay walked alongside Ellie as they headed to their cars.

"Hey. I just wanted to say thank you."

Ellie looked at her over the roof of her car. "For what?"

"For helping me get the community-service gig at your shelter. I like that I'll go in there on Monday kinda knowing someone. It'll make an unbelievably sucky experience a little less sucky."

"You're my best friend's sister-in-law. Of course I told her I'd help out any way I can."

Lindsay nodded and lingered, seeing if she could get more of a read on Ellie. She'd defrosted a bit while they played their spirited Jenga tournament, but then the castle drawbridge slammed shut immediately once it was over. "So are you all right to drive home?" She covered her mouth as a hiccup/burp combo tried to escape.

"I was about to ask you the same thing," Ellie replied.

"Why? You wanna take me home?" Lindsay joked.

"Uh…no, but your family has an extra bedroom right inside."

How did Ellie not even crack a smile at her cute little quip?

"I'm just kidding," Lindsay replied, laying the cool on thick. "I'm not even buzzed. I stopped drinking right after full meal number two."

"Okay, cool. Get home safe." Ellie got into her car and drove off.

Lindsay needed a minute to gather herself. Did Ellie Tuttle really just snuff out their chat like Lindsay was some creeper at a bus stop?

CHAPTER FIVE

Monday morning, Ellie breezed into Hope House with a couple of Starbucks coffees for herself and Rosa. Lindsay Chase was reporting for community-service duty, and Ellie had promised to meet her there and see her through the process.

After plopping into the chair in front of Rosa's desk, she noticed her hand shaking as she lifted the coffee cup to her lips. Rosa noticed it, too.

"*Qué pasa*, Mommy? Another three-cup morning for you?"

"No. This is my first." Ellie tried to seem unaware, but reality was setting in. The shakes weren't from a caffeine overdose. She was anticipating Lindsay's arrival.

"What time is our convict supposed to show?"

Ellie giggled at Rosa's dark humor. Lindsay seemed so put together that she had to remind herself that she was what Rosa said. And that her time spent here was not some grand act of altruism. "Nine sharp." She glanced up at the wall clock. "If she's not here in four minutes, they send her back to jail."

Rosa's giggling abruptly stopped as she stared ahead. Ellie whirled around to catch Lindsay sauntering in as though the shelter was her own personal catwalk.

"*Ay, dios mio*," Rosa mumbled.

"What you said," Ellie muttered back.

"Good morning. I'm Lindsay, and I'm a compulsive gambler." She extended her hand to Rosa but must have read the looks on their faces. "Sorry. I guess I'm still immersed in meeting mode."

"That's a good thing." Rosa received her hand. "Rosa Ortiz, Hope House director. Welcome aboard."

Lindsay seemed to loosen up at the greeting, warming her beautiful face. Clearly, this woman had had the world at her command before the gambling got out of control. Ellie had heard stories of what it felt like to be on top and then watch as your life plummeted to unimaginable depths. It must be such a humbling experience.

"So...when do we go out and round up the homeless?" Lindsay hiked up her jeans like she was the new sheriff in town.

Or not. Ellie turned to Rosa.

"That's not quite how it works," Rosa said. "Once the last of our guests leave, we have to change the bedding and sanitize the area."

"Where do the guests go when they leave here, the Ritz?"

The remark was cringe enough, but Lindsay's giggle afterward? Ellie closed her eyes and hoped Rosa wasn't going to kick Lindsay out and her, too, for bringing in this character.

"Ellie," Rosa said calmly. "How about you take Lindsay out on your first wellness check of the day and show her why sensitivity is the most important requirement in our profession."

"Yes, okay, good idea." Ellie looped her arm under Lindsay's and gave it a yank until they cleared Rosa's office and headed out the exit.

❖

Lindsay wasn't sure what to expect out of this community-service experience, but wandering around a smelly, bustling city hadn't entered her mind. Her lavish lifestyle in West Hollywood for so many years had apparently jaded her. As a teen, she and her friends used to spend Saturdays exploring downtown New Haven untouched by the poverty in some of the areas they'd pass through. They all had safe homes to return to at the end of the day. Now she was acting as though she hadn't needed to concern herself with this world. Ashamed for thinking that, she still would've given anything to be back in WeHo in her stylish townhouse living the life that had led to her downfall.

"Now who's this kid we're looking for?"

"Aiden Diaz," Ellie said. "He's a trans kid who's just aged out of the foster-care system."

"I'm assuming that means he's over eighteen."

"Yes. He's exactly eighteen. That's why he's on his own now."

"Well, if he's an adult and has disappeared, maybe he doesn't want to be found."

Ellie glared at her. "If that's the case, then fine. But I know if that's what he wanted, he would've reached out and told me of his plans. We have a relationship."

"Wouldn't it be a better use of your time to help the kids you can find? I'm sure there are a ton of them around."

Ellie's puckered face indicated that was clearly the wrong response. "Thank you, but at this point in my career, I don't need someone to tell me how to do my job, especially someone who's only here for three hundred hours."

"Sorry." Lindsay softened her tone. "I was just trying to make conversation."

"Well, for the sake of conversation, eighteen may be a legal adult in the eyes of the law, but Aiden and every other eighteen-year-old I've ever met is still a kid in all the ways that matter: mentally and emotionally."

"I'm not suggesting that you shouldn't try to find him. I just thought it would be easier for you to handle the kids who want the help."

Ellie stopped mid-stride, causing a brief backup of hurried morning pedestrians. "I have an idea. How about we table this topic of conversation for now and stay focused on our purpose."

"Sure." Lindsay followed as Ellie continued walking, quietly contemplating this very intense side of her. What a sharp contrast from the casual, seltzer-sipping woman at Kyle's picnic over the weekend. She'd been able to tell right away she was a serious person, but this version of her was a little intimidating. "So where are we headed?"

"We'll start at the Episcopal church over there. They have a fantastic LGBTQ outreach program." She pointed to an old colonial-era church on the west side of the expansive green.

"What do you do for a kid when they've aged out? I'm assuming they're completely cut off from assistance."

"Basically," Ellie said. "Imagine a teenager with no family connections, no way of providing for themselves being told, 'You're on your own now, kid. Good luck.'"

"I can't imagine it," Lindsay said. "Especially since said kid isn't even allowed to order himself a beer till he's twenty-one."

Ellie's swift pace showed she was on a mission, but her silence was making Lindsay uncomfortable.

"Don't ya just love our government?" She added a wry chuckle. "They'll toss them out on the street or send them off to war the day they turn eighteen, but heaven-forbid they try to buy a vape before they're twenty-one."

"Priorities." Ellie pursed her thin pink lips.

Hmm. At least she got one word out of her. Not that Lindsay ever shied away from a challenge, but *next level* hadn't even been invented yet for this girl. "So...uh, what do you usually do for them when you find them? Sorry for the questions. This is all new to me."

"It's okay. Community service is supposed to be a learning experience."

An ironic laugh bubbled out of Lindsay's throat.

"The first thing is to make sure they're safe," Ellie said. "And then get them into stable housing. Sexual assault and other forms of violence against street kids are disproportionately high. And that's counting only the cases reported."

Lindsay groaned. She had no words suitable for that one.

"In Aiden's case, I'm also working to enroll him in community college this fall. He's a brilliant kid. By the spring semester, I hope to help him get into a state university so he can live and work on campus."

"Fantastic. Let's find him and make it happen."

Ellie clutched Lindsay's arm and again stopped in the middle of the busy sidewalk, clearly having exceeded whatever reserve of patience she'd had earlier that morning. "One thing you need to know while you're killing time here is that *nothing* is ever as easy as it sounds. Yes, Aiden is exceptionally smart and capable, but he's a young adult emerging from a childhood of abuse and neglect. Add to that the fact that he's trans, and we live in a culture in which half the country's lawmakers are working to deny trans kids access to medical treatment, not to mention their civil rights and their dignity. In short, the kid's got serious issues, and if all I can accomplish today is finding him alive and okay, then it'll be a good day."

Ellie resumed walking up the street, almost as though she were trying to ditch her. After a moment to recover from that spanking, Lindsay scurried to catch up and make her point. "Look. I'm sorry. I didn't mean to sound so cavalier about this. The learning curve is way curvier than I'd expected. And I just liked what you had to say about college. It sounded so…hopeful."

"Hope is the golden carrot we dangle for our clients. But hope doesn't put food in their bellies or roofs over their heads." Ellie seemed to be intentionally avoiding Lindsay's gaze as they walked along in strained silence.

"What you said before about me killing time," Lindsay said. "Yes, I'm here because I have to be, but I don't want to waste anyone's valuable time." She studied Ellie's profile as they walked. Her eyes looked like they were floating. "Hey, are you okay?"

"Yes. Fine." Ellie swiped a hand under her eye as she straightened her shoulders. "Another thing you need to know is that I cry a minimum of twice a week on the job."

Her tears arrested Lindsay with a painful dose of reality. *Must dissociate. Must dissociate.* "Since it's only Monday, it looks like you're on the fast track to a new personal best."

When Ellie let out a small chuckle, Lindsay finally released the breath she hadn't realized she was holding. "I guess Rosa's right. I have a lot to learn about what you all do."

"And you will if you pay attention for the next two hundred and ninety-six hours."

"I will. I promise." Lindsay stiffened as though she were a military recruit standing before a drill sergeant. "I wanna pass with a good grade, make my probation officer proud."

"Let's start by finding Aiden."

Ellie's warm smile made Lindsay want to make that happen more than ever.

❖

Without success finding Aiden that day, Ellie and Lindsay returned to the shelter. Rosa was still contending with her usual mountain of paperwork when Ellie popped into the doorway of her office. "We're back. No sign of Aiden on the street."

"He hasn't shown here either," Rosa said. "We do, however, have a few newcomers for later tonight. Can you have Lindsay get to the linen changing?"

Even with only a glance from the corner of her eye, Ellie could tell Lindsay's demeanor had changed. "Sure. Nobody came in to help?"

Rosa finally looked up from her computer. "What do you think? I did the sanitizing after you left, but then I had a couple of new clients come in and a phone call from the State about a walk-through this week."

"Ugh. Okay. We'll take care of it." Ellie led Lindsay into the main sleeping quarters of the shelter. "Just start stripping the beds. I'll go into storage and get new sheets and blankets."

Lindsay's face contorted. "You mean I have to touch those beds?"

"How else are you going to change them out for tonight? Here." She tossed her a pair of thin rubber gloves.

As misfortune would have it, the bed closest to them had stains on the pillowcase.

"Eww," Lindsay uttered and, in dramatic fashion, seemed to be staving off vomiting. "Oh, God."

"Put the gloves on. You don't actually have to touch any of it."

"I don't actually want to be in the room with any of it."

Ellie sighed in exasperation. "You're supposed to be doing community service," she said with air quotes. "What did you expect? This is the kind of service we need you to do."

"But the smell." She seemed to be making more of an effort to restrain her gag reflex. "This is why I don't have a cat."

Ellie felt her cheeks begin to flush. "Lindsay, these aren't household pets. They're human beings. Young humans who don't always have access to basic necessities like a shower and toiletries. Maybe this whole setup isn't where you should—"

"Everything okay out here?" Rosa was smiling sweetly, but Ellie knew she'd overheard her voice as it escalated at Lindsay.

"Yes, yes," Ellie said. "I was just trying to—"

Lindsay stepped forward. "She was just explaining to me how important it is that I get the beds ready for the kids coming in tonight. We were just about to get the fresh sheets, weren't we, Ellie?"

"Excellent." Rosa nodded and slipped back inside her office.

"You didn't have to do that," Ellie said, still annoyed. "Why don't you go in and ask Rosa if she needs any help with anything? I'll take care of this."

"I'm sorry. I didn't mean to come off like I'm trying not to get my hands dirty."

"Really? Because that's literally exactly how you came off." Ellie stormed off to the supply room. She closed the pantry door, leaned against it, and exhaled. What was getting her so twisted up inside? Was it not finding Aiden? The mere knowledge that they would have yet another new klatch of kids in need of shelter?

Or was this solely about Lindsay? Lindsay and her gleaming Hollywood smile. Lindsay, who smelled so good, Ellie just wanted to take a bite out of her.

Wait, what?

"Sweet Jesus," she said, wiping beads of sweat off her forehead.

After shaking off those bizarre musings, she grabbed a new box of latex gloves and placed it on a pile of clean bed linens she intended to carry out into the main sleeping area. When she came out, Lindsay had apparently pulled on several pairs of gloves.

She held up her thickly encased hands. "I'm ready. Let's do this."

Ellie absorbed the smile that threatened to break out at Lindsay's stance and glanced at the large wall clock. "Your shift is over in ten minutes. Go home and come back locked and loaded tomorrow."

"Are you sure? You look like you need help."

"I really don't. Rosa and I can do this in ten minutes."

"All right," Lindsay said. "If you're sure it's okay."

Ellie nodded. "See you tomorrow."

❖

Lindsay sat on Blair's deck and stared at the sun twinkling on the calm water. Just as she finished the last sip of sauvignon blanc, Blair came out with a fruit-and-cheese board and a fresh bottle of wine. She refilled Lindsay's glass before sitting in the other wicker chair on her deck.

"I cannot tell you how much I need this right now. Thank you."

"Have some cheese and crostini." Blair's tone was nearly as soothing as the gentle waves of the Sound. She placed gourmet cheese slices and toasted squares on a plate, along with a small bunch of green grapes, and slid it over to Lindsay. "So, how was it?"

After a long sip of cold wine, she was ready to unburden herself. "How was it? It was awful. That's how it was. It made me think. And feel. And care." She shuddered as though an Arctic wind had just blown in off the water. "Please don't make me go back."

"It's not too late to choose the jail option."

"Fabulous. Call the judge." Lindsay took a nibble-size bite of the toast and cheese and dropped it back onto the plate.

"Kidding aside, I think this will ultimately be a very good experience for you, Linds. Of course, the first day was a massive culture shock, but social work has some positive outcomes, too. If you're lucky enough to experience one of those during your tenure, I'm sure it'll change your whole outlook on life."

"God. I'd kill for something positive to come of this."

"Go easy, girl. I don't defend murderers."

"I better inform Ellie that you're not available the next time I say something that makes her want to lunge at my throat with both hands."

"Well, you are kinda extra, Lindsay. Maybe you could dial it down just a tad during this gig." She pinched her thumb and forefinger together and held them up next to a sassy grin.

"I'm not extra. I'm ebullient," she replied with a flourish. "I'm high on life, and it's been a bit of a challenge trying to figure out how to adopt a humble approach."

"I'm not sure this environment is helping your cause." Blair indicated the top-shelf wine chilling in a bucket and their gorgeous view of the Sound.

"Well, it ain't hurting," Lindsay replied and sipped her wine.

"If you want, you can stay here while you do your community service. It might actually be a nice balance for your mental state as you get your wits about you."

Oh, no, here it comes, Lindsay thought. The shift from a casual good time to trying to lock her down with cohabitation. Why did women always want to do this to her?

Marcella Hughes was the last one to succeed at it, and it had been a hell of a task to untangle from her. Now Blair was breaking the sound barrier trying to nail them down into an actual relationship.

"Thank you, Blair. But that's a lot to put on you. I think things are working well the way they are."

"Okay. I'm not trying to push it. I'd just like to get to know the real you a little better."

"That's what dating is all about," Lindsay replied, trying not to sound flip. "I just think in our case, you know, with our attorney-client thing, getting to know each other should happen slowly, without the U-Haul truck."

Blair sucked at her teeth. "How I hate that lesbian trope. People should move at whatever pace they're comfortable with. If they both want to move in after six months, then go for it."

"I couldn't agree more, but you know, with me working on my gambling sobriety, it's wise to take things slow...*really* slow."

"Yes. I agree. Speaking of your sobriety, how are your meetings going? You never talk about them."

"That's an excellent question." Lindsay swallowed hard at the truth. She'd attended only two meetings and had done very few of the recommended readings. "They're going great. I really feel on top of my game. Excuse the pun."

"I'm glad to hear that," Blair replied. "The offer's still open if you'd like me to come to one with you for moral support."

"That's sweet of you, Blair, but I've gotten to know the guys and gals in group, and we have a nice groove going."

"That's wonderful, Linds." Blair got up and kissed her on the forehead. "I'm going to whip us up a little dinner."

"Let me help." Lindsay got up and realized she'd better make her meetings more of a priority. No need to give Blair any excuse for further scrutiny.

CHAPTER SIX

By the end of the week, Ellie headed to the shelter sullen with contrition. After an evening of thoughtful introspection, she realized she wasn't very patient with Lindsay on her first week of community service. Yes, Lindsay stank with bravado, but as Ellie knew from her experience with teenagers, that bluster was often just a shield that scared, damaged people hid behind to protect themselves.

Yes, Lindsay Chase deserved some grace, and Ellie was prepared to offer it.

When she walked in, she noticed Lindsay talking to a woman from the Child Advocate's office, a statuesque older Black woman who could've just as easily been in a commercial for age-defying makeup rather than working for the State.

"Well, you know how it is," Lindsay said, piercing the line of personal space with a knowing grin. "It's the same all over with these state agencies." She chuckled and added a gratuitous hair-flip.

What the hell? As Ellie approached them, she seemed to be a disembodied spirit floating by. It wasn't until she practically bumped into Lindsay that she became visible.

"Oh, hi, Ellie," Lindsay said. "You know Kimball Hayward. We were just discussing a new referral to the center today."

"Of course. Nice to see you, Kimball." Ellie shook Kimball's hand and glanced at Lindsay. With a smile plastered on, she said through gritted teeth, "Why didn't you show Kimball to Rosa's office? Since she's the director."

"Well, I just figured she's so busy, I'd take this one for the team." She shot Kimball that flirty wink of hers, and Kimball, a married grandmother, seemed on the verge of a swoon.

"Uh, Kimball..." Ellie glanced between them as her brain tried to process what her eyes were witnessing. "Let me take you to Rosa's office. She's never too busy to see you."

Kimball looked back at Lindsay. "You have my card."

Lindsay gave her the okay sign and another wink before Ellie led her away.

Upon her short stroll back to Lindsay, Ellie seemed to have forgotten her earlier pledge to be more gracious with her. "Must you turn every situation you encounter into a round of speed dating?"

"What do you mean?"

"You know what I mean. You were so flirting with her, and it was so unprofessional."

"Um, Kimball and I were having a very productive discussion about the pitfalls of working for state agencies. After we talked about placing a kid here until housing with a relative can be arranged."

Ellie studied her. "I don't understand any of this."

Lindsay shrugged. "She assumed I'm a social worker, so I went with it. And yes, there was a bit of flirting. She's a fine-looking woman."

"Lindsay..." She paused and took a huge gulp of air to calm herself. "You can't masquerade as a social worker so you can get into someone's pants. I don't know how to be any clearer about that. "

"I was going to correct her, but once she started talking, I couldn't get a word in."

"Ugh." Ellie stormed off but Lindsay followed.

"Hey, just so you know, I'm not trying to get into anyone's pants."

Ellie stopped and whirled around. "I guess there's a first time for everything." She walked off again, and again, Lindsay followed.

"You barely know me. How can you be so judgy? Isn't that the one thing you're not supposed to be in your line of work?"

"You're not my client," Ellie said, trying to ignore the effect of Lindsay's penetrating stare and full, glistening lips. "And I'm not judging. I'm just going by what's all over the internet about you."

Lindsay's grin was enormous. "You googled me?"

"Not for any other reason than I wanted to see what I was getting myself into with you coming into the shelter."

"I see. So it was purely for professional reasons."

"Absolutely. What do I care what you do in your personal life? As long as you're not doing it in here."

"Well, don't believe everything you read on the internet."

"Everything I've read so far checks out."

"Oh, so you've done an actual thorough investigation. Am I living up to all the hype?" Lindsay's eyebrows bobbed up and down.

"You don't want me to answer that."

"I can tell you what Kimball would say if you asked her to."

Ellie felt the blush heating her cheeks and hoped her complexion wasn't betraying her. This attempt to call Lindsay out was backfiring big-time.

"What. Ever. I have work to do."

She whirled away from Lindsay so hard, the ends of her hair could've sliced through a brick wall. For the sake of her sanity, she'd complete her reports remotely from a Panera before it was time to meet Gretchen for lunch.

Let Lindsay be Rosa's problem for a while.

❖

After ditching Lindsay, Ellie had spent the rest of the morning in peace sipping iced green tea and picking on an almond pastry as she worked. By lunchtime, as she headed for the little

Mediterranean bistro a few blocks away, she savored a bit of fresh air mixed in with the city fumes and a light breeze on her face as she walked.

She was excited to meet her best friend for lunch just like they had in the old days, in the middle of the workday and without small kids clamoring for Gretchen's attention. And the break for the day from Lindsay was exactly what she'd needed.

Until Gretchen got hold of the topic halfway through the meal.

"Ell, I get the whole thing about it not being prudent for addicts newly in recovery to dive into relationships, but life happens sometimes. You can't reschedule falling in love for a more convenient time."

"I know, but if you're—" Ellie grimaced at the suggestion. "Wait a minute. Who said anything about falling in love?"

"You know I'm being colorful when I say that. What I mean is if sparks are flying between you and Lindsay, stop fighting it."

"First off, no sparks. Not a one. The only things flying between us are grievances and thinly veiled sarcasm."

"Foreplay," Gretchen said before shoving a forkful of chopped Greek salad into her mouth.

"Gretch, I'm a social worker. If anyone knows the importance of following the recovery protocol to the letter, it's me. I don't want to interfere with anyone's growth through the steps."

"Why are you assuming it'll turn into something negative? You two falling in love could be the best thing that's ever happened to both of you."

Ellie studied her hope-smeared face. "You need to go back to work. Your days filled with baby talk and those godawful Hallmark movies have clearly compromised your ability to think rationally."

"It's not the movies. It's those goddamn kids' shows." Gretchen momentarily buried her face in her hands. "Thank God you were able to meet me for lunch today. My parents' strawberry-picking trip with the boys saved me from a complete mental breakdown."

"When are you coming back to work?"

"Three more years, when Evan is in pre-K."

"I'll pray for you," Ellie said and sipped her ice water.

"So, getting back to Lindsay…"

Ellie dropped her fork, and it landed with a clang on her plate. "Ugh. Why?"

"I'm just curious. When she's done with her community service, would you go out with her?"

"Look. In or out of this court-ordered situation, we are not each other's biggest fans. We bicker all the time, and she gets on every one of my nerves—last, first, and everyone in between. And worst of all, she compulsively flirts with every woman she meets. I'm quite sure that once she's no longer legally bound to be around me, she'll stay as far away as she can."

"Does she flirt with you?"

Ellie pulled a face. "Occasionally she'll try, but she knows I'm on to her. She's like a precocious toddler who's figured out how to use her cuteness to distract from her bad behavior."

"I'm familiar. I have two at home."

"But at least they're actual kids and not forty-year-olds with arrested development. I can have patience when kids are acting up. With adults, not so much."

Gretchen laughed. "Wouldn't it be hilarious if you actually ended up with her? I mean, how cute would that be for us? Two besties who fall in love with siblings."

"Adorable. I'd rather eat glass."

"Come on. Be honest with me, and I'll never ask again. You wouldn't go on a date with her if she asked?"

"Well, since you promised you'll never ask again, I guess one date wouldn't hurt. If nothing else, it would prove there's no way I'd ever become Lindsay Chase's flavor of the month. No, ma'am."

Gretchen dug around her salad with her fork and plucked out a black olive. "You know what I think? She's finally ready to pick a favorite flavor and stick with it."

"What makes you say that?" Finally something said about Lindsay that was worth listening to.

"Just something I've gleaned from casual conversation when she's been over for dinner. I really think this situation has rocked her. She wouldn't have come back to Connecticut if she wasn't committed to change."

"She had no choice. Isn't she penniless?"

"Lindsay always has a choice. She could've stayed out there in LA around all the bad influences. Someone would've come along and helped her get back on her feet. There's never been a shortage of women who've wanted to save Lindsay Chase. But she wanted to get away from it all and start over."

Ellie tried to absorb this new information with neutrality, but some part of her was counting on Gretchen's observations to be right. What if Lindsay did ask her out on a date? She'd say yes—just out of curiosity. But nothing significant would ever come of it. Why would Lindsay want to settle for Ellie the ordinary when she'd had wealthy, powerful women like Marcella Hughes and Blair Maddox and Lord knows who else?

"Well, this has certainly been enlightening." Ellie signaled for their server. "This is on me."

"No way. Let's split it."

"Let me treat my friend on her one-day furlough from motherhood. It will make me happy."

Gretchen smiled warmly. "I like to see you happy, Ellie. I'd also like to see you blissfully, happily, sickeningly in love."

"I'll just go with the joy of giving for now."

They laughed, but the idea of being blissfully in love stuck with Ellie for the rest of the afternoon. She'd been in love only once, for several years, with a woman named Cynthia she'd met through a college friend. But as many first loves do, it fizzled and faded until a third party stepped in and freed her from what would've been a mundanely-ever-after existence.

And then work became her focus. And remained it as she watched friends like Gretchen and others get married, start families, and build lives with their forever person. It was much easier and safer to view relationships as a spectator sport.

It was what she'd become familiar with anyway.

CHAPTER SEVEN

A fter brushing her teeth, Lindsay crawled into bed. She desired only to drop her head onto her pillow and drift off into an oblivious slumber—her father's obnoxiously loud TV be damned.

After she checked her phone one last time.

A number with a Los Angeles area code was lying in wait in the text bar. Probably a debt collector. She was tempted to delete it without even opening the text, but who does that?

I'm in New York. Call me.

Although the texter hadn't identified herself, Lindsay knew instinctively who was behind the directive. Of all the temptations Lindsay thought she'd had a harness on, the one that had launched her into all of them so many years ago had risen again.

The years of decadence, luxury, introductions to Hollywood elite, the incredible, unforgettable sex...Marcella Hughes.

After reminding herself to breathe, she continued to stare at those six words. Such simple, monosyllabic words, yet they held the power to recast the course of her life.

Her first thought brought her back to deleting the message. But how could she do that? Marcella might have been a demanding, oversexed diva, but she'd come through for Lindsay at a time when all her other LA friends were nowhere to be seen. Her massive gift for restitution had enabled Blair to strike the sweet probation-community-service deal that allowed her to return to Connecticut. No. Ignoring Marcella was not an option.

Her thumb hovered over the phone number. Maybe it wasn't even her. Maybe Lindsay was getting herself knotted up for no reason. She should sleep on it. Yes, sleep on it. Revisit the matter in the morning well-rested and with a clear head.

She shut off the light and lay motionless in the darkness, her arms folded across her chest, her impotent phone tucked under them.

She'd closed her eyes and attempted to sleep for about three full seconds before switching on the light and calling the number.

"Well, hello, stranger." The voice was liquid gold and poured over Lindsay with tingle-eliciting warmth.

"Marcella. What a surprise."

"A pleasant one, I hope."

"Always. I see that you're in New York."

"Yes. I'm the feature of the New York Film Retrospective in Midtown, all this weekend. Can I send a car for you to attend?"

"Oh, Marcella, I'd love to, but I can't leave the state. It's one of the conditions of my probation."

"Have they adorned you with an ankle bracelet?"

"No, but I do have a probation officer I have to report to. And he could hit me up at any time."

"I'm sure that overpaid, fancy-pantsuit lawyer could work something out for you."

"Uh, at this point, I don't really feel I'm in a position to be asking for favors, so—"

"I am. Give me their numbers. I'll make the calls."

"Marcella, my probation is only for two years. It'll go by in a snap. After that, I promise to fly right out to LA for a visit."

She shrieked with laughter. "I'm not waiting two years to see you."

"Well, I'm not going to jail to see you."

"All right, honey. You win. I'll book the Stamford Regency Sunday night, and we can have dinner. Just text me your address so I can send a car for you."

"Dinner as friends, right?"

"No. I'm going to throw you down on the table right after the first course."

How Lindsay adored her sarcasm. "I wouldn't put it past you."

"Hmm…I could use the publicity these days. But how I detest those women who become pen pals with and then marry jailbirds. So droll."

Lindsay laughed at her theatrics. "But I'm not a jailbird, and I intend to stay that way."

"You know I'm teasing. Since I'm on the East Coast, I'd just like to see you and chat, especially after the ugly way we ended."

"I think you paying my restitution more than squared things away for me."

"Lindsay. You're trying to shirk me, aren't you? Don't worry. I'm not calling in your debt with a hotel rendezvous."

She would if she thought she could get away with it. "Of course you're not, and I'm not trying to shirk you. It would be lovely to have dinner."

"Brilliant. See you Sunday, darling."

Lindsay ended the call without further protest. She couldn't help smiling. After all their time apart, Marcella still had the power to send her dopamine surging.

❖

Gretchen had invited Ellie to dinner later in the week, and she'd gladly accepted. The deal in their household was that after Gretchen cooked and cleaned up, Kyle would bathe and get the boys to bed to allow Gretchen time to unwind. That night Ellie was helping her plow through a bottle of wine.

"Okay, Ell. When you told Kyle earlier that Lindsay was doing great, I know you were lying."

Ellie popped a chocolate-covered almond into her mouth as she swirled her glass of pinot noir. "I wasn't lying. I just wasn't being entirely truthful."

"Then be entirely truthful with me."

Ellie huffed. "I don't wanna start anything. She's his sister, and I really shouldn't be broadcasting her business."

"You can to family," Gretchen replied. "I mean, I care about her. I want her to do well. But I also know how she is."

"She's obnoxious," Ellie blurted. "An entitled, manipulative brat who thinks she can bend even court-ordered community service to her will. Ugh."

Gretchen giggled. "If anyone can, it's her."

"But then she also seems to have this sweet side. Like maybe, just maybe, there's room for her to care about something other than herself."

"That's what I hope she's going to learn in her meetings and working with you. An addict just doesn't have the room to care about others when their worlds become about serving the addiction."

"I understand the mindset, but in this case, it's annoying, nonetheless. I don't have the time or mental energy to babysit her. She's supposed to be helping us and the people we provide for."

"Of course she is. Have you tried to talk to her about it?"

Ellie's expression let her know how outlandish the suggestion was.

"I know," Gretchen said. "I'm asking the most confrontation-avoidant person I know. Maybe the shelter director can do it."

"Yes. I thought of that, but wouldn't it be like I'm ratting on her if I tell Rosa?"

"Hmm." Gretchen caressed the stem of her wineglass as she pondered the question. "I have an idea. Why don't you ask her out for a bite to eat and then casually bring up what you're looking for in a volunteer?"

"Gretch, I thought we'd settled this the other day. Relationships for people starting recovery are too distracting."

"Who said anything about a relationship? I'm talking about a casual, friendly type of get-together. Get to know each other as people without the cloud of your very stressful job and her court order hanging overhead."

"That sounds exactly like how one would go about starting a relationship. And to be honest, now that I've gotten to know her, she's not for me at all—too self-absorbed."

"Well, you're right about that. I love my sister-in-law, but she definitely seems all about Lindsay. I was just thinking that establishing a friendship might make it easier for you to work with her."

Ellie shrugged. "Kyle was right. I don't know why I cross-contaminated by offering my best friend's relative the venue to pay off her debt to society."

"If she becomes too much of a problem for you, kick her to the curb. Kyle would understand. Nobody wanted this to be an extra burden on you."

As she finished the last sip of wine, Ellie suddenly felt inexplicably sorry for Lindsay. "Well, I don't know if it's fair to call her a burden."

Gretchen drained her glass as well. "Kick her to the curb."

"I see what you're doing, and I love you for it."

"I'm not sure what I'm doing. I've got a good buzz going."

Ellie giggled. "You're being a solid friend."

Now that they'd finished bashing Lindsay, Ellie reminded herself she should extend to her some of that indefatigable patience and compassion she reserved for her young-adult clients.

Her beauty, sex appeal, and arrogance shouldn't blind Ellie to the fact that Lindsay wasn't that different from many of them—homeless, struggling with addiction, and with an excess of sass that was more a coping mechanism than an aimless desire to be defiant.

"You know what? I don't know why I let myself get twisted whenever Lindsay is being Lindsay." She scoffed. "It's not on me if she fails miserably at her court-ordered servitude. Let her."

Gretchen grinned. "That's cute, Ell. But we both know you'd never let anyone fall on their face if you had a say in it."

Ellie sighed. "I know. I just wish I could get Lindsay to be less…Lindsay-like."

Gretchen was animated with amusement. "If you can pull that off, you will have truly earned the title 'miracle worker.'"

"It's important to have goals," Ellie replied with a smirk.

❖

On the car ride down to Stamford, Lindsay couldn't seem to make sense of what she was feeling. The thought of seeing Marcella again for the first time since they broke up a year ago excited her. Even at the end, their sexual chemistry had burned like a wildfire. While she hadn't wanted Marcella to call it quits, she also hadn't done much to fix her part of their problems before Marcella had reached her breaking point. Instead, they just careened toward an inevitable, messy, melodramatic demise.

Now sitting across from Marcella as the top-floor hotel restaurant slowly revolved around the Stamford skyline, she watched her talk through the candlelight between them. Her claret lips hugged her martini glass, but her expensive lipstick left not even a trace of evidence on the rim.

"So that's why I decided to leave our past in the past. There's no reason why we can't be friends."

"I'm glad you've come around to feeling this way, Marcella."

"Okay, so ultimately, we weren't meant to be together as a couple. Meaningful friends are essential in a woman's life."

"I couldn't agree with you more."

"Incidentally, I have a room upstairs, FYI," she said as she placed her glass on the cream-colored tablecloth.

"Marcella, we haven't even gotten our appetizer yet."

She shrugged. "You know me. I like to get the boring little details out of the way."

Lindsay studied the flawless face for signs of her true age. "You just got through making the case for why we're better off as friends. What makes you think I'd want to sleep with you tonight?"

"You don't find the idea appealing?"

"I didn't say I don't find it appealing. I just find your assumption that I will sleep with you audacious and, frankly, a little offensive."

She offered an alluring grin. "I like that word, audacious. It reminds me of salacious, which is how I feel whenever I'm near you."

Lindsay smirked and sipped her chilled wine to cool down the embers still predictably smoldering in her.

"I don't mean to be glib, Lindsay. Honestly, I haven't been able to stop thinking of you since we reconnected due to your unfortunate legal troubles."

The confession stirred a little more in Lindsay than she would've guessed. Or have preferred. But now wasn't the time to start caving. "Are you being sincere, or is this part of your little seduction vignette?"

"Fully sincere. You know I never wanted to end things with you. It was one of the hardest decisions I've ever had to make. But you pushed me into it."

Lindsay nodded. "I really am sorry. It's one of my few regrets in life."

"Oh, enough with the apologies. I've already said I've forgiven you."

"You're a gracious lady, Marcella. I never deserved you." Lindsay raised her glass to her.

Each time their older gay server brought something to their table, his gaze lingered on Marcella.

"Nonsense. You deserve the best, Ms. Chase, and I'm thrilled to see that you're finally vanquishing your demons."

"Well, I love that you're using a line from your most iconic movie role on me, but I have a long way to go before anything's vanquished."

Marcella grinned as her mind seemed to slip back in time. "Of all my roles, I do miss playing Queen Auriella the most."

"It's what made you a star."

"It got me voted 'Most Fuckable Movie Villain of 1990.'" Her reverie turned wistful. "Oh, youth really is wasted on the young."

"I respectfully disagree with that notion. You're still quite fuckable now. Women only get better with age."

"Tell that to my agent. Anyway, that leads us back to my initial announcement about having a room here tonight."

"Ah, yes. The room. Perhaps we should circle back to that after a few more drinks." Lindsay smiled, plucked a snail from its shell, and dredged it in a buttery sauce.

"Good God. Don't tell me you need to be pickled now to get aroused with me."

Lindsay pinned her with a charm-drenched stare. "Never in a billion years."

Marcella smiled demurely in the reassurance.

It came as no surprise that Lindsay still found Marcella extremely attractive, but what was surprising was that she hadn't wanted to skip dinner and run out of the restaurant straight into Marcella's bed. Was it a sign of maturity? Was she finally mastering the impulsiveness that had gotten her into so many predicaments in the past?

Suddenly, Ellie's face floated past her mind's eye. Ellie's wavy brown hair that must be perfect for pulling during sex, her ethereal blue eyes judging her for even considering banging Marcella just for banging's sake.

She put down her tiny snail fork and breathed in deeply. This wasn't the first time the image of Ellie had interrupted Lindsay while she was casually living her life.

"Is everything all right with your snails?"

"Yes. They're exquisite," Lindsay replied. "But I think I need something stronger than this." She finished her wine and signaled the server for the first of what would be a series of cosmos.

❖

As Ellie walked down Elm Street and appeared to be talking to the warm late-spring air, she was actually being talked down by Gretchen through her ear pods.

"Ellie, I'm sure she's not in Atlantic City on a weekend gambling junket."

"Calling in sick on a Monday to court-ordered community service? That seems more than a little sketchy."

"People get sick on Mondays. It happens. Did she report it to her PO?"

"She said she did."

"Then I'm sure she'll be back tomorrow morning bright and early."

Ellie's relief was almost audible.

"Unless she's been with Marcella all weekend..."

"Marcella Hughes? Her ex?" Ellie's stomach tightened from an unexpected spike of jealousy.

"Lindsay said she was in New York over the weekend for some film-nostalgia thing, but she never mentioned going to meet her."

"I hope she didn't, for her sake. She's not allowed to leave the state." Ellie's blood was simmering, and it wasn't from the humid air overspreading the city.

"Let me call her," Gretchen said. "I'll get right back to you."

Ellie dropped her phone in her purse's side pocket as she strode toward her car in a municipal parking lot. Her disgust turned slowly to concern. What if Lindsay had sneaked into New York to see Marcella, then something terrible happened to her? A stunning woman traveling alone in a big city, she was the perfect target for human traffickers. These days no one was exempt from being victimized.

She grabbed her phone to call Lindsay herself, but Gretchen was calling her back.

"She's not answering."

"Now I'm worried," Ellie said. "What if she's been kidnapped?"

"Now listen. From what I've been told, Marcella is a freak, but I highly doubt she'd go to that extreme."

"I'm not talking about her. Sex traffickers," Ellie shouted. She remembered herself when an old woman walking ahead of her turned around and stared at her.

"Oh, please. Lindsay would have them rethinking their career choice if they abducted her."

Ellie sighed at Gretchen's lack of concern. "Well, then she's probably just home sleeping. After all, she called out sick this morning, remember?"

"Don't worry. I'll get to the bottom of this," Gretchen said. "She can't possibly be with Marcella. They had such a nasty breakup."

"Speaking of that, I can't believe you never spilled the tea about that with me."

"I couldn't gossip about my sister-in-law. I'm like a vault with sensitive info. Besides, it's not that their entire relationship wasn't all over the internet."

"Whatever, Gretch. I gotta go. I have a home visit to get to."

"Okay. I'll keep you posted."

"No need," she snapped. "As long as she shows up tomorrow, that's all I care about." She ended the call and rounded the corner to State Street. She had more pressing matters to focus on than what or who Lindsay Chase was doing when she was supposed to be performing community-service hours at the shelter.

Catatonic in the king-size hotel bed, Lindsay was on her second bottle of water when Marcella emerged from the bathroom in a robe, her hair wrapped in a towel turban.

"It's alive, *alive*," she said with a slight rumble of laughter.

"Barely," Lindsay replied.

"Should I order you up a nice, greasy sausage biscuit from room service?"

Lindsay gagged. "Let me hydrate first."

"I tried to stop you after your third cosmo, but you weren't having any of it. Nobody tells Lindsay Chase what to do—at least not outside of a sexual encounter."

Lindsay groaned as she fell back into the pile of pillows. Why did she give in and go to bed with Marcella? She'd made so much personal progress in the time she'd been back in Connecticut. This would only further complicate her life. And it was just a matter of time before Marcella started making demands.

"If you can manage to get your bedraggled self out of bed in the next hour, we can go down and get some breakfast before I have to leave for the airport." She unzipped an enormous makeup bag and leaned toward the mirror.

"The way I feel right now, you may have to reserve this room for one more night."

"As tempting as that is, I do need to get home to my fur babies. They're already going to shun me for leaving them behind for the weekend."

Lindsay sat upright in bed, and as she reflexively pulled the sheet up to cover her chest, she noticed she still had her V-neck on from the night before. Strange. She had the presence of mind to get dressed after they'd had sex? Or maybe they were so caught up in their animalistic sexcapades, she'd never taken it off.

"Um, Marcella, even though I shamefully admit I don't remember anything about our night in bed together, I just want to make sure we're okay with it just being a one-night thing."

Marcella swung around with her mascara applicator still airborne. "You mean our night in bed with you passed out keeping me awake for hours with your snoring? Yes. I'm more than okay with it being just a one-night thing."

"Wait a minute. After we had sex, I snored all night?"

"What sex? When we got back to the room, we kissed for four seconds, you called me Ellie, and then you passed out cold. No curtain call. Just lights out."

"No. It couldn't have happened like that," she said, scratching through her hair.

"It did. And by the way, who the hell is Ellie?"

Lindsay scoffed. "Nobody. The social worker where I'm doing my community service."

Marcella studied her knowingly. "Oh, honey. A 'nobody' doesn't make you whisper her name while you're kissing an old flame."

"I'm sure you're not remembering the events of the evening accurately. You were hitting the bottle pretty heavily yourself." Lindsay got out of bed and gathered her pants and sandals from the floor.

"Not even. You power-drank way past me before the main course. I can assure you I remember every uneventful detail."

Lindsay groaned and sat down on the edge of the bed. "I'm sorry, Marcella. If I had known what a disaster our reunion dinner was going to turn into—"

"I can't fault you entirely. You didn't even want to meet me to begin with, but I did my usual bulldoze right over you."

"And, as usual, I let you." Lindsay smiled.

"So what does this mean?" She stared at Lindsay's reflection looking back at her in the mirror.

"It means it was really good to see you, Marcella. And I meant it when I said I would come out to visit once my probation is over."

"Visit, huh?" She smiled. "No chance of you moving back to LA?"

"With me, I can never say never, but given the one-day-at-a-time mantra I'm supposed to be living by, I'll just say a visit is something you can count on." Lindsay attempted to straighten out her mussed hair in the mirror before heading to the door.

"See if you can't stay out of trouble for a while, okay?" Marcella said. "I'm through being your hero."

Although Marcella was grinning, Lindsay knew her well enough to see her face backlit by a glow of sadness. After they shared a tight, lingering embrace, Lindsay closed the door and walked to the elevator.

CHAPTER EIGHT

Tuesday morning, Lindsay had arrived early at the shelter, propelled out of bed by a Jetstream of guilt. The last thing she'd intended when she'd gone to see Marcella was to miss a day of community service, especially since she and Ellie were finally tolerating each other on a semi-friendly, co-worker basis.

Rosa had also just pulled into the parking lot, so they walked in together.

"You're here early," she said.

"Yeah. I feel bad about missing yesterday, but it couldn't be helped. I'll make up the day though. Don't worry."

"I'm not worried. I know you will. Is everything all right?"

"Yes. I just had a personal matter to clear up. It's all set now."

"Good. We're getting a food delivery in about an hour. How about you make some room in that storage closet after straightening out the bedding situation?"

"Sure thing."

"After our coffee, of course." Rosa handed her the pot to fill with water while she scooped ground coffee into the filter basket.

Once it was done brewing, Lindsay poured Rosa's black, made her own, and sat by her desk. "Thanks for being cool about yesterday. I appreciate it."

"Listen. Life happens. We can all use a little extra coolness when it happens to us. If you need anything, I'll try my best to help."

Lindsay sipped her coffee. "Thanks."

"How are your meetings going?"

"Okay. I just need to be a little better about getting to them."

"If you can't make them in person, you can always attend the virtual ones."

"Uh, yeah. I'm going to buy a laptop soon, so I'll check them out once it's up and running."

"If you need one, I'm sure I can find you a loaner."

"Thank you. I'll let you know." Lindsay checked her watch. It was time to get out of this "helpful" conversation. "I better start getting those beds ready."

While all the support and compassion was nice, part of her hated that she was viewed as a lost woman in need of uplifting. Not so long ago she'd been living in Los Angeles as an O.G. She'd enjoyed wealth, status, and more friends than she'd had time for. Not to mention an on-again, off-again B-list-celebrity girlfriend.

No one would've imagined her on the receiving end of anyone's sympathy. Now here she was changing bed sheets for the lowest of the low.

Early in the afternoon Ellie popped in, something she'd been doing more and more lately. After checking in with Rosa, she meandered over to where Lindsay was organizing the supply closet.

"Feeling better?"

"I wasn't sick. I had a personal matter."

"With Marcella Hughes?"

Lindsay's head whipped around toward her. "How did you know?"

Ellie smirked. "I didn't. Just a wild guess."

"Yeah, right. My wild guess is that Gretchen told you."

"I don't think hookups with your ex fall under excusable absences in community service," she said with a playful grin.

"You gonna narc on me?"

"I would never do that. It's none of my business how you spend your weekends. Or if you want to stretch your community-service ordeal out longer than necessary."

"I didn't intend to miss yesterday. I had dinner with Marcella Sunday night. Well, actually more martinis than dinner, and I passed out till morning."

Ellie snorted. "As I said, what you do on your off time is your business, but you don't have to lie about it."

"I'm not lying."

She narrowed her eyes in doubt. "You didn't rekindle your romance?"

"No. That's not why I met her for dinner. We ended on bad terms, so I wanted to set things right, especially after what she did for me."

"Not that I care, but does she want to get back with you?"

"To be honest, I don't remember much of the conversation. That may have been part of it."

"Do you want to get back with her?"

Lindsay was amused. "For someone who insists they don't care what I do, you certainly have a lot of questions about what I did."

"Pffft. Pardon me for trying to have a friendly chat."

"You're funny. Why don't you tell me what's going on in your personal life for a change?"

Ellie glanced around as if they were in a crowded room. "Nothing's going on. Why do you think I'm curious about yours? And come on. You're involved with an eighties movie icon. You have to excuse a little nosiness when it comes to that."

Lindsay chuckled. "Okay. Fair enough. I'm just glad you're not mad at me for playing hooky yesterday."

Ellie shrugged. "It's not like I'm your boss."

"No, but I'll be honest. I do care what you think. A little." She offered a saintly smile.

"Don't worry about what I think. Your hands are already full with Marcella Hughes and Attorney Maddox."

"The only thing my hands are doing these days is tying up loose ends."

"Okay. Good."

"Yes. It is good." Lindsay assumed Ellie would walk away, but she just stood there looking at her. "Are we okay now?"

"Fine. We were never not okay."

"And if you're wondering, I already told Rosa I'll be making up the hours for yesterday."

Ellie smiled politely. "I wasn't wondering."

Lindsay studied her for a moment, trying to get a read on her. For some odd reason her intuitive skills weren't working with Ellie. It was as if she had some force field of uptightness around her preventing anyone from gaining even a sliver of insight. "Well, I have work to do so…"

"Yeah, me too, so…"

Lindsay darted to the safety of the supply closet to try to slough off the awkwardness of their chat. What was all that passive aggression about anyway? Was Ellie that uptight about her taking one unanticipated day off, or had Lindsay detected something else in her tone? A little jealousy over Marcella?

Whatever it was, Lindsay didn't have the headspace for any mystery-solving.

❖

After her meeting with Rosa, Ellie chose not to hang around longer than necessary, as she had been doing. She'd developed a major case of the "ick" recounting the flare-up of jealousy she'd felt learning that Lindsay had spent the night with Marcella Hughes. She hadn't believed for one second that two smoking-hot women who used to be involved would share a hotel room overnight and not engage in anything sexual.

Even worse, why had she reacted that way in front of Lindsay? The last thing she wanted was for her to think she had her feeling some type of way, like she'd lured another hapless fly into her web.

She got Gretchen on the phone. "On a scale of one to ten, if Lindsay spent the night with Marcella Hughes, how likely is it that she's lying if she said they didn't sleep together?"

Gretchen guffawed and then immediately cleared her throat to apparently cover her reaction.

"I'm being serious."

"Yeah. I'm getting that. Oh, Ellie, have you fallen for her already?"

"Get out of here. I just like knowing the content of a person's character if we're going to be friends. I detest liars."

"We all know she's capable of lying when it comes to her gambling problem, but I don't think being a liar in general is part of her character. This is probably more of a question for Kyle."

"Whatever. Who cares?" Ellie sighed in exasperation. "Anyway, she probably won't even want to stay friends once her community service is over. I don't know why I'm giving this any thought at all."

"I think because you enjoy her friendship. I think you enjoy her."

"Please don't start with this falling-in-love business again."

"Ell, I just mean you like her as a person. Yes, she's flawed, frustrating, and quite irritating at times, but she's also fun and charismatic, and let's face it. That level of self-confidence is intoxicating to be around."

"Wow. You weren't joking when you said you married the wrong Chase."

Gretchen laughed. "Yes, I was…a little…maybe not."

They laughed together, and Ellie's feeling of safety in Gretchen's unconditional friendship guided her back down to earth. "I have the best friend in the world in you, Gretch. If Lindsay doesn't want to hang out when she's no longer forced to, it's her loss."

"That's right," Gretchen said. "You just do your thing, girl."

When they ended the call, Ellie picked up her stride, her confidence in her worth as a friend restored.

Still, she couldn't deny how disappointed she'd be if Lindsay moved on from her after logging her three hundred hours.

❖

After a month of doing as she was told, complying and kowtowing as necessary, Lindsay felt edgy. The humble-servant routine was tired and totally uninspired. So was playing video poker on a free slot-machine app on the sunken twin mattress in her dad's spare bedroom.

She'd tried to create accounts on the two legal sports-betting apps in Connecticut, but Attorney Maddox had already signed her up for a yearlong ban on each site. Not that she couldn't go to the lengths of creating a fake identity to sign up, but that would require way more time, cash flow, and stealth than she could arrange in her present condition.

That was when, after putting in her hours for the day, she found herself driving to the casino. With her hair tucked under a baseball cap and wearing a pair of Dollar Store cheater glasses, she was sure to beguile any security cameras trained on the entrances.

With some of the cash her brother had loaned her to purchase a preowned car of her own, she moseyed up to the bar laden with video slot machines. Tingles ran up her spine as she fed a crisp hundred into the machine and selected her bet amount. She gently poked the deal button, and her brain gushed with dopamine at the row of red, black, and white cards in the first hand. In no way did it match the ecstasy of being seated at a felt-covered poker table hidden behind sunglasses and surrounded by a dealer and four other players. Or the slap of the cards on the table, the smoothness of the chips between her fingers, the smell of booze and cigarette smoke. It was all so intoxicating. Luckily, she got none of it sitting at a bar looking down at her cold, unfriendly machine.

On her second deal, she hit a full house, which sent her dopamine surging again. As lame as it was surrounded by old ladies tapping away on their keno games, she basked in the glimmer of that old familiar high rushing in.

The machine was hot. Soon after a four-of-a-kind added a nice cushion of extra funds, she increased her bet. Lindsay ordered a bourbon on the rocks—the club sodas with lime just weren't cutting it. It had been months since she'd felt so present, so exhilarated. She'd so badly craved the total abandon, the adrenaline rush as the cards flipped each time she slapped the deal button.

She increased the bet again, this time to max bet per hand, a move she knew was leading her out of the realm of tempered rebellion. She had the machine up six hundred dollars from her original hundred. Now was the time for the proverbial take-the-money-and-run.

But now was also the time she felt the best. She was being bad, doing all the wrong things, and it felt so good.

With another sip of bourbon, she held two aces and slammed a fist down on the deal button. Two more aces. A cool thousand-dollar hit. Lindsay was invincible.

She played hand after hand, cashing out a ticket each time she won, a strategy she'd convinced herself would keep her in check and prevent her from losing everything. See? She wasn't a true degenerate gambler. Would a real degenerate pace herself, employing a carefully thought-out plan to keep within healthy limits? This was her chance to prove to herself that she'd finally developed boundaries.

Then out of nowhere, she heard the voices of Barb and Angie, talking about how their endless rationalizing had led to them destroying their chances to retire at a reasonable age. She knew as well as anyone how insidious gambling was, how easy it had been to form a habit of it, especially as a way to blunt whatever emotional stresses that were vexing her.

She then flashed to Kyle and Gretchen, who'd been so supportive and helpful to her through all the stages of her downward spiral. Lying to them via text or phone call from across the country was one thing. But fibbing to their faces after they'd dug her out of her deepest hole—that was just trash.

She cashed out the ticket from the machine and stuffed it in her pocket with the others. After locating a ticket-cashing machine, she folded up the twenty-four hundred-dollar bills and headed straight to the parking garage. First thing she would do was give Kyle five hundred as a good-faith gesture in repaying the money he'd loaned her.

No. The first thing she'd do after her shift at the shelter was head to a meeting. As she drove the interstate toward home, her hands trembling for the first several miles, she realized how much she needed one. What a strange phenomenon—to have the high of a poker win contaminated by the angst of guilt.

❖

By the time Lindsay arrived home from the casino, she had a few hours in which to cram some sleep and a shower before she'd be late for the shelter. While giving her hair a quick blow dry, she smelled coffee brewing. Shit. Her father was already up and at 'em. The bitter irony of retirement: when you finally can sleep in, you're waking up with the chirping birds. How was she going to explain where she'd been all night and why? She was supposed to be on a short leash.

Left with the choice of presenting to her father as a degenerate gambler or a slut, she knew which one was the only option. Slut.

"Morning," he said with a smile as he stirred a small pot of oatmeal. "Hungry?"

"No, thanks," she said suspiciously. "I just have time for coffee." She studied his face as she poured herself a cup and sipped it black.

"Sleep okay last night?" he asked as he sat at the table.

"Sort of." She tried to decipher what was happening.

"Yeah. I know that mattress isn't the most comfortable. How about this weekend we go to the store and pick out a new one for you?"

Unbelievable. Not only had he not heard her sneaking out as he snored during a baseball game, but he also didn't hear her roll in. Who knew there was a third option?

"Sounds like a plan, Pop." She smiled victoriously, kissed him on the cheek, and headed out for the strongest cup of coffee she could find.

❖

By mid-morning, a lack of sleep was hammering Lindsay hard. Her eyelids felt like cinderblocks as she struggled to enter monthly demographic data into Rosa's laptop.

"Rough night?" Ellie's voice jolted her alert.

She eagerly received from Ellie the paper cup of motor-oil coffee from the shelter's ancient Mr. Coffee machine. "Uh, no. Just didn't sleep that well."

"Mmm," Ellie said casually as she sat at the desk opposite her. "That's right. You're dating Blair Maddox."

"Well, I don't know if dating is the right word…"

"Or did you hook up with Marcella Hughes again?"

Lindsay choked as the bitter coffee slid down the wrong pipe. "What do you mean again? We didn't hook up the last time I saw her."

"So you say." Ellie shrugged. "The other day you said you were tying up loose ends. Maybe the ends weren't tied tight enough, especially after that massive favor she did for you."

Lindsay withered, recalling the leaked story about Marcella paying off her restitution. The things that gained traction in the news these days.

"Uh, no. She's just an old friend."

"Very old," Ellie muttered. She seemed to enjoy watching Lindsay squirm.

"She's only in her sixties. And in case you hadn't noticed, she's still wickedly attractive."

"Oooh, *wickedly* attractive, huh?" Ellie said, clearly teasing her. "Lindsay, we're friends. You can tell me if you're seeing her again. I promise not to sell the story on the dark web."

"That's kind of you." Lindsay rolled her eyes. "I'll say for the record, I'm not in a relationship with anyone, nor should I be at this particular juncture in my life. Sell that on the dark web."

She leapt up and walked away with a dramatic flourish. She wanted Ellie to think she'd offended her, but in reality, she just really needed to splash some cold water on her face.

As if on cue, Ellie crept up behind her in the ladies' room while she was drying her hands.

"I'm sorry if I upset you. I didn't mean to. I really do consider you a friend, sort of, so I thought we were just kidding around."

Lindsay smiled. Ellie was so sweet and sensitive. Sometimes Lindsay didn't know what to do with her. "It's okay," she said, playing up the pouting. "I guess I'm just a little hypersensitive these days."

"Cool." Ellie looked at the floor.

"Did you mean what you said before about us being friends?"

Ellie nodded. "I think so, but I mean if you want to be."

Lindsay smiled. "Yeah. I wanna be."

Ellie backed up to let Lindsay out of the bathroom. "I just wanna say I admire the way you're handling your situation."

"Really?" Lindsay was surprised by Ellie's sudden burst of sincerity.

"Yeah. A lot of people lose faith and relapse by this point in their first attempt at recovery. But look at you. You're doing great."

Lindsay glanced at the wall as her senses replayed her casino jaunt the night before. "Well, you know, it's a daily struggle but..." She caught herself sounding like a jerk. "I mean, thank you. That means a lot."

"So if there's anything I can do for you in that regard, just let me know."

"I appreciate that. And I have to say, I'm learning more about addiction with you letting me tag along and meet some of your clients."

Ellie's face lit up. "I have an idea. How would you feel about speaking to a young-adult addiction group? You could share your insights with them, show them that recovery is possible at any age."

The offer was equal parts flattering and horrifying. "It's a neat idea, but I don't think I'm nearly far enough along to be giving anyone advice."

"You wouldn't be giving advice. You'd be sharing your experience and listening to them share theirs. It would be just like your meetings but from a different perspective, for you and for them."

"I promise I'll give it some thought."

"You should. Talk to your sponsor about it." She flashed that beaming smile that had been growing on Lindsay like moss in a forest.

Lindsay couldn't think of anything she'd rather do less than talk to a bunch of adolescents about her gambling problem. She'd feel like a fraud. The only problem she had with gambling was getting stupid and cocky about her skills. But then if she refused, Ellie would be so disappointed.

She could see only one option: don't refuse. Just keep deflecting.

CHAPTER NINE

After several days of going through the motions at the shelter, Lindsay was tempted to text Ellie to see if she was all right. Of course she was all right. It was just unusual that she'd been MIA for so many days after weeks of making excuses to pop in almost daily at the shelter. Had their conversation about Lindsay's lady-juggling put her off? That couldn't be it. Why would she even care other than it being fodder for her apparent love of gossip?

Whatever. Enough time spent musing about Ellie Tuttle. She had her own work to do at the shelter with the three adolescents who'd wandered in that rainy afternoon.

When the kids were done with lunch, Lindsay cleaned and sanitized the table area and then gathered them around it again to play cards in the afternoon. She'd become so immersed in teaching them how to play that she hadn't noticed that Ellie and a young trans man had come up behind her.

"What the f—" Ellie's face was distorted with rage. "What are you doing, Lindsay?"

"Teaching them to play poker."

"You can't do that here. It's not a saloon."

"We're not playing for money. Just for fun."

Ellie shook her head in what appeared to be disgust and walked away. Lindsay shrugged it off for the moment and returned to the game.

Ellie, on the other hand, wasn't as adept at responding to Lindsay's antics with merely a shrug. She ushered the young man into Rosa's office, and before she finished her first sentence about Aiden, she felt Lindsay's smarmy presence behind her.

"And by the way, this one's turning your safe haven into a casino." Ellie flicked her thumb over her shoulder. "She's teaching them to play poker right under your nose."

Rosa reclined in her chair. "Last I knew they were playing Go Fish."

"It was a little too pedestrian for these kids," Lindsay said casually.

Rosa nodded as though it were the obvious response, and they both looked at Ellie.

"That's it? Once she's done with her tasks around here she gets to corrupt an already vulnerable group of kids?"

"They're all over eighteen," Lindsay said. "At least that's what they told me."

"No money's changing hands, correct?"

Lindsay guffawed. "Who has money in this building?"

"All right," Rosa said. "Why don't you wrap up your game out there, and then you can help Ellie get Aiden settled before you go."

"Aiden?" Lindsay glanced at Ellie, then back at him. "You're the missing Aiden? Nice to meet you." She reached out and shook his hand as he parroted the greeting back to her softly. "I'll get your space ready for you."

When Ellie came back into the main room, the cards were gone, and the three shelter guests were dispersed into separate sleeping areas. Lindsay showed Aiden to his cot and handed him a bottled water and a couple of granola bars.

"Congrats on finding Aiden," she said when she returned to Ellie. "That's some A-plus detective work you accomplished."

"He called me and told me where he was."

"Oh." Lindsay seemed disappointed. "Well, don't tell anyone that. Be the hero. I can keep a secret." She pretended to lock her lips with an invisible key.

"I have no doubt about that," she replied, her eyes still on Aiden.

"So shouldn't you be relieved that he's safe? Or at least not look like you're in line at a wake?"

"His grandmother's flying up from Florida in a few days to take him down with her. He doesn't want to go, so I'm afraid he's gonna peace out and disappear again before she gets here."

"Yikes. I don't know what's worse, being homeless in Connecticut or a trans kid in Florida."

"Aiden wasn't on the street all this time. He was staying with someone in her thirties. He called her his girlfriend, but people were in and out of the apartment, and he realized he wasn't safe there."

"Someone in their thirties was having sex with an eighteen-year-old? Gross."

Ellie shrugged. "Gross, yes, but it's not illegal as long as he consented. And if he was safe and off the street, that's what mattered most. But in this case, he wasn't. Drug activity, and I'm sure other unsavory things, were going on."

"That poor kid. Maybe living with Grandma in Florida for a while is the best thing for him."

"If we can get him there before he vanishes again," Ellie said as she opened a bottle of water.

"I can keep him with me for a few days."

Ellie almost spit out her sip. "What?"

"He can crash on my dad's sofa for a few nights and come with me here in the morning."

After another sip of water, Ellie found the idea a little less ridiculous. "And your father won't mind?"

"He's seeing someone. Sometimes he doesn't even come home. Besides, it's just for a couple of nights. He wouldn't mind either way."

Ellie studied her for a moment. Where did this woman get the ability to make the biggest problem seem like the easiest thing to solve?

"Let's run this by Rosa. I'm pretty sure there's something on the books that says we shouldn't drop our clients in the hands of people on probation."

"I'm not a sex offender, and Aiden isn't five."

"Still," Ellie said. "I'm going to get clearance from Rosa first."

"Suit yourself," Lindsay replied.

Ellie walked to Rosa's office smiling inside. It was the craziest idea, but something told her Lindsay was the person who could actually pull it off.

❖

That evening, they arrived at Lindsay's father's apartment. Earlier she'd verified that he would be at his lady friend's place again and that it was okay for Aiden to stay for two nights. Ellie was looking around at the small, tidy apartment as though she were the health inspector.

"Are you sure you're both okay with this?" she said.

They both nodded as if they were siblings getting dropped off at summer camp.

"Do you need anything before I go? I can run out and get some dinner for you."

"We're fine," Lindsay said. "Aiden and I've already decided on pizza." She looked at her watch. "It should be here any minute."

"Okay. I guess I'll be heading out then. Text me if you need anything. Either of you."

They nodded again. "We'll see you tomorrow," Lindsay said. "Unless you want to stay and have pizza with us."

"Oh, no thanks. I'm beat. I'm going right home after a stop at the grocery store." She turned and opened the door. "Are you sure you don't need anything?"

"It's cool, miss," Aiden said with a smile. "Go home and have a relaxing night."

Ellie returned his smile, finally seeming assured.

"Ciao," Lindsay said with a wave as Ellie slowly disappeared behind the door.

As soon as the pizza delivery arrived, they settled on the sofa and dug into the box as they watched TV. Aiden chose reruns of some real-housewives show, and Lindsay didn't object. She was just contented to know her unconventional idea to take in Aiden seemed to be working out. Not that she'd ever needed to dabble in brown-nosing, but she was all about the added bonus of scoring points with Ellie.

After scarfing down his first piece of pizza in silence, Aiden wiped his mouth with a paper napkin and blurted, "Are you Ellie's girlfriend?"

Lindsay acted appalled. "What? No. Why do you ask?"

Aiden shrugged. "You volunteering to keep your eye on me is a key move if you want to be."

"I have enough women problems right now, thank you."

"She's cute," he said as he slid a slice of pepperoni from the box to his plate. "I kind of have a little crush on her."

"Now there's a news flash."

Panic flashed in his eyes. "Don't say anything to her."

"I would never violate the bro code, Aiden. And you're not wrong. She's super cute, but I'm afraid she's too old for you."

Aiden broke open a true smile for the first time since she'd met him. "Thanks for letting me stay here till my grams comes up. Ellie's right. I probably would've dipped if I'd stayed in the shelter."

"She mentioned that you don't want to go and stay with your grandmother. Do you guys not get along?"

"Nah. We're good. But it's Florida. Would you wanna go live there?"

"Fuck no. But it's only temporary. Ellie's going to try to get you into school up here in the fall. Or the winter semester at the latest."

That news didn't seem to help. His expression faded into the dour, hopeless look he'd had when she met him earlier in the day.

"Aiden, I didn't offer up my dad's place so I could kiss up to Ellie. I want to help you, too."

"You live with your dad? Aren't you like forty?"

"I'm forty-one, if you must know. And for your information, teenagers aren't the only ones who find themselves temporarily unhoused."

That tiny tidbit of info brought back a twinkle to his eyes. "Do you like it here?"

"No. I don't like it here. I used to live in a townhouse in Santa Monica overlooking the Pacific Ocean, but sometimes life gets a little unpredictable."

"Were you a drug addict?"

She shook her head. "Gambling. I wasn't even aware there was such a thing as a gambling addict, but next thing you know, I'm embezzling money from the firm I was a star at, so I wouldn't lose my house." She leaned over with her hand on the side of her mouth. "Spoiler alert: I did anyway."

"Wow. You're worse off than I am."

Lindsay dropped the pizza crust into her paper plate and stared at him. "My god. You're right. I'm so fucked." She placed the plate on the coffee table to run her hands through her hair. "How do I even find the motivation to get out of bed in the morning?"

"Hey. You're gonna be okay," Aiden said. "You seem to have a lot of supportive people around you."

Lindsay searched his eyes for a shred of hope. "I do?"

"Yeah. Your dad lets you live with him, and you're friends with Ellie. She's the best. She'd do anything to help someone."

"It just seems like I'll never get back the awesome life that I screwed up. It's so depressing." She buried her face in her hands.

Aiden put his plate on the coffee table and patted her back. "Hang in there, Lindsay. Don't lose hope. It's always darkest before the dawn."

She picked her head up. "Is that what they're feeding at-risk kids in the system? No wonder you all have crippling anxiety."

He shrugged again.

"Thanks, Aiden. I needed some perspective." She patted his back in return. "You're going to be okay, too. Ellie and I will make sure of it."

"I really wanna believe it. I hope she can help me get into college. I want to become a social worker like her."

Linday exhaled as his words filled her with warmth. "You'll be absolutely great at it."

He replied with a shy smile. "Thanks."

❖

The next afternoon, Ellie came in to see how Lindsay and Aiden were doing with her own eyes. All the texts from her had painted a lovely picture of Lindsay stepping up to the role of "big sister," as it were, but Ellie still wasn't able to decipher when or if Lindsay was doing good as a part of her being or if she was trying to score some kind of advantage.

When she walked in, Lindsay and Aiden were involved in a game of Ping-Pong. *I swear if they have money on this game, I'll lose my shit right here.*

"You little stinker," Lindsay shouted when Aiden's return whizzed past her. After chasing down the ball, she noticed Ellie as she returned to the table. "Hey."

"Hey." Her arms were tightly folded across her chest. "Teaching Aiden the finer points of the Ping-Pong hustle?"

Lindsay wiped the sweat from her forehead. "There's no money involved here. Just the joy of spirited competition."

"I'm kicking her ass," Aiden said.

"Wow. That's rude." Lindsay glared at him playfully, then turned to Ellie. "He actually really is. Care to play doubles with us? I'll go wake up that kid over there." She indicated a young man rumpled up on a cot across the room.

"Uh, no, no. Let him sleep. I just came by to drop some forms off to Rosa, and then I have to head out for a home visit."

"Do you need me to come with? I've heard those can get kinda dicey."

"No, thank you. I've worked with this family for a while now. They're good people."

"Roger that." Lindsay assumed her defensive stance at the table with her back hunched and legs spread apart. "Come on, punk. I'm done letting you win."

Ellie turned to Aiden, feigning a serious look. "Show no mercy." When she turned and started walking to Rosa's office, Lindsay delivered her reply.

"Oooh. Sounds like someone's still bitter about their cornhole defeat."

Ellie kept walking but allowed herself to break into a smile. Before she reached the threshold of Rosa's office, Aiden called her from behind.

When she turned to him, his cheeks were rosy with exertion and a tinge of shyness.

"So, I just thought you should know that Lindsay didn't step up for me just to impress you. She's the real deal."

Ellie tried not to show her surprise. "Um, okay. I'm glad everything's working out. We don't usually do things this way."

"I know," he said. "But I like Lindsay. We had some good talks, and she really listened. We kinda helped each other because she's homeless and screwed up, too."

Ellie barely caught the gust of laughter at Aiden's assessment before it escaped. He wasn't wrong. "It's not fair to refer to either of you like that. You're both on new paths that require some adjustment and patience and commitment to yourselves."

He nodded. "It just felt really good to have someone hear me and not just nod while they're filling out more paperwork about me."

Ellie smiled and gently squeezed his shoulder.

"By the way," he said. "If you and Lindsay became a thing, you could do a lot worse. Just sayin'." He grinned and scurried back to the Ping-Pong table.

If they became a thing? What on earth had they talked about at their senior-housing slumber party?

As Ellie turned to leave, Lindsay trotted up to her. "Hey. I may be going against protocol again, but what do you think about us taking Aiden out tonight for a farewell dinner?"

"Well, we've pretty much heaved protocol out the window for this case, so sure. What the hell?"

"Fantastic. I'll go tell him." Lindsay jogged back to Aiden's side of the table, and then they both waved at her before she left.

That evening at the restaurant, Aiden's words recurred in her head. More like taunted her. *If she and Lindsay became a thing...* She watched Lindsay interact with Aiden, seated next to her in the booth. The vision conflicted with that self-obsessed version of her she'd both heard about and witnessed in the recent past. The way she'd opened up her whole life to Aiden over the past two days was so antithetical to the Lindsay she thought she knew.

Her physical attraction took on a new pull as her traits of patience and compassion started to show. She was physically beautiful—that could never be denied—but combine that with a giving and open heart. How could anyone resist her?

"Did you hear what Aiden said?" Lindsay said.

"I'm sorry. My attention was elsewhere."

"Come on. This is Aiden's last night. We're celebrating," Lindsay said. "He wants to tell you something."

He sipped his soda as if preparing to give the speech of a lifetime. "If, I mean when, you get me into school, I want to major in social work. Because of you."

"Aiden." The tears immediately, predictably pooled in her eyes. "What a perfect career for you."

"Thanks." He smiled and glanced down. "I want to be there for other kids the way you've been there for me."

"Before Ellie waterlogs her chicken fettuccini, a toast to the titans of social work both present and future." Lindsay raised her lemon water and smiled warmly, mostly at Ellie.

"You guys." Ellie squeezed Aiden's hand and smiled warmly in return. Mostly at Lindsay.

❖

When Lindsay suggested they walk down the street for ice cream after that big Italian meal, the button on her jeans screamed at her audacity. Although she was stuffed from dinner, she wasn't ready for the night to end.

The three of them sat at an outdoor bistro table indulging in ice cream cones and gelato.

Lindsay leaned toward Ellie. "You think people walking by think we're lesbian moms and this is our kid?"

"Aww. I wish," Aiden said as he licked his cone.

Ellie delicately scooped out a spoonful of gelato. "I used to consider being a foster mom, but I always imagined doing it while in a stable relationship."

"Do you need to be in a relationship to do it?" Lindsay said.

"No, but I've witnessed the struggles of single working moms. I'll stick with my role of helping young adults transition into an independent life for now."

"You did a good job with me," Aiden said and shoved the cone stump into his mouth.

"Thanks," Ellie said. "But I beg of you. While you're in Florida, please stay away from thirty-year-olds who date teenagers."

"Yeah. We'll be checking up on you," Lindsay said, feigning a stern attitude.

"You're not even a social worker," Aiden said.

"No, but I'm your friend."

"Lindsay, where the heck did this sweet side of you come from?"

When Ellie sucked the gelato off her spoon, she seemed almost—enticing.

She grinned. "I like to keep the ladies guessing."

"So I've heard." Ellie checked her watch. "It's almost nine thirty. We better get going."

They walked down to their cars parked along Main Street. When Ellie stopped to take a call from her mother, Aiden pulled Lindsay aside. "Can I have the keys?"

"You don't have your license, do you?"

"Don't you want some privacy to say good night to Ellie?" He made a smoochy noise with his lips.

"Get out of here," she whispered and gave him a gentle shove. "Go wait in the car." Suddenly stricken with nerves, she shoved her hands into her pockets and swiveled at the waist as she heard Ellie wrapping up the call.

"Where's Aiden?" Ellie said as she approached.

"In the car. He doesn't want any emotional good-byes."

She looked puzzled. "I'll see him in the morning when I drop him at the airport to meet his grandmother."

Lindsay chuckled. "You know kids. Go let him have it."

"Don't worry. I will." Ellie sighed and then looked at her. "Thank you for tonight. And for coming through for Aiden. It means a lot to both of us."

"It was really nothing. Aiden is a cool kid, and he's great company. He's got this depth of wisdom that…"

Ellie helped her out. "Only a kid on the streets could develop?"

Lindsay pointed in agreement. "Exactly. Well, I guess we better…"

"Yeah," Ellie said, and they walked to their cars.

Lindsay got in the car and started the engine, apparently unaware of her face.

"That's a pretty big smile for someone who didn't even go in for the good-night kiss."

She chuckled. "Aiden. The anticipation leading up to the first kiss is the best part. Make a note of that."

"Noted," he said as they drove off.

CHAPTER TEN

When Lindsay left the shelter Friday night, she was almost bummed that it was the weekend. She'd had such an amazing week and was so jazzed telling Blair about how she was actually enjoying her community-service work that she hadn't noticed the scowl forming on her face. She shifted on the barstool at Blair's kitchen island after she stopped talking.

But Blair remained silent, focused on chopping cilantro across from her.

Lindsay slurped at the ice cubes left in her glass of cucumber water. "So, anyway…I'm really glad I went with the shelter for my community service after all."

Blair finally looked up. "Clearly."

Lindsay could no longer pretend something wasn't eating at her, as much as she wanted to. "Rough day?"

"What makes you say that?"

"Only that you're mincing that cilantro into the size of molecular particles."

"It needs to be small for the gazpacho."

"Okay. As long as nothing's bothering you." Lindsay went to the fridge to retrieve the pitcher of water. As she refilled her glass, the words that Blair tossed out behind her filled her with dread.

"Now that you mention it…"

After a deep breath to mentally brace herself, she returned to her stool. "You were saying?"

Blair's face hardened as though she were confronting a hostile witness. "What is it that you suddenly love so much about the shelter?"

"Well, they help people. Help kids. And as you know, I got to be part of that experience for one specific kid. What's not to love?"

"Especially when a beautiful social worker comes along with the package."

"Yeah. She's cute. So what? She's a total professional."

"Hmm. I just wonder how gung ho you'd be about this gig if she wasn't so attractive. You are, after all, a self-professed womanizer."

"That was a joke, Blair." She stared down her accusatory glare, but if pressed, several women in the LA area might side with Blair on that one.

"Whatever," Blair said as she attacked a cucumber. "This is just a casual thing with us anyway, right?"

Oooh. She was baiting her, trying to lure her into a trap. *Don't fall for it, Lindsay, old girl.* "That's what we said at the start, isn't it?"

Blair continued glaring as she uncorked a bottle of chilled white. "I don't know. Is it?"

For fuck's sake. Here we go. "I don't remember our exact words, but I do recall us both agreeing that it was a terrible idea for us to sleep together, given our attorney-client relationship."

"A thousand percent."

"So we just ignored it and kept having dinner and sex."

"That's all this has been to you, dinner and sex?"

"Not at all, Blair. I care about you and really enjoy being with you."

"But?"

Lindsay parted her lips to speak but couldn't find the words she knew Blair wanted to hear. Or at least ones she wouldn't pounce on her for.

"But you like spending time with Ellie more."

"What? I never said that. As you well know, I'm required by law to spend three hundred hours with her."

"Technically, you're required to spend those hours at the shelter. But you'll often tag along with her outside the shelter."

"I don't know if 'often' is accurate, but Rosa sends me out with Ellie occasionally because I think she feels bad for me always being stuck inside that joint. Sometimes she wants me to give Ellie a hand on certain cases."

"And I'm sure you and Ellie just hate every minute of it."

"Blair, I'm not involved with Ellie in any way other than her overseeing my community service."

"And the family picnic. And the dinner out with the kid."

"I can't help that she's my sister-in-law's best friend. And we went to Chili's to celebrate Aiden, her client."

"Isn't all that convenient?"

Lindsay pushed her water aside and poured herself a glass of wine. This line of questioning was beginning to irk her. "If I'd have known you were serving me a deposition along with dinner tonight, I would've gone to the diner with my father and watched helplessly as he put ice cubes in his cabernet."

"We're having a conversation. Can you not be so defensive?"

"Maybe if you didn't come across so confrontational…"

To Lindsay's relief, Blair placed the knife down. She seemed to gather herself the way she would if she were switching up her tactic during cross-examination. "Look. I know you're a little lost at sea right now, and understandably, you're looking for a friendly port. But that role isn't for me, especially given my feelings."

Feelings?

"Blair, I thought we were keeping this light. I thought we were having fun."

Blair chuckled. "Come on, Lindsay. How long have you been a lesbian?"

"What are you trying to say? Are you ending this?"

"I'm afraid so."

An unnamed darkness lifted from Lindsay like a cloud. Her lips tickled with the slightest sensation of a smile.

"You're relieved." Blair's eyes bulged, and her voice echoed throughout the kitchen like a demon was escaping from her soul. *Funny. She was so calm a second ago.*

Lindsay stuttered. "Na-na-no. That's not true. I'm—"

"Yes, it is. You're relieved that I'm cutting you loose. You want to be free so you can pursue Ellie."

"I don't want to pursue anyone. I'm in no position to get seriously involved romantically." However, the idea of pursuing Ellie wasn't entirely unpleasant.

"You're right." Blair was suddenly, eerily composed again. "You're not in a position to be with anyone. You're an addict, and you need to focus on your recovery."

"Which is why you and I were enjoying a casual relationship of dinner and sex." She then mumbled from the side of her mouth, "At least I thought we were."

"I'm sorry, but I don't want to be Lindsay Chase's latest dalliance. I expect, no, I demand better than that."

"Wow. Okay." Lindsay let that sentiment wash over her. "I just want you to know I never viewed you as only that. I was just going with the flow...the flow you started."

"Well, now I'm closing the valve. No more flow. We're just wasting valuable time at this point."

Lindsay lightly tapped her fingers on the counter for a moment as she gathered her thoughts. "So, should I still stay for dinner?"

"I think you should go."

"That would make more sense."

"I'm sorry, Linds."

"Yeah. Me, too," she said as she slowly climbed off the stool. "Will you still be my lawyer?"

"I have to. I'm paid off."

"If it's any consolation, I'm more than halfway done with my community service."

Blair nodded, her mind clearly elsewhere. "Once the shelter director signs off, I'll submit the paperwork to the court, and you're free from the horrors of forced altruism. As long as you keep your nose clean."

"It'll be cleaner than a Puritan's liver. That's a promise."

"Fantastic," Blair said dryly.

"Do I at least get a hug before you shove me out?" She held out her arms and smiled innocently.

Like all those who came before her, Blair clearly fell into the Lindsay Chase charm vortex. She smiled in spite of herself and walked into Lindsay's open arms.

Once Lindsay shut her car door, she exhaled deeply. Blair was spot-on. She was relieved. It was a good thing to be out of whatever she and Blair had and not only because it was best for her recovery.

She was always talking about Ellie. That was another thing Blair had been right about. Ellie had been occupying way too much of her headspace for it not to be something more than friendship.

But now wasn't the time to move forward with that either. First off, she couldn't imagine how she would ever get Ellie to see her as something more than an overgrown punk. Lindsay had the impression that Ellie would be as excited not to see her anymore as Lindsay would be sad once she'd completed her required service hours.

She needed a major overhaul to her image. She wanted Ellie to see her as the woman she truly was, with so much potential, and not just biding her time through a court-ordered penitence.

❖

The next morning, after snagging a rare unmetered parking space on a side street, Lindsay enjoyed the fresh morning air as she walked toward the shelter. She stopped in a gourmet-baked-goods shop and ordered breakfast sandwiches for herself, Ellie, and Rosa. They'd both been so great to her on so many levels that she wanted to express her gratitude.

But during their entire twenty minutes of noshing and sipping, something was off. She'd restrained the urge to reach for dark humor in asking *who died*, because in their line of work, they might've had an actual answer to that question.

As Ellie stood, she crumpled the wrapping her sandwich came in. "I have to head out to a placement. But Lindsay, thank you again for breakfast."

Lindsay rose and followed her to the door and out to the sidewalk. "Hey, are you okay? I wanted to ask you the whole time we were in there, but I didn't know if it was personal or not."

"You can ask me anything in front of Rosa. She's one of my best friends."

"So…are you?"

Ellie exhaled deeply. "It's this place. I know they're going to close it down. It's been on the fiscal chopping block for years now, but I think it's finally going to happen."

"Oh, no. I'm so sorry, Ell. I've come to see how much these kids and this place mean to you. You must feel horrible."

Ellie seemed to study her for a moment, as though Lindsay's sentiments had come out in a foreign language.

Finally, a "Thank you. I really appreciate that."

"I mean it. If you ever need to talk, you have my number."

Ellie smiled and consulted her Apple watch. "I have to run, but thank you." She hurried off down the street.

Lindsay headed back inside as a feeling of cringe crept over her like a vine. She seemed to have forgotten that she was a convict serving out community-service hours, yet there she was, serving up what came across like an offer to counsel a trained social worker.

Rosa met her outside her office. "Don't worry about her. She's the queen of the bounce-back."

"I hope so. I've never met anyone who cares so much about something. It sucks that this place may shut down."

"Not may—will. But for now, we're open. Let's go rearrange the cots and set up the new divider. We have about five new kids coming in today."

"More? Where will they go if the State padlocks the doors?"

Rosa shrugged. "They'll go somewhere. But that's a worry for another day."

As she followed Rosa, her brain launched into the mental gymnastics it took to process all the fucked-up things Rosa had thrown at her in a matter of seconds. She worked quietly alongside her as they prepped the quarters. Until she couldn't.

"Can I ask you a question?"

Rosa nodded as she worked the washers on the large partition with a wrench.

"How do you guys...turn it off? The bureaucratic bullshit. The homeless kids? After my arrest and they seized my townhouse, I was homeless for all of ten minutes before my dad got involved and said come home and stay with him. I mean, I'm an adult, and it scared the living shit out of me. How do these kids survive? And how do you, knowing your hands are tied every time you wanna reach out and help them?"

Rosa stopped and let her wrench hand drop to her side. "You just have to. There comes a point early on in your career that you realize either you learn to shut it off when you go home at the end of the day, or you leave the profession. And leave the kids behind. Some people just can't do it. They just can't develop the mental toughness."

"Has Ellie been able to? She seems to have a pretty low meltdown threshold."

Rosa chuckled at her assessment. "There are days I question that myself, but as I said, she always bounces back. I've never known a colleague more dedicated to these kids than Ellie Tuttle."

"You both do such crucial work. What a shame that you have to deal with all this fiscal uncertainty."

"I've been through this before. If the shelter closes, we'll move on to another one. It's not ideal for the clients we serve, and some will probably slip through the cracks, but that's the way it is."

"I wish I could do something to help."

"Hey, no pouting. One Ellie is enough," Rosa said playfully. "Whatever you're here to do today helps. The present is what matters most."

Lindsay nodded. "And presently, I can unpack the food-delivery boxes and get the pantry shelves stocked."

Rosa smiled. "See? You're already being proactive."

Lindsay returned a smile and headed over to her morning project. Rosa made an important point about being proactive. Rather than being mired in defeat, why not step up and take on whatever task she was capable of accomplishing?

As she slit open the boxes of canned goods and other non-perishable food items, she contemplated how she could help in a more substantive way than just stocking shelves with garbanzo beans and elbow macaroni.

She focused on one particular way that could, if she was having a lucky day, result in a sizable cash payout.

CHAPTER ELEVEN

Although Lindsay wasn't the biggest fan of beer, she was curiously excited to meet Kyle, Gretchen, and Ellie at a local craft brewery. Just shy of being on time, as usual, she caught herself at the sight of Ellie sitting at the high-top table in pink shorty shorts and a scoop-neck tee. She smiled as she sipped from a glass of orange-colored beer, prompting Lindsay to wonder, for a second, if Ellie had a relaxed, carefree twin she'd sent in her place.

Kyle consulted his watch playfully. "Not bad, Linds. Only twelve minutes late. That's a record."

"Give the people what they want, and they'll show up for it." She winked at Ellie.

"I'm happy you agreed to come out on a weekend, given that you have to take orders from me all week." Ellie's delivery sounded almost...flirtatious?

"Taking orders can be fun, given the right context." Lindsay couldn't resist.

"Well." Gretchen seemed a tad disconcerted by their banter. "I'm not sure what's going on here, but if my mom is willing to take the kids on a Saturday afternoon, I'll show up for anything."

"Amen to that, honey," Kyle said as he clinked his mug into hers.

After ordering a lager, Lindsay absorbed the beauty of their outdoor surroundings on the patio overlooking a verdant wooded area. "I'm glad we were all able to do this today. The summers fly by so fast these days."

"And you're almost done with your indentured servitude with Ellie, so who knows where you'll be off to next."

Ellie shot Kyle a look, then immediately trained her gaze on Lindsay.

"I'm not going anywhere," Lindsay said, on the defensive. "I reconnected with a friend from high school who runs an accounting firm. I might be doing some freelance work until something more permanent comes along."

"Gotta love you, sis. You always land on your feet."

"Really? Have you seen me lately?" She huffed. "Anyway, the true test of that statement will be if I can get back my SEC license someday."

"Are you planning to move back to California if you do?" Ellie asked.

Lindsay sighed. "Connecticut is my home. I think I'm here to stay. Besides, too many bad influences out in West Hollywood."

"Yay." Ellie offered her famous delicate finger clap to show her approval.

"Aww. I didn't know you cared." Lindsay gave her a little nudge in the shoulder.

"Of course I do. You've become a friend," Ellie said as she returned the gesture.

Gretchen and Kyle exchanged grins. "I'd love to be able to see my super-cool sister-in-law more often," she said.

"Holy crap. I'm about to drown in estrogen over here," Kyle said.

"Oh, come on, Kyle. Your feminine energy is bigger than all of ours."

"Bullshit." He leaned back, adjusted his baseball cap, and spread his legs wider to take up more space.

Gretchen casually leaned toward him. "By the way, honey, we're getting our manis and pedis at five."

Lindsay locked eyes with Ellie as they shared a good-natured laugh at Kyle.

"Anyway," Gretchen said. "I can't tell you how surprised I am that you two didn't kill each other during this whole experience."

"Ellie, I don't know how you didn't," Kyle said.

"It's not like I hadn't thought about it once...or twenty times." She grinned at Lindsay as she pushed the empty glass aside and sipped her fresh beer.

Ellie was, without question, flirting. "You think I didn't? You were the Nurse Ratchet of social work for at least the first two hundred hours."

"I had to be. You were that Jack Nicholson character—"

"McMurphy," Lindsay said.

"What?" Ellie seemed flustered.

"The Jack Nicholson character in *One Flew Over the Cuckoo's Nest* is McMurphy."

"Oh. Whatever. You were the McMurphy of community service."

Gretchen chuckled at them. "From where I'm sitting, it sounds like two flew over the cuckoo's nest."

Lindsay smiled with self-consciousness. The vibe between her and Ellie outside of the shelter was so different, so magnetic. The looks exchanged between Kyle and Gretchen proved she wasn't the only one who noticed it.

As the afternoon turned into early evening, Ellie was ecstatic when Lindsay suggested they split a flatbread pizza and more apps before leaving the brewery. When Kyle and Gretchen got up to leave for their salon appointments, Ellie had feared Lindsay would take it as an opportunity to bail herself to who knew where. Blair Maddox's? A secret rendezvous with Marcella Hughes? Some new woman who'd fallen under her spell?

As much as Ellie refused to acknowledge or encourage it, Lindsay had the 'rizz like nobody she'd ever known. What a power to possess. And she clearly knew how to use it.

"Thanks for staying a while longer," Lindsay said. "It's such a beautiful night, I didn't want to head home to my dad's yet."

"Your dad's?" Ellie hadn't even considered that scenario. "On a Saturday night?"

Lindsay nodded in obvious resignation.

"How many times a day do you think about jumping on a plane and heading back to the excitement of LA?"

"When I first got back, I'd lose count by noon, but these days, it's not as often as you might think. Sometimes even I'm surprised."

"It must've been nice to see Marcella Hughes again. You two looked like you were enjoying dinner together—judging by what popped up on the internet," she added with a smirk.

Lindsay chuckled. "Marcella says one of the things she misses about the 80s is at least you could usually see the cameras out in public. Nowadays, any fool with a cellphone can be a paparazzo for a minute, and you never get the chance to prepare for the shot that'll be seen around the world."

"Well, you guys made a stunning couple."

"Thanks. Emphasis on 'made.' But I'm glad we're on friendly terms. She really pulled my ass out of the fire with that restitution money."

"I'll say. Talk about forever indebted."

Lindsay nodded. "It would be cool if she and I can reach a point where we could be friends because she's such a great person. I feel like it's starting to happen."

"Do you think about trying to get back with her?"

Lindsay pondered the question, and for the first time she felt confident in her answer. "No. It ran its course."

"She's also part of the world you needed to leave to get well again."

Lindsay winced. She didn't want Ellie to view her as "sick" or needing to become well. She'd never been okay with showing weakness of any kind, and certainly not to a woman she wanted to impress. "Not that I want to change the subject from such an intriguing part of my past, but do you think you'd like to go out to dinner sometime?"

Ellie pulled a slice of pizza from the tray. "It's after five. Isn't this dinner?"

"I mean a real dinner, with forks and knives—one where we're not just eating to soak up an excess of beer."

Lindsay's smile was mesmerizing. "Did you have braces? Your teeth are perfect."

"Yeah, but the rest of me is fucked."

Ellie nearly spit out her beer as she laughed. Dry wit had always been a turn-on, and Lindsay had it in mega doses. "That is a totally inaccurate statement."

"Well, okay. I guess you're a reliable-enough judge in that category."

"What category? Being fucked or perfect teeth?"

"Now I don't even know," Lindsay said, joining in on the giggling. "Both."

They needed a moment to recompose themselves after falling into giddiness. Lindsay was the first to get it together.

"So, listen. There's something I've been wanting to tell you, but I've been putting it off. For obvious reasons. But I think now is an appropriate time to fill you in."

"Okay." Ellie leaned forward as though preparing to take in all the scalding-hot tea Lindsay had to spill.

"I had a relapse." When Ellie said nothing but continued to stare at her, she elaborated. "I was in a really low, dark place a few weeks back, and I took a ride."

"To the casino."

Lindsay nodded, feeling her shame ooze from every pore.

"Did you get yourself in trouble, financially or otherwise?"

Lindsay shook her head. "I actually won, but the high didn't last. On the long drive home, I just felt like shit. I wanted to tell you the next day, but I couldn't bring myself to. I reasoned that after feeling so guilty, I would be able to resist next time I got the urge, so I said nothing, afraid you'd think less of me if I told you the truth."

Ellie sighed, seeming to temper her disappointment. "I've never thought less of anyone who's told the truth, no matter what it was. I'm glad you finally let it go. And that you trusted me."

"Thanks."

"Have you discussed it in your group?"

She nodded. "They assured me it was normal to have a misstep in the beginning and that I should stay focused and do some journaling about the experience."

"Good."

Needless to say, their smooth, flowy conversation all afternoon had ground to a halt.

"So, I'm guessing that's a no on dinner now?"

"No," Ellie said with a warm smile. "It's a yes...one hundred percent a yes."

❖

On her drive home, Ellie had to call Gretchen.

"You're just leaving the brewery now?" she asked. "I hope you're not driving after six hours there."

"I'm fine. We ate a bunch of apps and just talked the whole time after you guys left."

"I knew it," Gretchen said. "I knew it," she repeated in a shout. "What did you talk about?"

"What *didn't* we talk about? She's actually very funny and sweet. It's like she totally let down that obnoxious guard she had up during most of her community service."

"Sounds like you're letting yours down, too."

"I don't know about that, but I really had a nice time with her. And she asked me to go out to dinner."

"Get out," Gretchen said. "You said yes I hope."

"I did." She felt the caution in her reply. "It's just dinner."

"It's a dinner date. She asked you on a date."

"It could just be as friends. You've been pushing a friendship between us since she got back from California. Once her community service is officially over, we can have one without our current complicated dynamic."

"Ellie, you and I have been close friends forever. Would you just admit to me how you really feel about her?"

"What do you mean?"

"I know I've been teasing you about it all along, but you really do have a crush on her. Just own it."

"So what if I might have a teeny-weeny crush? You have one on Bradley Cooper, and you're a married woman."

Gretchen sucked her teeth. "Okay. I can see this isn't going anywhere. I have to hang up now. Kyle is signaling me for sex since my mother kept the kids overnight."

"How romantic," Ellie said in a drawl.

"Keep me posted on the details of your dinner date," she said and ended the call.

As she drove home, Ellie replayed her engaging time with Lindsay and the quasi-confession to Gretchen that followed. She hadn't planned to blurt out any secrets that day. She hadn't even been aware that she had been crushing on Lindsay. But it did sort of track. And now there it was, out there like a zit on school-picture day.

❖

Lindsay was antsy all morning at the shelter. She occupied her brain by clearing out the breakfast setup and then entering intake forms into the state database, but after she completed those tasks, her mind again drifted to Ellie. What a drag on those days when

Ellie was working outside the shelter, and she was stuck inside. How she loved the "take your felon to work days," when she could tag along and assist Ellie in her do-gooding out in the field.

Luckily, Rosa was an exceptionally cool woman. Lindsay tapped lightly on her open office door to avoid startling her. "Anything else I can help you with?"

Rosa removed her reading glasses and rubbed the bridge of her nose. "You're done with that stack of forms already?"

Lindsay nodded, her pride blooming into a smile.

"I am certainly gonna miss you when you're gone."

"What's not to love about free labor?"

Rosa chuckled. "Have a seat for a bit. I may have an errand for you to run."

She sat in the chair next to Rosa's desk. "An errand, huh? Sounds mysterious."

"Not really. Ellie needs a file, so rather than have her schlep back here, I figure you could take it to her and get some fresh air."

"You're an idea woman, Rosa. I like that."

"From one idea woman to another." Rosa lifted her coffee mug. "I meant it when I said I'll miss you around here. Your efficiency as a volunteer has been unmatched."

"That's high praise. Thank you."

"Well, you're working with the best. I swear I think some days Ellie could squeeze actual blood out of a stone."

"I don't doubt that one bit. She's great."

Rosa smiled. "I can tell you're fond of her."

Why was that observation making her feel flushed? What the hell kind of vibe was she giving off? "I'm sure everyone who gets to know her is."

"I hope you two will continue your friendship after you leave us. Having you around has been good for her."

"Really?" Lindsay sipped her coffee slowly as she reflected on Rosa's comment. "It's been good for me to be around her. I'd forgotten about how being in the company of grounded people brings a sense of peace."

"She's grounded all right. Too grounded. Some days this job is like an anchor, and we're fighting just to keep our noses above water."

"I know, man. She's so intense. I can't imagine going to a job that makes me cry at least once a week."

"That's just Ellie. We watched *The Notebook* once, and she went through half a box of tissues."

"Aww, that's so cute." Lindsay was loving this impromptu fact-finding mission. And the more she learned of Ellie from others, the more she wanted to experience these brilliant facets on her own.

After a moment, Lindsay looked up and noticed Rosa's telling grin.

"So, yeah. I think having you around to help Ellie get out of her own head has been a good thing."

Lindsay cleared her throat and sat upright in her chair. "So where am I supposed to meet her?"

❖

After Ellie and Lindsay left the courthouse, they walked to the green and took their lunch break outside. They hit up a falafel food truck and chose a spot on the north side of the green to plop down in a patch of lush grass.

"What happens now that the paperwork has been filed?"

"I pick up my newest young client tomorrow, take her to her new foster family, and pray it works out."

"Works out as in they adopt her?"

Ellie stared at her with obvious frustration. "Fifteen-year-olds rarely get adopted. Best-case scenario is that the family keeps her while she attends and hopefully finishes high school. Then I can transition her into a dorm at Southern, so she won't graduate high school into a life of degrading herself to survive."

Lindsay uttered a cynical laugh. "Is that your go-to with these foster kids? Just enroll them all in a State college, so they'll have a place to live for four years? I gotta say, it's pretty goddamn genius."

"My success rate is fairly decent, too. I've been doing it for about six years now, and as of this moment, twenty-one percent of the kids actually finished with a bachelor's degree."

"Wow," Lindsay said. "That's a remarkable feat."

Ellie shrugged, clearly trying to be modest. "It's my answer to the government's school-to-prison pipeline they started in the eighties."

"How are you not running the Connecticut State Department of Children and Families?"

"Maybe someday, but I like being in the trenches with the children and families, not pushing their names through on paper. I love to see the looks on the clients' faces when they learn they're going into a stable home situation or to college. No fancy title or six-figure salary could beat that sense of accomplishment."

"Don't knock a six-figure salary till you've tried one. It's been a struggle learning to adjust."

Ellie narrowed her eyes playfully. "What struggle? Having to drink coffee at home versus an eight-dollar Starbucks mocha-douchie latte? Wah wah."

"Oh, the harshness," Lindsay said, feigning seriousness. "I like that. That's what these kids today need, a swift kick in the ass."

"I know more adults that need one than kids." She stared straight at Lindsay.

"Seriously though, it's crazy that you figured out a way to solve the teen homeless problem, but your name isn't known all over the country."

"I appreciate your enthusiasm, but what I'm doing is nowhere near as definitive or as easy as you're making it sound. The majority of teens don't qualify. They have to at least have the skills to pass the remedial math and English courses before they're accepted into the program. When you're homeless or in foster care as a child, education is rarely your first priority."

Lindsay sucked her teeth. "We had a really positive momentum going here. Why'd you have to crush it?"

"Okay. Forget all that. Here's something positive. I was invited to speak at a national social-workers' conference in July in Chicago."

"What?" Lindsay said, dragging out the word. "That is awesome. You must be so psyched."

"I am. And nervous. Attendance is usually in the thousands."

"I'll go with you for emotional support. Nothing like Chi-town in the summer."

"Better clear it with your probation officer, or we'll be adding extradition to the list of non-conference activities."

"Oh yeah. There's that. Hey, speaking of my sentence, can you believe I've almost finished my community-service hours?"

"Wherever did the time go?"

Lindsay smirked. "Ha, ha. I'm sure you're relieved to send me packing. But I, for one, have greatly enjoyed keeping you company."

Ellie regarded her with the sincerest of smiles. "I'm just teasing. I've enjoyed your company as well. It's been...well, an adventure."

"I can't thank you enough for shepherding me through this whole ordeal. Of all the grandiose dreams I had for myself when I was younger, none of them included court-ordered anything. It's been humbling."

"If I've learned anything from this job, it's that life can take the wildest of turns in a flash, and many good people have landed in places they'd never imagined. Look at you: a fun, occasional indulgence turned into an addiction that decimated your entire world. And the only thing you were able to control is your response to it."

Lindsay forced herself not to tear up. She wanted to jump into Ellie's lap and give her the kiss she'd been dreaming of for the last several weeks. But a "wow" was all the reaction she allowed herself.

"Wow what?"

"Oh, nothing. I mean I was just a little overwhelmed by what you said. In one simple yet profound statement I felt that you totally got me. I don't think anyone's ever met me there before."

"That can't be. I'm sure your sponsor must get it."

"Yeah, he does, but that's his job. You…" Lindsay stared into her big, beautiful, soulful eyes. "You said it because it's who you are. And I just find that amazing. I find you amazing."

Ellie looked like she was about to melt, and it didn't seem to be from the summer heat. "Oh, Lindsay. I've never seen you this vulnerable before. Thank you for sharing this side of you with me."

"Thank you for digging it out. I can't remember the last time I felt comfortable being this authentic with anyone. Maybe never."

"I…"

Before Ellie could form another word, Lindsay leaned in and silenced her with a gentle kiss on her warm lips.

"Okay then," she replied as Lindsay pulled back.

"I'm sorry," Lindsay said. "I mean, I guess. I don't feel sorry at all except that it was kind of a little inappropriate."

"Completely inappropriate but also kind of sweet," Ellie replied. "It's been a long time since someone kissed me." Her endearing shyness came back hard.

"I find that hard to believe. Your lips are so very kissable."

"Thank you for saying that." Ellie rose and packed up her lunch bag. "Well, we should probably head back."

"Oh, okay." Lindsay wasn't used to this, women freezing her out after one hot kiss. It baffled her. "I haven't made things weird, have I?"

"What? No. It was fun."

Fun? Ellie's forced smile along with her lame assessment of their kiss stung. Was it finally happening? Was Lindsay finally on the downslide from the glorious pinnacle of irresistibility she'd perched atop for decades? How the mighty had fallen.

"Okay. Cool."

❖

Lindsay had spent far too much time dwelling on her kiss with Ellie. More like Ellie's reaction to it. She'd thought it was spectacular. It had touched her in all the right places, including her heart, which she found most astonishing of all. It was clear evidence that her attraction to Ellie was more than physical. Meanwhile Ellie had reacted like she'd simply tried out different flavors at a Gelato shop.

"Hello, Linds. Are you with us?" Gretchen was waving a hand in her face.

Lindsay picked up her wineglass and waved Gretchen off with her other hand. "Why are you being so obnoxious?"

"You're zoned out. I'm so excited that the three of us finally have a night out together, and you're not even paying attention."

"Yes, I am." She totally wasn't. "I thought for sure you'd ask Ellie to join us."

"I did," Gretchen said. "She had plans."

"Oh." Lindsay shrugged but caught Kyle catching her reaction. What was on her face? Jealousy? *Oh, God, please don't let it be jealousy.*

"I hope you're not too disappointed," Gretchen said.

Lindsay leaned back in her chair. "I believe relieved is the appropriate word."

Kyle snorted into his phone.

"Wait a minute," Gretchen said. "I thought you two were getting along really well. You have a dinner date with her coming up free of any legal obligation." Gretchen plucked Kyle's phone from his hand and dropped it into her purse, an act that elicited a whimpering "Hey" from him.

"I know, but I'm getting mixed signals from her now. Has she said anything to you about me recently? Like out of the work context?"

"Like a true Sagittarian, she doesn't leave much on the table when it comes to what she's feeling, but I will say she's given me the impression that she likes you." Gretchen grinned as she sipped her sparkling rosé.

"How so?"

Gretchen shrugged. "She may or may not have admitted that she might have a little crush on you."

Kyle looked at her as though she was being diabolical. "What are you doing?"

"What?"

"If your friend tells you something like that in confidence, you don't tell the person she said it about."

Lindsay glared at him. "I'm family. It's okay to tell me if I swear I'll pretend I don't know anything. Isn't that the code, Gretch?"

Gretchen nodded. "She's right. It's like after you tell your bestie about a surprise, you make them swear they'll act like they had no clue when it happens."

"I will never understand women as long as I live." Kyle stood up. "I have to hit the head."

"Did something happen between you and Ellie?"

"You might say that."

"A fight?"

"No, actually. A kiss."

"Are you kidding me? That's awesome…isn't it?"

"One would think, but I may have jumped the gun. I should've waited till our first real date, but something came over me when I was staring at her delectable mouth."

"Was she grossed out or something?"

Lindsay nudged her hard. "No. She wasn't grossed out. She was into it. But you know how straight-laced and rule-oriented she is. The slightest whiff of impropriety sends her into a tizzy."

"I could've told you that," Gretchen said. "I worked with her for seven years."

Lindsay pulled a face. "Well, it would've been really nice if you'd clued me in."

"I wouldn't worry about it. You only have a few days left, and then you'll go on your date and see how things develop from there."

"Or I could just cancel the date and put this whole weird community-service experience behind me."

"And do what? Keep going in circles with Blair? Keep falling back into bed with Marcella? I'm sure you know from your meetings that you can't create new, healthy habits while still holding on to the old, familiar ones."

"Yes. I'm aware of that fact. But change is hard. And scary. I'm still learning in group how to deal with the fear."

"Then stay neutral. Talk to Ellie about the kiss before your CS is over, and then see how you both feel about the date next weekend."

"Thanks," Lindsay said. "It's nice to see you can still get some use out of your marriage-and-family-counseling degree."

"Marrying into the Chase family, it's gotten more use than you know."

They shared a good laugh on that one. In an uncharacteristically tender move, Lindsay leaned forward, took Gretchen's hand, and said, "I'm so glad you did."

CHAPTER TWELVE

The next day at the shelter, Lindsay was on a mission to follow through with Gretchen's advice and be preemptive about the tricky situation she'd created. By early afternoon, Ellie finally made it back from court. Lindsay swallowed hard, remembered who the fuck she was, and called after her.

"Ellie, can we talk for a sec?"

Ellie walked over to meet her at the pantry door. "What's up?"

"Um. Listen. I just want to apologize for the kiss the other day. Sincerely. I made light of it when it happened, but now I realize it was a bad move."

"What made you realize that?" She seemed ambivalent about the whole thing.

"The vibe between us seems off now. You haven't been yourself, and I'm sad about that if I caused it."

Ellie snickered. "I'm sure it's hard for you to grasp, but this isn't about you."

Lindsay stared at her for a moment, lost for words. New snark level achieved. What duality.

"I'm sorry. I didn't mean to snap at you." Ellie frowned. "It's just that Rosie says it doesn't look good for us in this location. That we need to start preparing for the real possibility of Hope House closing."

They were practically nose to nose. "Oh, no. I'm so sorry." Lindsay was trying to ignore Ellie's enticing sandalwood perfume. Her glistening lips…

"It's not your fault, and here I am taking it out on you." Her eyes were glassy with sadness.

"That's what friends are for sometimes." She clutched Ellie's wrist hanging by her waist.

Ellie melted into a smile. "We are friends, aren't we?"

"A thousand percent." Lindsay studied her face. Her cute button nose, her big, gleaming-white teeth, those expressive eyes.

Something was happening between them in that tight pantry as they stood locked in a stare. Lindsay wanted so badly to kiss her again, to taste her sweetness, but she chose better judgment this time and held back.

"I wish this wasn't your last week." Ellie finally broke eye contact and let her gaze fall to Lindsay's mouth.

Lindsay lifted Ellie's chin to meet her eyes. "That doesn't mean the end of our friendship."

"I don't want it to mean the end of seeing you every day. I've gotten quite used to it."

"Me, too…as weird as that sounds. But I think—"

Before Lindsay could complete her sentence, Ellie's lips were on hers, sending a thrust of exhilaration rocketing through her. They kissed slowly and sensually, Lindsay closing her eyes and savoring the feeling. When she peeked at Ellie, her sky-like eyes were peeking back.

After they pulled away from each other, Ellie was smiling. "Thank you" she whispered.

"For what?"

"For allowing me to distract myself for a moment from my anxiety over this place closing."

"Glad to be of service." Lindsay absently resumed the shelf-stocking she was doing before Ellie came back. "We still have some time to try to figure something out, don't we? What does Rosa say about it?"

Ellie sat on a large case of toilet tissue. "Ever the realist, she says things always work out the way they're supposed to. Not terribly helpful to an anxious mess like myself."

"I'm pretty good at revenue management by trade. Do you think Rosa would be offended if I talked to her about shelter finances?"

Ellie's smile illuminated the entire storage closet. "She appreciates any offer of help she gets, no matter what kind."

"Cool. I'll check in with her before I leave tomorrow."

"Thank you, Lindsay."

After Ellie walked away, Lindsay couldn't believe how much deeper the satisfaction of helping someone was than the adrenaline rush of a straight flush or four of a kind. Their conversation at lunch the other day was making so much more sense now.

Not that she'd entirely forsaken her passion for a hot hand in poker. Wouldn't it be something if she could use her passion for poker to help Rosa save the shelter?

Once Lindsay's shift was over and Ellie watched her drive off, she ran to Rosa's office and stood in the doorway wringing her hands.

Rosa never took her eyes off her computer screen. "Are you just going to stand there and melt into a puddle, or do you want to come in and sit?"

"I don't know what's happening to me," she said as she sank into the chair by Rosa's desk.

Rosa finally turned toward her and lowered her glasses. "You mean about the kiss?"

If Ellie had pearls on, she would've clutched them. "You saw that?"

Rosa smirked. "I don't miss much around here."

"Are you going to report me? Can I get fired for that? I mean that's like sexual harassment, isn't it?"

"Only if it was unwanted, and from the look on Lindsay's face afterward, it was wanted. Very wanted."

Ellie shuddered at the embarrassment hitting her on multiple fronts. "I don't know what came over me. I just totally let myself get swept up in the moment and went for it."

"You initiated it?"

Ellie nodded.

Rosa considered her response. "Now that I never saw coming."

"I felt so...I don't know, weak in the knees? That sounds corny, but I don't know how else to describe it."

"That's the kind of thing people say when they're falling in love with someone."

"No. That's not what I'm feeling." Ellie's nerves were making her itchy. She scratched through her hair. "I don't know. Maybe it is. Rosie, what if I'm in love with her?" Her knees were now bouncing independently of each other.

Rosa cradled her forehead in her hand and muttered, *"Dios mio."*

Ellie felt like she was about to sail away like a deflated mylar balloon. "That's bad, isn't it?"

"As long as I've known you, you've never backed down from a challenge. But I thought that was just a professional trait."

"You think Lindsay is a challenge?"

"Look. I've made a career out of giving people the benefit of the doubt. You know that in our profession that comes with as much disappointment as it does success. Lindsay's an addict. While it's not anything as physically destructive as drugs or alcohol, she still managed to screw up her life. Three hundred hours of volunteer work isn't going to make that go away."

"But she's really committed to changing. She's only missed one day here, which she made up, and she goes to GA meetings."

"Every day?"

"Well, no—"

"Truly committed people go to meetings daily, at least for the first year."

Ellie opened her mouth to formulate another rebuttal but stopped herself. What was she doing debating this subject with

Rosa armed with nothing but rationalizations? She was starting to sound like all the partners and enablers of addicts she'd met and tried to counsel over the years.

"You're right, Rosie. I don't know what I was thinking. I know the rule about staying clear of romantic relationships during that first year. I guess I ought to remind Lindsay of it."

Rosa squeezed her hand. "Don't look so sad. The rules are meant to be guidelines. But there's no rule about being friends with someone who's working on their sobriety. Just don't take her to the casino."

A little levity filtered into the tight room. "I'm a civil servant. Do you think I have money for the casino?"

After a chuckle, Rosa grew somber. "Just don't get your heart broken, okay?"

Ellie sprang from the chair, still mildly charged from the kiss. "That's been the plan my whole adult life."

"Look. I'll say this." Rosa swung around in her chair and tapped her pen against her lips. "In all the years I've worked with you, I've never seen you get googly-eyed over anyone. I didn't even think you were interested in dating at all. So if this woman's got you thinking you might be in love, she must be something."

"Oh, Rosie, she is."

"Just take it slow and give her the space she needs."

"Of course. I mean I don't even know for sure if she likes me like that. A kiss doesn't really mean anything."

"Oh, but it does, *mija*. From the right person it means everything."

Ellie surged down the street to her car, electrified as Rosa's words replayed in her head. She was right. Lindsay's kiss was everything.

CHAPTER THIRTEEN

On Lindsay's last day of community service, her insides were roiling, and she couldn't understand why. Completing this significant step was the first major hurdle in moving forward and reclaiming her life. She should be deliriously happy. The strip of photo-booth photos from that day they took a few tweens to a local carnival tucked into her mirror frame explained it all.

Ellie.

Ellie was the reason for her angst. Ellie was the reason she'd put in more than three hundred hours at the shelter. Ellie was the reason that maybe moving forward wasn't so exciting if it meant moving on from her.

"Good morning." Ellie's eyes glimmered like the sun on the Sound as she pulled a coffee cup from the cardboard tray and handed it to her. "You must be ecstatic."

"I am. Very." Lindsay read the cup. "What's this? A mocha-douchie latte? With almond milk? You can afford this?"

She chuckled. "Today's a special occasion, too special for ordinary coffee-pot coffee."

"You're too good to me." She moaned with pleasure on her first sip.

"I hope you don't have any plans after work, because Rosie and I are taking you to happy hour at the Noodle House."

"Aww, you guys." Lindsay squeezed her hand in appreciation but apparently didn't let go soon enough for it not to trigger a slight look from Ellie. "Uh, yeah, that's really sweet of you, but this wasn't supposed to be fun, remember? This was supposed to be a grueling punishment."

Ellie grinned. "It *was* a punishment, certainly for me in the beginning."

"Well, I admit I'm not everyone's cup of tea but…"

"You know what I think? I think you've been a model example of how community service should be."

"I have?"

"I'm serious. You've shown tremendous growth in your empathy for others. I've watched you interact with the kids. This hasn't just been about counting down the hours to freedom for you. You care about the plight of the people we serve."

Lindsay's cheeks felt hot with humility. "I really do. I guess I've always taken for granted the fact that my parents were decent when I came out to them. Not every kid is that lucky, especially trans kids."

"Exactly. And with that new insight you have to share, I'd say your community-service hours were truly time well spent."

"Thank you." The boiling in Lindsay's stomach had cooled to a slow simmer. She was looking forward to happy hour later, but what she really looked forward to was their date this weekend. She'd been daydreaming for weeks about a romantic evening of dinner in a classy restaurant, stimulating conversation, and after-dinner drinks in a dark, cozy wine bar or maybe even at Ellie's place.

How unfamiliar that feeling of anticipation, the uncertainty of whether the woman she was into was just as into her. All of her past romantic interests had never left a trace of doubt—either they were sycophants hanging on her every word, or in cases like Marcella and Blair Maddox, they'd made their designs on her clear from the start. But Ellie was so different from the women in her past, so hard to read. And it made her nervous.

Now seemed like the perfect moment to feel out if Ellie was looking forward to their date as much as she was. "So, I was wondering—"

"Ooh. Look at the time. We have to get going." She sprang into manic-Ellie mode, gathering her purse and an accordion file. "Jenna's emancipation hearing is at nine."

"Yes, okay," Lindsay said.

She trailed Ellie as she'd done for the last nine weeks or so. She was really going to miss that view.

❖

Later that afternoon, Ellie, Lindsay, and Rosa gathered at the popular Noodle House downtown in a small corner booth, small enough for Ellie and Lindsay to be bumping shoulders the whole time.

Not that Ellie minded. Lately, just the proximity of Lindsay's body to hers was quietly, deliciously titillating. She couldn't even bring herself to think of their date tomorrow night. An actual, official date.

She must've zoned out so deeply entertaining fantasies about a good-night kiss that she hadn't heard anything Lindsay was saying.

"Don't you remember?" Lindsay said, nudging her out of her haze.

"I'm sorry. What was that?"

"How many of those did you have?" Lindsay teased her, indicating her cocktail. "I was telling Rosa about when we took the group to the carnival down at Long Wharf. And our ride got stuck?"

"Oh, please. Don't remind me," Ellie said. "I'm going to relive that mess in nightmares tonight."

"I'm shocked you were able to coax her on a giant Ferris wheel in the first place," Rosa said. "Her knees knock if she climbs to the top of the folding stepladder."

"I didn't coax her on to anything. How was I supposed to know you have a fear of heights? You should've said something."

"I didn't want to make a name for myself as a carnival coward, so I just plugged my nose and jumped in. How the hell was I supposed to know the ride would get stuck…with us at the top?"

"You were very brave," Lindsay said, lovingly. "You set quite an example for those kids by mustering up all that courage."

"It was temporary insanity. You can tell by how pale I look in the photos we took."

"You look like a movie star in them. Don't play coy with us."

Ellie giggled. "Aww, thanks." She absently let her head fall against Lindsay's shoulder and then immediately sat up when she noticed that Rosa was keenly observing them.

"You two were quite the team the last few months," Rosa said. "I hate to ask this, but what are you both going to do without each other every day?"

Ellie groaned. "Rosie. Why? We were having such a lovely time here." She glanced at Lindsay, who had a flair for making even the act of slurping noodles from chopsticks seem sexy.

"Yeah, Ro." Lindsay dabbed her mouth with a napkin. "We're supposed to be celebrating."

"I'm sorry," she replied. "I'm projecting. I'm getting a little misty-eyed myself thinking about how you won't be back on Monday."

"Rosa, mamacita," Lindsay said. "Get in here, you kooky kid. You, too." She threw one arm around Rosa's shoulder and the other around Ellie and squeezed them both to her sides.

"I can't breathe," Ellie said.

Lindsay released them, and they broke into laughter. "This isn't the end, ladies. It's just the beginning."

"We're going to hold you to that statement," Ellie said.

Lindsay's wink sent a shiver through Ellie. Their date couldn't happen fast enough.

CHAPTER FOURTEEN

As Lindsay applied the finishing touches to her makeup in the mirror, she heard her father pick up his keys from the kitchen counter. She assumed he'd just shout out a good-bye, but next thing she knew, he was standing in the hallway at the open bathroom door.

"You look lovely," he said with a smile.

She put down her blush brush and turned to him. "So do you." She tugged at the collar of his dress shirt to even it out inside his blazer. "I'd forgotten how well you clean up."

"Gloria likes to dress up for dinner sometimes when we're not eating at the Elks Club."

Lindsay smiled. "A night out on the town is good. A couple can eat only so many chicken wings and cheese cubes before their arteries clog up."

"You have a good time tonight with…Ellie, is it?"

Lindsay nodded, happy he remembered the little details of their conversations. "How about us? Both all spiffy for our dates."

He grinned and suddenly grew shy. "I, uh, won't be coming home tonight. Gloria doesn't like me to drive at night after a couple beers. So, if you want to bring your date back for a nightcap…"

She tried not to embarrass him with a smile. "Gloria's right. No sense in taking any chances."

He tossed his keys in his hand with another tight grin. "See you tomorrow."

"You betcha."

She waited until she heard the door shut to allow the smile of all smiles to break free at a scenario she never could've predicted—she and her dad like dorm buddies briefly chatting about their hot dates. He so deserved to be happy, and she would have to check out this Gloria person soon to see if she deserved him.

But until then, she had her own lady in waiting.

❖

After an alfresco seafood dinner along the Branford River, they'd dropped into a trendy wine bar in the town center. Lindsay wasn't ready to say good night to Ellie, and it seemed as though they weren't even coming close to running out of conversation topics.

Nestled on seats at the end of the bar, Lindsay still couldn't stop staring at Ellie all done up for a date. Seeing her at work every day, she'd just assumed Ellie didn't wear makeup. She was so wholesomely beautiful without it. But with a little mascara, her long lashes fanned across her glacial blue eyes, and with a mauvy gloss, her lips became even more tempting.

"Thank you for this beautiful night." Ellie smiled warmly as she swirled her chilled glass of Riesling.

"It's not over yet. This place has the best dessert menu. How does New York-style cheesecake and a pistachio martini sound?"

"Divine," Ellie replied.

Away from the steady influx of patrons, Lindsay drank in Ellie's aura. She was beginning to understand "divine" beyond the abstract.

Lindsay cupped her stemless glass of red. "It's my turn to thank you, Ellie."

"You've already thanked me a hundred times for getting you through your community service."

"No. I mean for seeing me as more than just the jerk I was when I first waltzed in. I don't want to sound cheesy, but I really began to feel like you believed in me, and that motivated me to want to do better. And then when I confessed that time that I went to the casino, you never judged me."

Lindsay stopped when she saw Ellie's eyes start to water.

"Aww, Lindsay." Ellie flicked away a tear in the corner of her eye.

"I'm sorry. I didn't mean to make your mascara run."

Ellie chuckled. "I'm sure I'm not the first woman you've done that to."

"Sitting here with you, those other women might as well have never existed. I'm having the best time with you tonight."

"Even better than when you were with the legendary Marcella Hughes?"

"I had my time with her, and we certainly had our highs and lows, but that's in the past. The new Lindsay doesn't dwell there anymore."

"How long were you together, if you don't mind me asking?"

"On and off for about six years."

"Wow. The longest I ever made it was four years. But then again, I never dated a movie star."

"Her A-list movie-star days were pretty much over then, but she was and still is a force. That's for sure."

"I don't mean to sound like a geek, but do you think you could you get me an autographed pic?"

Lindsay giggled. "Really?"

Ellie nodded. "*Kingdom of the Goddesses* is still my go-to guilty pleasure on a lazy Sunday afternoon."

"Sure. I think I can squeeze one more favor out of her."

"Yay. Thank you. If you're sure she won't mind."

"Mind? She may be a diva of the highest order, but she's always appreciated her fans."

"That's sweet. Thanks. Now what should we order for dessert?"

"Let's see." Lindsay picked up the menu card and, in her periphery, noticed a figure heading toward them. She glanced up and her stomach sank. *No. Please, dear God, no.*

"Well, hello, Lindsay Chase." The disdain in Blair's booming voice clearly alerted Ellie. "Blair Maddox. Ms. Chase's attorney," she said, all business as she power-shook Ellie's hand.

"Ellie Tuttle. I've run into you several times at the courthouse. I'm a social worker."

"Sorry I didn't recognize you. I run into lots of beautiful women in the course of a day."

Lindsay fought not to emote her fury toward Blair. She knew very well who Ellie was. Lindsay had talked about her any chance she got while they were seeing each other. Now Blair was going to stand there in her space and flirt with her date?

It would take more than that to rattle Lindsay. "I'd invite you to join us, Blair, but I'm sure you're meeting a date here."

Blair almost cackled. "We don't all go from one woman to the next as fast as you, Lindsay. Last I knew you needed to remain unattached for the benefit of your recovery."

Now Lindsay was starting to unravel, especially when she caught the look on Ellie's face. "Well, it was great seeing you, Blair," she said. "Don't let me keep you."

Blair eyed her up and down. "Hmm. Says the woman who'll never be kept." She turned to Ellie and cocked an eyebrow. "Good luck."

After Blair sauntered away, Lindsay sheepishly returned her full attention to Ellie. Fucking Blair. Why couldn't Lindsay ever choose a woman to date who'd handle breaking-up with a little maturity?

"Well," Ellie said calmly. "Some people certainly know how to make an exit." Lindsay let out a chuckle, only somewhat relieved. "She didn't take the breakup too well."

"You don't say?" Ellie clearly did not hold back her eyeroll.

"Technically speaking, it wasn't even a breakup since we never labeled it as anything or discussed exclusivity."

"Why didn't it become exclusive? You guys made a stunning couple."

"I just wasn't there. And at the start she said she wasn't either. Neither one of us made it clear we were looking for something serious."

"I have a certain criteria I go by to determine if it's a relationship. I don't care about words or labels," Ellie said.

"I'm intrigued. Go on."

"Sex."

"Oh. Okay. Just sex? Does a one-nighter count?"

"I've never had one of those."

"Are you kidding?" Lindsay cleared her throat. "I mean, me either."

Ellie smirked knowingly. "No. Of course you have to have established a pattern of communication, but if you've also had sex with the person on at least two separate occasions, that's a relationship, whether you call it one or not. Hence, Blair's obvious hurt feelings." She extended her arm as though Blair were still standing there.

Lindsay found the impromptu seminar compelling. "But not everyone subscribes to that very specific list of requirements."

"Okay, but it's just common decency. You know when you've created a connection with someone. Apparently, when it comes to dating, you're the president of the Hair-splitters Club of America."

"I love it," Lindsay said through laughter. "You call people right out on their shit. I think that's my new favorite thing about you."

"In my profession, I've had a lot of practice learning how to sift through people's shit."

They bumped shoulders as they shared a laugh.

Lindsay signaled the bartender and ordered their choice of dessert: pistachio martinis and a piece of cheesecake they'd share.

After their silliness settled, Ellie looked at her and said, "You said 'new' favorite thing about me. That means you had another?"

"I've had a few, if you must know. Do you have a favorite about me?"

"Oh, so we're doing this?"

"I said one about you. It's only fair that you reciprocate."

"Okay. Let's see…" Ellie seemed to pretend to mine for an answer, tapping a finger against her chin.

"Come on. It can't be that hard to come up with one."

Ellie was playing it out as she waved her hand. "Give me a minute."

"Aww, you're not being nice," she said as the bartender brought them a slice of cheesecake. "You're not getting any of this." She slid the plate in front of her and pretended to block Ellie from it.

"All right, all right. I have one."

Lindsay slid the plate back between them.

"I would have to say my favorite thing about you is when you let down that Lindsay Chase rap and let me glimpse the real you, the vulnerable part I bet most people don't get to see." She then slid the plate in front of herself and cut off a chunk with her fork.

"I don't even allow myself to see my vulnerable side that often. You're the only one who's gotten to know the post-rock-bottom me." She sipped her pistachio martini before she revealed anything more.

"I believe you," Ellie said. "Which is why I'm not letting Blair's little performance ruin our night."

After another sip, Lindsay let out a sigh. "You are a true humanitarian."

Ellie smiled, then leaned closer and stole a tender kiss that rendered Lindsay defenseless. "You had a little pistachio foam on your lip."

"Oh. Thank you," Lindsay said.

"No. Thank you."

❖

It was almost eleven o'clock, and judging by the glare grenades the coffeehouse baristas were tossing, they could no longer tolerate Ellie and Lindsay's casual lingering. They'd moved from a restaurant to a wine bar to the coffeehouse, but the night was still thrumming with possibility. Ellie didn't want to go to another bar and have more alcohol, but she absolutely didn't want to say good night to Lindsay. She was about to make the lame suggestion that they stroll around the green when Lindsay's innocent question about her condo steered the night in an unexpected direction.

Next thing Ellie knew, they were approaching her front steps.

"Your condo complex is gorgeous," Lindsay said.

"Thanks. The groundskeepers do a fab job with the landscaping." Ellie felt her standing closely behind as she unlocked the door, and they entered.

What was she doing? Why had she invited her over? Lindsay had only asked how far she lived from the center of town. Now there they were, standing in the middle of Ellie's living room, and she was trying to hide her trembling hands from Lindsay.

"I can open a bottle of wine if you'd like," she said.

"Actually, I could just go for a water if you don't mind," Lindsay replied.

"Thank God. I'm so alcohol-ed out for the night."

Ellie scurried into the kitchen to grab a couple of bottled waters and to calm herself. This was such a stupid idea. She'd never taken a woman home after a first date. But then again no woman had ever made her feel the way Lindsay did after a first date. She took a deep breath and held it to stave off hyperventilation, then proceeded into the living room, where Lindsay had made herself comfortable on the sofa.

"I love your taste in decor," Lindsay said as Ellie sat beside her. "The modern-farmhouse style suits you perfectly."

"Thank you. I cultivated it through an HGTV obsession. What's yours?"

"Under normal circumstances, it's minimalist with a touch of Pacific beachcomber, but at present, it's old-man-retirement-community apartment."

"Oh." Ellie wasn't sure if she should laugh or sign Lindsay up for Meals on Wheels.

"That was a joke, Ell."

"Oh. Yeah." She produced a laugh. "Your delivery was so deadpan, I almost couldn't tell."

"I guess I should be clearer when communicating my intentions." Lindsay gave her a smoldering look as she licked her lips.

Ellie thought she might melt into the sofa cushions. "Yeah? What exactly are your intentions?"

Lindsay slipped the water bottle from Ellie's cupped hands and placed it on the coffee table. As Lindsay's lips came toward her, arousal throttled through her. Tender kisses from those soft lips gave way to a delicate flicker of her tongue against Ellie's.

A kaleidoscope of warning signals flashed around Ellie as she felt herself falling into Lindsay's sway. And it wasn't just her physical hold.

"I've thought about this for weeks," Lindsay whispered as she nudged Ellie back onto the sofa.

A whimper of pleasure escaped from Ellie as Lindsay fit her body into the curves and grooves of hers.

"Same," Ellie said. "You feel even better than I've imagined."

At last Ellie gave in to the desire for Lindsay that had been steadily building since they'd met. She'd done her best to heed the red flags and to keep it professional during her community service, but now Lindsay's sensuality was too powerful to resist. She throbbed as Lindsay's body physically overtook hers.

She cupped Lindsay's firm ass in her hands as Lindsay's tongue worked its way around her neck, driving Ellie into fits. She clenched her teeth as the words I love you began climbing up her throat. She couldn't allow the physical euphoria to make her become emotionally sloppy.

And it was working, too, until Lindsay's hand roamed up her shirt and attempted to unclasp her bra. Ellie groaned at the thought of Lindsay's fingers grazing over all her sensitive parts. But then she thought of the aftermath. Would Lindsay want anything to do with her after carving yet another notch in her headboard?

Panic rushed in. "Stop."

"What's the matter?" Lindsay whispered.

"I think we're going too fast."

"Uh, okay." Lindsay shifted off her and to her side. "I didn't mean to push—"

"No, no. You're fine. Maybe we should say good night and regroup."

Lindsay smiled. "Oh, that's right. If we made love, it would put us halfway into a relationship. According to your standards."

"I'm sorry. I'm just thinking about what Blair said, how you told her you weren't ready for one."

"That was before you swept me off my feet."

Ellie grinned. "I did that?"

"You did that." Lindsay gently brushed some strands of hair off Ellie's face.

"Oh, Lindsay. It's not that I don't really, *really* want to do it with you. I'm just afraid."

"Of what?"

"That if we move too fast, you'll spin out, and I'll get my heart broken."

Lindsay looked as though she had more to say, but she kissed her tenderly and sat up on the sofa. "I get where you're coming from, and you're right. Let's not rush this."

Ellie sat up with her. "Are you mad?"

"Not at all," she said in a soft voice. She took Ellie's hand and held it in her lap. "This gives me an excuse to ask you for another date."

Ellie could not even take how sweet and romantic Lindsay was being. "It's so late though. Will you stay over in my guest room? Breakfast is included."

"Oh, well, if breakfast is included, how can I refuse?"

Ellie stood and stretched. "I'll put some towels and a toothbrush on the bed in the guestroom. Let me know if you need anything else."

Lindsay stood with a yawn. "This is some tier-one service. Thanks."

"Anytime."

They stood staring at each other for a moment until Ellie broke the imaginary bond tethering her to Lindsay. With the heat rising between them, one more kiss would have them back on the couch and the decision to take it slow disintegrating beneath them.

❖

The next morning Lindsay awoke from the most luxuriating sleep she'd had in ages. As she lay on her side watching the show of dancing shadows the sun made through the swaying trees, she felt curiously cozy and insulated from the wreckage of her past.

Then she realized why. Ellie was big-spooning her. Startled, she whipped her head across the pillow. "Hi?"

"Good morning," Ellie whispered and then stretched out the arm that was curled around Lindsay's stomach. "I hope you don't mind. I could not fall asleep last night. I sneaked in here with you around four a.m."

"Then we didn't…"

"No. We didn't." Ellie sounded playfully offended. "I would certainly hope it would be good enough for you to remember."

"Well, I had some freaky dreams last night, so it's hard to tell."

"I dreamed, too, but mine couldn't top the reality of waking up next to you. You're way cuddlier than my body pillow."

"I can't tell you how relieved I am to hear that." Ellie giggled and sprang out of bed in her cute little shorty summer pajamas. "I'm going to grab a quick shower and then start breakfast. What would you like?"

"I'd like you to stay in bed with me a little longer, if that's on the menu."

Ellie sat for a moment in suspenseful silence. "Mmm. That's on the list of specials. We won't have those available until next weekend."

Lindsay laughed. "Good one. Then I'll have whatever you're having."

"Feel free to stay in bed and relax." She tossed her the TV remote. "Would you like a cup of coffee? I have pods."

"No, thanks. I'll wait for you."

"Okay. I won't be long."

Lindsay watched her legs as she flitted out of the room. Her soft breasts had felt amazing as they grazed her back, even if the moment was fleeting. Suddenly, her morning dry mouth was gone. If only it had woken her when Ellie slipped into her bed. How could she have missed that opportunity?

Then she remembered that Ellie wasn't some hell cat she'd picked up at a West Hollywood nightclub or movie-industry party. Ellie wanted to take it slow, and Lindsay was all for respecting her values.

After a couple of cups of coffee and a savory spread of lox and bagels, Ellie got up and tidied up the kitchen in seconds.

"Do you ever give yourself a minute to be lazy?"

Ellie giggled. "I never know when I'm going to get bursts of energy, so I just go with them. I'm not at all trying to hurry you along. It's Sunday, after all."

"Let me guess. You're thinking about going for a hike later."

"Kayaking, but close enough."

Lindsay smiled and got up. "Well, I won't keep you from your paddles."

"Will you come with me? I rent the kayaks and launch from the marina."

"Your friends won't mind someone new tagging along?"

"I was going alone, so if you'd like, I'd love it if you joined me."

"You're giving me an awful lot of offers I can't refuse."

Ellie beamed as she clapped her fingers together.

"Okay if I take a quick shower?"

"Of course. Help yourself to whatever you need in the linen closet."

With her hair balled up on her head, Lindsay picked a tropical-smelling body wash and smiled absently as she rubbed it over her body. Kayaking on a gorgeous sunny Sunday. How fun. Then they'd probably grab a late lunch at the marina and enjoy more flirty banter and some deep, penetrating conversation. She could envision no better foreplay than that.

Suddenly, the glass shower door opened, and Ellie dropped the towel that was around her and stepped inside with Lindsay.

"Does this mean you're ready to go halfway there with me?"

"I'm ready to go all the way." Ellie draped her arms around Lindsay's neck, and the shower rained over both of them.

Lindsay squeezed the body wash into her hands and then spread it across Ellie's back and around her waist, all while kissing her slowly and gently flicking her tongue against Ellie's. When she slid her fingers between Ellie's legs, Ellie gasped and pressed herself hard into Lindsay.

She glided them slowly, back and forth, in and out, in a sensual rhythm as the shower droplets danced on Ellie's eyelashes.

"This feels so good," Ellie whispered. She then grabbed Lindsay's hand and ground against it, tilting her head back under the cascading water.

As Ellie climaxed, her moans were rising in Lindsay's ear, and she thought for a moment she would come with Ellie.

Lindsay shut off the water, wrapped a large, fluffy bath towel around them both, and they scuttled over to the unmade bed.

Ellie sat on top of her, unwrapping Lindsay from the towel like she was a decadent treat she'd been craving all day. She descended onto her, tantalizing Lindsay with kisses all over her neck and collarbone.

Lindsay was throbbing in anticipation as Ellie slowly made her way down her, stopping to nibble on her stomach before she reached her final destination. Ellie's skill and enthusiasm had her reaching it in near record time. Lindsay had had more than her share of lovers over the years, but Ellie was different. She had a soulfulness in her eyes and in her touch that made their intimate connection feel that much deeper. She'd felt that way with only one other woman, Stephanie, in her early years in LA.

Since they'd parted, Lindsay had been chasing Stephanie's elusive qualities in other women, only to come up disappointed in the end. None of them could make her feel the way she did when she was doing anything with Stephanie.

Until Ellie. Being in her arms and making love with her was elevating Lindsay to a level of emotional consciousness that felt utterly exquisite. And terrifying.

When they'd finally run out of physical energy to expend on each other, they snuggled into a midday movie while still in bed. The sunny Sunday was calling to them, but Lindsay was content to stay right where she was.

❖

"I can't believe it's four o'clock, and we're still in bed," Ellie said as she stretched.

"It's not like we weren't productive. Two Meryl Streep films and an afternoon round of sex sounds like a fine Sunday to me."

"Are you disappointed we didn't go kayaking and have dinner at the marina?"

"We can go kayaking next weekend. And let's go to dinner right now. I'm starving."

"Me, too. We burned off a lot of calories today." Ellie grinned and pecked her on the lips.

Lindsay got up and put on the silky shirt Ellie let her borrow, then wound her tousled hair into a messy golden bun. Stealing glances at Ellie as she threw on some eye makeup, Lindsay had to force herself to calm down inside. And to stop subconscious comparisons to Stephanie. Ellie was an entirely different person, and if they were to become something serious, it wasn't going to end the way it had with Stephanie.

"So, I know your Sunday nights usually include one of your GA meetings. We can take two cars so you can go there directly after dinner."

Hmm. This was the second time a woman had reminded her about her meetings. She'd better take advantage of the opportunity Ellie was offering her and get back on her recovery track.

CHAPTER FIFTEEN

L indsay bounded down the steps to the church basement later that evening and pushed open the door to the usual crowd of three. Justin had his clipboard resting on his knees, and Barb and Angie had their paper coffee cups cradled in their laps.

"Look what the cat dragged in," Angie said playfully. "Where the hell you been?"

"I went to another meeting in North Haven," Lindsay lied. No reason to get anyone worked up.

"Remember, Angie," Justin said in a soft tone. "We don't shame people for not attending weekly. We welcome them back."

"Welcome back," Angie and Barb said halfheartedly.

"Thank you. One of the reason's I came tonight is because I wanted to share some fabulous news."

"We'd love that," Justin said. "Did you complete another step?"

Momentarily taken aback by the reminder of steps, Lindsay regrouped. "Yes, sure. But I wanted to tell you guys that I've fallen in love."

"With what?" Barb asked.

Suddenly, three sets of eyes were trained on her like snipers looking through their crosshairs. "With, uh…with Ellie, the social worker I did my community service with."

"Does she know?" Angie asked.

"Yes. We've been spending time together outside of the shelter, and last night we sealed the deal, if you catch my drift."

"Yes. Yes, we do," Justin said. "It's obvious she's a special person by the way you've spoken of her before but—"

"She's really remarkable," Lindsay said. "So different from anyone I've ever been with. That's good, right?"

"For sure. Going back to the same personality types you attracted prior to starting your recovery journey is highly discouraged."

Angie chimed in. "I thought having any new romantic relationships in the first year is highly discouraged."

"It's not ideal," Justin said. "Your first year of sobriety requires you to focus primarily on developing a sense of identity without relying on anything else to replace the source of the addiction."

"So you're saying I should just walk away from this near-perfect woman and how great it feels to be with her?"

"What do you wanna be tied down for?" Angie asked. "You're still young and attractive. Go out and be a whore. If I could do it all over again, I would."

Barb stifled a laugh as they all whipped their head toward Angie.

"You don't necessarily have to walk away from her," Justin said, then turned to Angie. "Promiscuity is also highly discouraged." Back to Lindsay. "We suggest that people explain to that special someone that the first year of recovery should be entirely about recovery. New relationships are full of emotional pitfalls."

"But she's a social worker. She can help keep me on track."

"Hmm. That's sort of a problem, Lindsay. If you need someone to keep you on track, then you're clearly not ready to shift the focus away from your daily learning journey."

Lindsay knew it was time to stop debating with Justin. Especially after noticing the hot twin glares coming from Angie and Barb.

"Listen, Lindsay," Barb said. "You're going to do what you want, but ultimately the choices you make are your responsibility.

If you're just here going through the motions to satisfy your probation officer, you'll probably relapse anyway, and then you'll lose this wonderful girl in the end."

"Uh, thank you for sharing, Barb," Justin said. "I'm just going to go ahead and assume that Lindsay is sincere in her desire not to gamble anymore."

"Thank you, Justin. I am." Lindsay glared at the ladies.

He acknowledged her with a light nod. "That said, if you want to pursue a healthy relationship with Ellie, you need to set a clear boundary that your recovery is your priority."

"Of course." Lindsay spoke as though his words were just a collection of no-brainers.

"And be more diligent in your 12-step meetings. And most important, work on developing coping skills that don't involve gambling in case the emotional swings of new love become overwhelming."

What a bummer this had turned out to be. Talk about the importance of knowing your audience. "Well, I want to thank you all for your input. I'm sure Ellie and I will be taking things slow."

From there, she recognized that if she was smart, she'd spend the rest of the meeting just listening.

As Lindsay drove back to her dad's, resentment rose in her over the group's egregious lack of enthusiasm for her news. This was the first time in years she'd felt genuinely good about something in her life. Ellie was a healthy person, and their connection was wholesome. How dare they toss turd missiles at her for being happy about something in the midst of a miserable experience?

And then Blair's phone number came across the screen.

"Shit," Lindsay said to no one. Should she answer? Blair was her lawyer, after all. But why would a lawyer contact a client at nine thirty on a Sunday night? "Fuck it." She pressed *answer*. "Hi, Blair."

"How nice that you actually answered this time."

"I'm driving home from a meeting. What can I do for you?"

"Oh, good. Glad to hear you're actually taking my professional advice about something. How are you?"

God, this was excruciating. "I'm fine. How are you?"

"Missing you." She slurred her words. "Can you drop by… like you used to after your meetings?"

"Uh, that's not a good idea, Blair. Remember how I'm supposed to avoid complicated entanglements?"

Blair scoffed into the phone. "You're just using that as an excuse. To avoid me, so you can fuck Ellie."

"That's not true," Lindsay said, despite it being totally true. "Blair, you're a vibrant, beautiful, intense woman, but now isn't the right time."

"Well, just how long do you expect a beautiful, intense woman such as myself to wait? I mean, what kind of timeline are we talking here?""

"You know that the experts say a year."

"A year?"

"At least."

"Then let's just be friends for a year. With benefits."

"As tempting as the offer may be, I don't think that will work either."

"You know what else isn't working? Me being your lawyer. I resign." Blair ended the conversation before Lindsay could reply.

Fucking fantastic. Luckily, Lindsay hadn't planned to do anything further that would cause her to need one.

CHAPTER SIXTEEN

Ellie walked into work the next morning wearing what had to be a smile bright enough to illuminate the shelter for a month. Good. No electric bill. That would help their fiscal crisis. She chuckled to herself but then halted as she heard shouting coming from Rosa's office.

She rounded the corner just in time to see Rosa slam down her office phone. "Good morning," she said meekly. "Should I have ordered you decaf?"

Ellie's attempt to lighten the mood fell flat.

Rosa removed the lid from her black coffee and took several sips before responding. "It's happening. They're closing our doors."

"What? No." The "no" trailed off like she was falling down a well.

Rosa's face remained contorted in disgust. "At the end of the month. That gives you exactly twelve business days to contact the clients you know you can find and let them know."

"Where are they sending you? Can I still work out of your facility?"

"Lower State Street, I'm assuming."

"That's an adult shelter. What about our kids?"

"Our kids are mostly between eighteen and twenty-four or thereabouts. They're adults. They can move on down to State Street."

"About a quarter of them are under eighteen. What happens to them? DCF? That'll be really effective."

"What do I always say, Ellie? It's not ideal…"

Ellie joined in the duet. "'But it's the best we can do.' I hate that empty phrase. It feels like such a cop-out. There's really nothing we can do to save Hope House?"

"I told you before. The landlord will extend the lease for another year, but we have only enough funding to cover operating expenses for the next couple of months. My superiors are saying shut it down now and move to State Street."

"Sure. Just pack it up and worry about it next fiscal year. But our kids don't have a year to lose."

Rosa sat back and folded her arms across her chest. She was apparently settling in for one of Ellie's long-winded rants of grievous indignation.

Instead, Ellie sighed and leaned against the wall. "I know that look, Rosa. I'm done ranting. What's the point? If I have twelve business days, then I'm going to use every one of them to figure out a way to save this place."

Rosa reached for her coffee. "Do not rob a bank."

"I thought about it for a moment, but a few grand and an exploding ink pack will not be worth the jail time."

"It's a setback, Ellie. Take it as that and not the end of the world. Our clients are quite familiar with them."

"For some of them, their whole lives have been one long setback. We're an agency meant to help. We shouldn't be part of the problem."

"We have enough in the budget for extra bus passes."

"Bus passes?" Ellie studied Rosa's impassive face. "That's the solution?"

"It is for now."

"I'm so over this," Ellie said, shaking her head. "I have to head into the office."

"Don't lose hope, mamacita."

"No. We're just losing Hope House." Ellie headed out and waved to Rosa.

She got into her car and headed across town to DCF, seriously contemplating a career change. She'd love more than anything to work for a lobby group on behalf of child welfare. Maybe then she wouldn't feel so mired down and helpless in the trenches with the kids.

Her mood instantly brightened when a call from Lindsay appeared on her car's navigation screen.

"Hi there."

"As hard as I've tried, I cannot stop thinking about you," Lindsay said. "Do you have plans for dinner?"

"If microwave mac and cheese counts as dinner plans, then yes, I do."

Lindsay chuckled. "It certainly does not. Would you be opposed to me coming over and making you homemade mac and cheese?"

"That would be a perfect way to end this shit storm of a day."

"Oh, no. What's wrong?"

"Rosa got the official word. The shelter is closing at the end of the month. That gives us like two weeks to get everything in order with our clients."

"Ugh. That's terrible. How can they let that happen?"

Ellie smiled, comforted by Lindsay's outrage. "We can talk about it later over dinner. Or not talk about it. I'll get the wine on my way home."

One of the recent discoveries Ellie had made about Lindsay that she absolutely loved was her appreciation of a one-plate dinner on the couch in front of the TV. Ellie had assumed that her years in West Hollywood hobnobbing among the rich and famous had spoiled her for the simple things in life.

Sitting closely beside her watching TV and feeling so comfortable, she realized how wrong she'd been.

"Would you like seconds?" Lindsay asked as she got up with their empty plates.

"I couldn't fit another bite of that cheesy goodness inside me. I'll have more wine though."

When Ellie got up with her, Lindsay gently touched her forearm. "No. Sit. I'll bring in the bottle."

"Thank you." Ellie watched Lindsay walk into the kitchen, paying special attention to her long, toned legs extending from her little gym shorts. The view from the front when she returned with the bottle of chardonnay was even more appealing, as her V-neck T-shirt allowed a teasing peek at her luscious cleavage.

Lindsay sat and refilled their glasses. "Not that I want to kill this idyllic mood, but did you want to talk about what happened at work today?"

"Not really, but I guess I should just purge it once and for all. Despite Rosa exhausting all her efforts, this time she couldn't stop the shelter from getting axed. The clients will be moved to the State Street shelter, but most of them won't go. I'm afraid of what's going to happen to the kids when Hope House isn't within a reasonable walking distance for them."

"I've never understood how homeless shelters close," Lindsay said. "These agencies get millions of dollars in state and federal funding. What are they doing with it?"

"Leasing space, paying a director, lights, heat…all those operating expenses add up. Rosa does a great job managing the budget, but the funds just don't stretch far enough."

"I could stretch those funds with some investments into aggressive, high-performing mutual funds," Lindsay said. "It would take about a year to get it off the ground, but if they'd let me manage the money, they'd cover operating costs and then some."

Ellie couldn't help smiling. "You'd probably have to wait till your probation is over before the State would let you handle the money."

Lindsay nodded. "Despite my current situation, I really was good with money, professionally and in my recreational activities. I used to kill it in poker. Then I started going to Vegas on the weekends and got sloppy. It wasn't about strategy and self-control anymore. It was just reckless abandon."

"If you were always winning in the beginning, why did you change and become reckless?"

Lindsay sat back and seemed to grow pensive. "It's like any addiction, I guess. The longer you do it, the more you need to do to feel that original high. The thrill of using calculated strategies dwindled away. Plus, things were starting to go awry with Marcella, too."

"Really? What happened?" Ellie caught herself and tamped down her excitement. "I mean, if you want to discuss it. You don't have to. I'm not trying to pry."

Lindsay giggled. "Don't worry. Everyone wants me to talk about my relationship with the famous Marcella Hughes. I get that. But she's really just a person like any one of us, especially when it comes to being in a relationship."

"Yeah, but she's so extra on her social-media accounts and when she did that reality show. You couldn't have felt like you were dating a regular woman."

"Regular? Definitely not. She had plenty of diva moments, but she had her dreams and insecurities like the rest of us."

"So why did you guys break up? Was she making outrageous movie-star demands on you?"

"Yeah. Totally outrageous. She wanted me to stop partying so hard and commit to a normal life with her. She even talked about marriage."

"No way." Ellie was riveted.

Lindsay nodded as if stretching out the suspense.

"You could've married a movie star, and you didn't? Didn't you love her?"

"I did love her, but at the time, I didn't realize how much. I was in my early thirties, and she was early fifties. I was having a great time and thought she was trying to shut it down on me."

"Makes sense. You just weren't ready for a big commitment."

"So we stayed in this on-again off-again pattern for almost seven years before she finally had enough of my shit."

Ellie's heart was swelling with empathy for her. In that moment, Lindsay was letting herself be honest and raw, and it was sadly beautiful. "It's funny now when I think how Kyle and Gretchen said you were such a party girl that Connecticut wasn't big enough to hold you."

Lindsay smirked as though the assessment made her self-conscious. "For a long time that was true. Now it all seems so far away. I just know that wherever I am, I feel most comfortable when you're there, too."

"Oh, my gosh, Lindsay." She reached over and took her hand.

Lindsay gazed into her eyes with vulnerability. "I'm sorry if I'm saying too much too soon. I just love the way I feel when I'm with you. It doesn't have to mean anything more than that."

Ellie shifted so she was facing Lindsay. "I feel the same exact way. But I know you're early on in your recovery journey, so I'd never want you to feel any kind of pressure. I just like hanging out with you."

Lindsay smiled and leaned closer for a kiss. One became two—soft, sensual. Three became four, and soon they lost count. Ellie pushed herself against Lindsay until they were prone on the couch, their kisses growing deeper, hungrier by the second.

"I want you to stay with me tonight," she whispered.

"I want that, too," Lindsay replied. She grazed her thumb over Ellie's lip as she stared lovingly into her eyes.

It was still early, but Ellie couldn't stand the desire Lindsay aroused in her any longer. She needed her touch. "Let's go get cozy." She jumped up and pulled Lindsay with her.

When they reached the bedroom door, Lindsay was throbbing. Ellie already had Lindsay's top off as she led her toward the bed, kissing her and sucking at her lips. Sexual aggressiveness in women wasn't new to Lindsay, but Ellie had kept hers so well hidden she felt a little like Persephone when Hades had plucked her from the fields.

"Ooh. Who are you, and what did you do with Ellie Tuttle?"

Ellie giggled. "Shut up and get out of these shorts."

"You first." Lindsay spun her around to the edge of the bed and playfully hopped on top of her.

They kissed passionately as Lindsay ran her hand up the back of Ellie's smooth thigh and over her taut rear end. Ellie groaned and undulated under Lindsay's touch. Lindsay slid her fingers across her legs, and it was obvious Ellie was ready.

Suddenly, Ellie opened her eyes and clutched Lindsay close. "I'm so glad you're here."

Normally, Lindsay would be miffed if a lover took her out of such a passionate moment, but the sweet vulnerability in Ellie's eyes made her soul tingle.

"Aww, baby. There isn't anywhere else I'd rather be."

"Really?"

"Cross my heart—which, by the way, is now in your hands."

A tear dripped down from the corner of her eye. "Oh, Lindsay. I love you."

"I love you, too, Ellie." Not since Stephanie had those words resonated so deeply within her.

"Please stay with me tonight."

"I'm not going anywhere." When Lindsay kissed her, Ellie's tears dampened her cheek. "Hey, are you okay?"

"Yes, yes," she whispered. "I'm just feeling a little overwhelmed…but in a good way."

Lindsay smiled to reassure her. "I can't believe we just said 'I love you.'"

"Neither can I. But I meant it, Lindsay, with all my heart."

"So did I. It's not like I needed to say it to get you into bed."

Ellie giggled. "No, you didn't. You turn me on so much I couldn't have refused if I tried."

"Speaking of that, here we are both crazy turned on by each other, and all we're doing is talking about it."

Ellie clutched the back of Lindsay's neck and kissed her as though she were about to devour her.

When she felt Ellie's wetness slide against her thigh, she knew neither one of them could hold out any longer.

CHAPTER SEVENTEEN

They'd enjoyed about a week of being madly in love, no longer bickering, just tucked into an insulated bubble of pure bliss before the gray cloud descended, turning Ellie's mood to soot. Curiously, Rosa had chosen the morning they were to board the flight to Chicago for Ellie's big weekend at the National Association of Social Workers' annual convention to drop the news that she'd received their transfer date from the State.

Was she kidding, Lindsay wondered. She couldn't wait till Monday and let Ellie have a carefree weekend?

As they Ubered to the hotel, Lindsay couldn't bear the silence any longer. "Come on, Ell. I know you're devastated, but don't let that ruin our getaway."

Ellie's head swiveled toward her.

"Yes. I heard it," Lindsay said. "You know what I meant. It's Friday. Nothing can be done until Monday anyway. You're speaking at a national conference tomorrow night. This is the highlight of your career. Let yourself enjoy it."

"This is not the highlight of my career. A highlight would be if I could create a program in which every kid transitioning out of foster care had a safe, reliable exit plan."

"Sure," Lindsay mumbled. "Why don't you just part the Red Sea while you're at it."

"Lindsay!" Ellie swatted her leg. "How can you be so insensitive?"

"I'm just trying to inject a little much-needed humor. You're the most caring, compassionate person I know, and it makes me sad to see you be so hard on yourself."

"Haven't you ever felt totally powerless in a situation you care so much about?"

"You mean aside from this very minute seeing you in such anguish?" She held her chin pretending to think. "Uh, yeah. That's been my whole entire life for the last eight months or so."

Ellie let out a heavy sigh. "I guess you do know the feeling. Thank you. And you're right. This is supposed to be a fun-packed weekend of professional camaraderie and romance, and I'm bringing it down before it's even started."

Lindsay squeezed her hand. "Nonsense. It's on and we're here. And look at that skyline." She glanced out the window at the skyscrapers glistening against a backdrop of blue space and billowy white clouds. She turned back to Ellie, still clasping her hand. "It's going to be okay, Ell. I promise."

Ellie rested her head on Lindsay's shoulder. "Somehow I believe you."

❖

After the morning conference sessions, the attendees were free to spend Saturday afternoon exploring before the dinner and awards banquet at six p.m. The gorgeous weather made planning their brief time easy. While Ellie was thrilled to visit a culturally rich city she'd never been to, her traveling companion was the most thrill-inspiring. And although their time as tourists was brief, she could appreciate Lindsay for the person she was in the moment, without probation and community service and a future of uncertainty overshadowing the sheer bliss of being in the moment.

They headed over to Northalsted to take in some LGBTQ history and view the Legacy Walk.

"I hope you don't mind that I'm a history nerd," Ellie said. "When I'm in a new city, I just love experiencing exhibits like this."

"No, it's great," Lindsay said as she scanned a tourist pamphlet. "It says that the Legacy Wall is interactive. We have to check that out."

"I'm so happy you're into this. I was afraid you'd find me a boring travel companion."

"Ellie, there is nothing boring about you. I have a feeling I wouldn't find something even if I searched for it."

"Not even my unwavering love for touring musty old historic homes?"

"I'll even take 'musty' if it's with you."

"Okay then." Ellie grabbed her hand, and they continued walking. "Thank you for coming with me this weekend. I feel less nervous about my speech tonight knowing you'll be there."

"Don't thank me. Thank my probation officer for giving me clearance. He said what could be a more productive way to spend a weekend than being at a conference full of social workers?"

"This is one way to keep you out of mischief," Ellie said. "Can we look in the Jane Addams Hull-House Museum?"

"Sure, but only if we can visit the Leather Archives and Museum, too. That could give us some interesting ideas for the good kind of mischief later tonight."

Ellie returned Lindsay's naughty grin. "Are you into bondage?"

"I can be into anything you want, you dirty girl."

Ellie chuckled and threw an arm around her waist as they walked. "Let's take a selfie over by the fountain."

"Another one?" Lindsay teased.

"I want memories from this trip, lots of memories."

"You're gonna need a fat photo album down the road. This is the first of many, once I complete my probation, of course."

"I would love that." Ellie stopped her and gave her a tender kiss.

"I'm loving what a vacation brings out in you. Do you think my probation officer would believe the next social-worker conference is being held in Turks and Caicos?"

"It wouldn't hurt to ask."

Lindsay consulted the map inside the pamphlet. "Hey, there's an art exhibit at a lesbian café a few streets over."

Ellie smiled at Lindsay's enthusiasm. "Could it be that we have two travel nerds in this relationship?"

Lindsay switched over to viewing her phone. "I'll be honest. While I love lesbian art exhibits, this place had me at 'gourmet grilled-cheese Panini.'"

"Let's do it."

❖

Seated at a large round table with a "Connecticut" sign sticking out from a floral centerpiece, Lindsay carefully observed as Ellie revealed a new layer of her personality throughout dinner. As Ellie exchanged stories with colleagues from around the country, sharing her successes and disappointments in her advocacy for LGBTQ young adults, she had a confidence and conviction mysteriously missing in her personal interactions. She was like Bat Girl or something, morphing into a superhero whenever she threw on her social-worker-ID lanyard.

As Lindsay sat quietly in awe of the stories and struggles all of the social workers shared, she realized this was one of the few instances in her recent history that she wasn't the center of the conversation. Her shoulders relaxed and she exhaled softly. What a novel experience to learn about other people from different walks of life. She began to comprehend why Ellie was so devoted to her profession—why, when things went wrong in her line of work, the consequences were so dire.

In Lindsay's line, when things had gone awry, the worst that happened was a multi-millionaire lost one or two of their multimillions, only to get it back once the market had an upward surge, or Lindsay was able to reroute a portion of their remaining millions into different, better-performing funds.

Ellie's profession touched people in the profoundest of ways.

As the serving staff cleared away the dessert dishes and refreshed coffees, the master of ceremonies returned to the podium.

Ellie clutched Lindsay's hand, painfully squeezing her knuckles together. "Oh, my God. Oh, my God. It's time for my speech."

Lindsay put down her coffee cup and used her free hand to extract her fingers from Ellie's grip. "You are going to be fabulous, honey. You've rehearsed for days. Just go up there and be your delightful, captivating self."

Ellie sucked in several deep breaths and seemed to be calming down.

Lindsay patted her leg. "Are you okay now?"

"I'm going to throw up."

"No, you're not."

"I'm going to go up there and throw up all over the podium, right in front of the entire ballroom."

Lindsay briefly flashed to the black-and-white gangster movies her father watched on TCM, where a guy in a pinstriped suit always seemed to have reason to slap the hysterics out of his female costar.

She opted instead to gently rub Ellie's back. "You're not going to throw up. Just breathe. Breathe."

"Friends and colleagues, please welcome to the stage Ellie Tuttle, from Connecticut's Department of Children and Families."

Lindsay's knees were smacking together under the table like small boats in a storm as she watched Ellie make her way to the podium. She glanced around the ballroom at the ocean of heads representing nearly every state's department of social services and commenced deep-breathing exercises herself.

"As we've all come to accept in our field," Ellie said, "we often have more bad days than good, and sometimes the agencies that are supposed to be our allies become our adversaries, miring us down with bureaucratic red tape and, at worst, systemic racism that fosters apathy and results in reduced funding and lack of belief in the communities we serve.

"But I refuse to accept the toxic ideology that many of our at-risk young adults are on an inexorable trajectory toward prison, thanks to government privatization. That's why it has been my life's work to help build a new bridge for our nation's at-risk youth. One that leads them from high school into career training and educational paths on which they can learn life and trade skills that lead to a product, independent life as adults. And not become another statistic that we all lament about after they've fallen through the cracks."

After Ellie concluded her speech, the audience of her peers roared with approval, and Lindsay was still standing applauding as she returned to her seat.

"You were outstanding," she said as they sat.

"Thank you," Ellie replied. "I'm so glad it's over and I can finally relax."

"Don't lose that mojo you've got going. They're having karaoke later at the afterparty."

"What are your thoughts on a duet?"

"I thought you'd never ask."

They sealed the deal with a kiss and sat closely together as they listened to the rest of the program presenters.

Once their romantic weekend in Chicago ended, reality again drifted over Ellie, sucking the happiness out of her disposition. While Lindsay might have created problems when it came to her own life, she'd had a longstanding reputation in the financial world as an innovator, a problem-solver who had helped folks plan for comfortable retirements and many others weather the market-tanking recession years earlier.

How could she just stand by and watch the refuge that Ellie and Rosa had manifested be closed down like a failing gas station? The kids they served needed that place. It wasn't like they could just hop into their cars and drive to another gas station.

When she got in the car and headed toward the casino, she engaged in some heavy mental bargaining with herself during the hour-long ride. It hurt her heart to see Ellie so anxious and upset over the shelter's fate. She worried that it might affect her physical health, as she wasn't eating or sleeping well lately. Also, the emotional stress might make Ellie shut down and need to put their relationship on ice for a while. Things were so promising for them, Lindsay couldn't allow that to happen.

Load on to that Lindsay's frustration in trying to find full-time employment in the midst of her legal troubles, and it was all weighing heavily on her. Now that she and Ellie were officially a couple, she wanted to do more things with her, to take her to trendy places, show Ellie she was much more than all the drama she'd brought back from LA.

One afternoon. That's all. Just a few hours. She was feeling lucky, and if she could walk out of there with several thousand in her pocket, no one had to know.

She needed to release some of the mounting stress, and deep breathing and yoga poses just weren't cutting it.

Once she finally secured full-time employment, hopefully in the finance sector again, she'd leave the frivolous days of cheap thrills at a card table behind her.

She adjusted her baseball cap, tucked up the stray hairs, and strolled into the poker room. She found a table with a low buy-in and a bunch of scruffy amateurs who looked like they'd been gaming since the night before. A little Texas Hold'em with these poor jerks who'd probably learned how to play the game on a phone app.

This was going to be easy.

After about an hour or so of playing, her initial stack of chips had turned into four stacks. The guy next to her checked his watch, pushed his small stack toward the dealer, and announced that the tournament was going to begin soon.

Tournament?

After the dealer told her that the tournament had a prize of one hundred and fifty thousand, she cashed in her four grand in chips and headed over to the ballroom to check it out.

While her performance in the poker tournament had exceeded her wildest expectations, she knew that confessing this one to Ellie was out of the question. She'd already made that classic solemn promise to her that her first relapse was a one-and-done transgression. Ellie's thinly shrouded warning that one more relapse, and Lindsay would be done—with her—had lingered in her consciousness ever since.

Yes. This was going to be her final secret from Ellie. And with an outcome like they were about to experience, one more harmless little secret was no big deal.

A few days later, after the funds had cleared at her bank, Lindsay parked her car several blocks down from the shelter at sunrise. She couldn't risk it being connected to her if any random passers-by were out that early on the quiet streets. She'd wrapped wads of bills tightly in elastic bands and stuffed them into a small, used, Amazon delivery box.

She pulled the strings on the hood of her black sweatshirt and casually strolled toward the employee entrance of the shelter with the box tucked under her arm. Hopefully, porch pirates wouldn't notice the side entrance in the murky dawn.

CHAPTER EIGHTEEN

After Rosa summoned Ellie with a seven-a.m. text, Ellie made the shelter her first stop of the day. Rosa was at her desk leaning over a small, open box with a look of exuberance that Ellie had never seen before on anyone, let alone Rosa.

"What are you grinning about?"

She plucked a note from inside the box and handed it to her. "Read this."

"*Dear Hope House Shelter.*" Ellie read aloud. "*Thank you for all the good work you do for the young people in this neighborhood. We hope you can stay here forever.*" When she looked up, Rosa had the box tilted so she could see that it was full of cash.

"Oh, my God. Are you serious? What is this?" Ellie plunged her hand inside and stared incredulously at the fistful of hundreds she retrieved.

"When I came in this morning, I found this taped-up box right outside the entrance. All it says on it is Hope House."

"How much is in there?"

"One hundred and two thousand."

"Did I hear correctly? Did you say one *or* two thousand?"

Rosa laughed. "You heard me right when I said one hundred *and* two."

"I can't believe this. An angel heard our prayers."

"Clearly some nocturnal philanthropist read about the shelter closing, but I like your version better. I'll take angels around us any day."

Ellie flipped the note over. "And no name or anything?"

"Nothing," Rosa replied. "I'm going to call the local news, though, and give them this update. If they run the story, maybe the angel will see it and come forward so we can thank them."

"It might even inspire others to give. Oh, Rosie, I'm so happy I could cry. We don't have to close."

Rosa stood up and ruffled her hands through the heap of bills. "No, we don't, mama. Not this year."

Ellie ran toward her, and Rosa enveloped her in her arms.

Once Rosa finally let go, Ellie pulled her phone from her pocket. "Oh, I have to call Lindsay and tell her this incredible news."

❖

At dinner, Lindsay couldn't stop smiling as Ellie recounted the story of Rosa coming to work and finding that miracle in a box outside the shelter.

"Linds, I cannot describe how good it feels to have my faith in humanity restored like this."

"I can see how good it feels. You're positively beaming."

"I mean, I don't know if this is a case of an actual prayer being answered or if it was one major random act of kindness. Didn't Einstein say something like there are no coincidences?"

Lindsay placed her hand over Ellie's. "Why overthink it? You should just accept this wonderful gift from the universe and eat those oysters before I steal them from you."

Ellie took a deep breath and then giggled. "I need to chill for a minute. I've been off-the-charts excited all day." She sipped her wine.

"I'm so happy for you and Rosa, Ell. You guys so deserved this."

"I just wish I could thank the person who did this, shake their hand. Let them know what a huge difference they've made."

Lindsay grabbed one of the remaining oysters on Ellie's side of the platter. "Anyone who donates that much to an organization understands the impact it will have. I'm sure Rosa will stretch those dollars as far as she can, and then all's well that ends well. Now, what are you going to order for your entrée?"

Ellie picked up the small menu and scanned it for a minute. "Linds, we're splitting this tab." She leaned in and whispered. "Everything here is so expensive."

"Well, we're paying for the view." She smiled as she indicated the boats docked outside in the Quinnipiac River.

"It is stunning," Ellie said. "But you're not paying."

"Of course I am. I'm working now."

"You're helping out your brother landscaping—part-time."

"I also have a side hustle. My dad hooked me up with a bunch of his friends at the Elks Club. I'm helping them all with retirement planning. It's easy money."

Ellie grinned. "Your brother was spot-on about you always landing on your feet."

"He loves saying that," Lindsay said. "Makes it seem like my life's been nothing more than a series of lucky breaks." She leaned back in her chair with her martini in the air, satisfied with herself. "I like making things happen. And I love that I made this happen with you." She leaned forward and tapped her martini against Ellie's wineglass. "I love you, Ell."

If Lindsay thought Ellie was beaming before, those four words had her lit up like a comet.

"I love you, too, Linds." She stretched over the bistro table for a kiss. "This all just seems too good to be true. Tell me it isn't."

"Listen, Ellie Tuttle. Whatever good fortune comes your way, you've earned every bit of it. You're a gorgeous human, inside and out."

"So are you, babe. If anyone proves that a person shouldn't be judged by their past, it's you. I'm so lucky you're mine."

"I'm the lucky one."

Just when Lindsay thought Ellie had finally put aside her mission to find out the donor's identity, Ellie leaned forward, apparently still mulling it over.

"It just puzzles me that nobody's coming forward to take credit for that massive donation."

"It wasn't that massive," Lindsay said, more concerned with dressing the last oyster in the plate. "It's not like you guys got a million-dollar endowment."

"It was a hundred and two thousand dollars," Ellie said. "That's kind of an odd amount. I wonder how they settled on that figure."

"It's the after-tax amount," Lindsay said absently as she picked at a few rings of fried calamari.

"What?" Ellie said, clearly confused.

Shit. "What?" Lindsay repeated.

Ellie continued, obviously undeterred from her line of thinking. "Anyway, it's going to help Hope House immensely, and Rosa will make sure this gets the publicity it deserves."

The oyster shell slipped out of Lindsay's hand and crashed onto her plate. "She is?"

"Hell, yes. Stuff like this usually triggers copy-cat donors once the community hears the story behind the donation. Something like this could go nationwide. Or worldwide even."

"It could?" Lindsay pushed her plate away and signaled their server for another cocktail.

"What's the matter? Was that last oyster no good?"

"No, no. It was fine. That's, uh, a clever idea Rosa has, but it was so dark, I'm sure nobody saw anything."

"That area has traffic cameras, so I bet someone at the local news could zoom in and screenshot an image of the person."

Traffic cameras. How did she not think of that? There really was no such thing as the perfect crime.

"Wouldn't it be so cool to find out who did it and nominate them for like a Good Samaritan award or something?"

"Not if they don't wanna be found." Lindsay began scrambling into damage-control mode. "Some people don't want that kind of attention. A lot of fanfare might embarrass the person, who obviously didn't want the credit. Otherwise, they would've done it in the daylight. Or at least signed the note."

"Hmm. I guess I didn't think of it that way."

"That's okay, babe. You were just caught up in the excitement of it all. You know what I would do about this if I were Rosa?"

"What?"

"I'd share a big, gawdy, thank-you post all over Hope House's social-media accounts and leave it at that."

"Really? Just a general thank-you post? It seems so anti-climactic."

"It covers all the angles. You get to publicly thank the benefactor and let the world know that some important person thought that shelters for unhoused teens matter enough to be saved."

Ellie sat back and appeared to be coming around to her side. "That makes a lot of sense. It also protects the generous donor's privacy."

Lindsay exhaled. She finally felt like the oysters had stopped trying to slither back up her throat. "Exactly. It's a matter of safety for them as well."

"I love how you can be my voice of reason when my optimism starts making me go off the rails."

"If there's anything I'm good at, it's tamping down other people's optimism."

Ellie's eyebrows furrowed.

"I mean by being a voice of reason. So, after dinner, why don't we skip dessert here, go back to your place, and have each other."

Ellie bit into a buttery slice of crusty bread. "Oh," she said through a moan. "Your ideas just keep getting better and better."

As soon as they got into Ellie's bedroom, Lindsay pushed her against the wall and kissed her hard. Ellie wrapped her arms around Lindsay's neck and held on as her legs grew weak beneath her. Lindsay's firm, skillful touch ignited a fire in her she'd long forgotten was possible.

She lit some candles, drew down her bedding, and pulled Lindsay toward her. They stripped each other of their clothing and fell into bed, Lindsay on top.

"I spent the whole day dreaming of this moment," Lindsay said as she gazed at Ellie. "Having you in my arms is the best feeling."

Ellie held her face and kissed her sensually. "Now that's the best feeling to me."

"I love loving you, Ell. And making love to you," she said as she pulled down Ellie's underwear. She then unhooked Ellie's convenient front-clasp bra and squeezed and kissed her breasts.

Ellie threw her arms back onto her pillow and offered herself to Lindsay. She writhed with desire as Lindsay caressed her from the back of her leg, up her torso, to her waiting nipples.

When she began tugging at Lindsay's thong, Lindsay sat up on her, removed her own bra, and then came back down, molding her naked body into Ellie's. They kissed as they ground together, with Ellie pushing Lindsay's hips closer to her.

"You feel so good, Lindsay. You make me feel so good."

"I want to make you feel amazing."

Lindsay kissed her lips, then her neck, and slowly made her way down her chest, her stomach, until Ellie arched into the pleasure Lindsay was giving her. After an explosive climax, Lindsay crawled back up and held her tenderly.

"I love you so much, baby," Ellie said as she caught her breath.

Lindsay brushed the sweaty strands of hair off Ellie's forehead. "I love you, baby."

Ellie hugged her as tightly to her as she could. She'd waited her whole life to experience a love like this. She only hoped Lindsay's feelings were as deep and as steady as hers.

CHAPTER NINETEEN

L indsay had set up her makeshift office in the back room at the Elks Club, a laptop and folding chair behind the plastic table they served their weekend happy-hour snacks on. Galaxies away from her days in her high-rise office with its stunning view of the Los Angeles skyline, it still made her grateful for the opportunity to get her fingers back into the world of financial planning and leave behind her days of scratched-up legs and green toes from landscaping for Kyle.

"Okay, Wally," she said. "I've got you set up in an annuity fund with that ten grand." She tapped away on the keyboard as she glanced at the mound of paperwork beside her. "And you're officially retiring next year, correct?"

"Yep," he said proudly. "Forty-six years at the gas company."

"Fantastic. So, if you're paid bi-weekly, I'll arrange to have two fifty go into the fund each pay period for the next year."

"And it's safe?"

"Very. Annuities are guaranteed income streams, perfect for retirees," Lindsay said as she closed her laptop and gathered his paperwork. "A lot safer than your money's gonna be in about a half hour." She looked at her watch and winked at him.

"We'll see about that." He tossed a deck of cards onto the table and handed her a roll of twenties for her services.

Later, as the game was underway with four of her father's fellow Elks, Lindsay observed how everyone's stack of chips was much lower than hers. Waves of guilt splashed her from all sides of the wobbly table. She'd helped all four of them create and/or tweak investment plans that would make their retirements more secure, and here she was winning some of their money right out from under them.

Not to mention the fact that Ellie knew nothing of this weekly underground senior poker klatch that had just sort of happened. Lindsay was viewing it as public relations. What better way to convince these seniors that she was good with money?

"Why is this table so wobbly?" Lindsay asked. "I'm sitting here with four tradesmen, and none of you can figure out how to level this?"

"Where's the matchbook I stuffed under there?"

She glared at him. "Really, Dom? A matchbook?"

"I'll make a wedge for it in my workshop this weekend," Wally said.

"Why don't you just make a whole new table," Sal said, and they broke into laughter.

"Why don't you shut up and deal the cards," Wally replied. "I'd like to try to win some of my money back before I go home."

"Not today, Wally." Lindsay enjoyed teasing the guys. "Mama needs a new pair of sensible shoes."

"Hey, when you were out in California, did you ever play cards with DeNiro?"

Lindsay shook her head regretfully. "He didn't exactly run with the same crowd I played with."

"Did you and your Hollywood crowd play high-stakes?"

"Sometimes. Especially if they got drunk and stupid."

"You never drink when you play?"

Lindsay shook her head again. "Not anymore."

"What's that you got there?"

"Diet Coke."

"No wonder you've been wiping the floor with us. Have a man's drink."

"I hate to break this to you, Johnny, but that's not why I'm wiping the floor with you."

The other guys roared with laughter and took jabs at Johnny as well. What a crew this was. To go from playing with WeHo's lesbian elite to these goofy old straight dudes. It's all she had now, so she was nothing if not grateful.

After getting away with that brazen tournament caper at the casino, she was finished with any kind of gambling besides this. The old adrenaline rush from being reckless and taking ridiculously unnecessary chances just didn't hit like it used to. Now that she'd fallen in love with Ellie, the risk outweighed the rush.

When her father and his girlfriend, Gloria, came in, she immediately walked over to Lindsay. "Hey, honey. Any news yet on the identity of the Hope House Angel?"

"Hi, Gloria," Lindsay replied as she tilted her hand of cards toward her chest. This is exactly what she hadn't needed. "Nothing yet. They won't find out unless the person comes forward."

"I don't know about that," her father said. "They have some decent video from the store across the way."

Not helping, Dad.

"It's too grainy."

"They've got all kinds of advancements now," he said. "The FBI has the technology to make it clearer."

"Well, I'm sure nobody is going to pay to put the FBI on the case."

"Let's call and see if someone from there will volunteer to do it," Gloria said. "Dom, don't you know a fella who retired from there?"

"You guys are going to kill this heart-warming mystery," Lindsay said. "If you launch an investigation and find out that the 'Angel' is some pasty old white billionaire, you'll ruin all the romanticism of this beautiful story. Then it's just another case of a rich person looking for a tax write-off."

"She has a point," Sal said. "Leave it alone and just be grateful."

Lindsay pointed at him with enthusiasm. "Exactly, Sal. That's what I'm saying."

"I just love mysteries," Gloria said. "I watch 'em all the time on the TV. Have you seen the new Matlock with Kathy Bates yet?"

"That's the shelter you worked at for two months," her father said before she could reply to Gloria. "Aren't you even a little curious?"

"Not really," she said. "Not enough to call in the FBI."

Wally looked up. "You worked there? Any idea if anyone there could be the culprit?"

"Well, I can tell you who it isn't...anyone who takes home a social worker's salary. Hey. Maybe one of the homeless kids won the lottery and wanted to give back." She lowered her head and pretended to study her cards, through with the conversation.

"Wouldn't that be something," Sal said casually.

"I thought we're here to play cards," Johnny said gruffly.

"That's what we're doing, loudmouth," Dom said.

"Who you calling a loudmouth, Mr. Matchbook?"

As the arguing continued, Lindsay tuned out and sent up a silent prayer that this curiosity pandemonium surrounding Hope House would soon die down.

When Lindsay pulled into her father's street, Blair's Porsche was already in the driveway. After she'd texted earlier that she needed to see her right away, Lindsay had assumed it would be just another ploy to get back with her.

"What's up?" Lindsay sauntered toward Blair, who was leaning against her car like Jake Ryan in *Sixteen Candles*.

Her jaw muscles pulsed as she apparently ground her teeth in angst. "It's you, isn't it?"

"The problem? Yes. Hi. It's me. I'm the problem. It's me." Lindsay was joking, but Blair's face remained on the verge of splintering.

"Where did you get that kind of money?"

Lindsay grimaced. "Oh. That's what you meant."

"Of course, that's what I meant," Blair snapped back. "I'm still on record as your attorney, so I want to be prepared when all this explodes in your face."

The humor in Lindsay's mood vanished. "It won't. I was very careful."

Blair's expression only grew more intimidating.

"It won't blow up on me," Lindsay insisted. She turned away and then back again. "Do you really think it's going to?"

"It's inevitable for two reasons," Blair said. "One, the footage is all over social media, thanks to the hashtag Hope House Angel. Secondly, the money. Where did you get it? I'm assuming you didn't find it under a rock."

"The casino." Lindsay whispered like they were under surveillance.

Blair shook her head. "I fucking knew it."

"How is that a problem? I wasn't caught in there. I was just an average tournament player with my hair up in a baseball cap wearing aviators."

"You *won* the poker tournament?"

Lindsay beamed. "Hundred and fifty grand. Pretty fucking impressive, huh?"

"Un-fucking-believable." Blair closed her eyes, apparently trying to regulate her response. "And you gave the casino your ID and social, correct?"

"I had to. They wouldn't give me the money without it."

"If your probation officer gets wind of this…"

"How will he? I wasn't recognized. It's over and done with, as long as someone doesn't identify me in that footage."

"And what if your girlfriend doesn't keep her mouth shut? She's responsible for most of the posts."

"Ellie doesn't know." Lindsay shuddered at the thought. Ellie would be done with her for sure if she knew she'd gambled again. "I haven't told a living soul except you, and that's because we have attorney-client privilege."

"Your own girlfriend couldn't recognize you in a video clip?" Blair's smirk dripped with satisfaction.

Lindsay fired back. "Neither did my previous girlfriend."

"Oh, so now I was your girlfriend, when the whole time we were fucking you didn't believe in labeling it?"

"Uh...my point was you had intimate knowledge of me as well, but you didn't know it was me in the video either."

"Not at first, but I made the obvious connection." Blair's hands were flailing at this point. "Your girlfriend's shelter is closing down; you're a degenerate gambler..."

"Then I guess I'm just lucky my girlfriend isn't a terrible cynic like you."

Blair studied her for a moment. "Okay. I've wasted enough of my time on this. Just continue to keep your mouth shut. And don't get any ideas about grabbing the spotlight over this."

"No problem," Lindsay said as Blair got into her car. "And don't you worry. This little social-media blip will run its course and be over in a week. It's had its fifteen minutes."

"I hope you're right. But in the likely event that you'll need an attorney over this, call me."

"Aww, thanks, Blair. That's sweet."

Blair backed out into the street and rolled down her passenger window. "I have a list of public defenders I'll give you."

Her tires screeched on the pavement as she drove off.

CHAPTER TWENTY

Lindsay had tried to block out her unpleasant encounter with Blair a couple of days earlier, but the real possibility of the donation being traced back to her had been menacing her. Nowadays, with social media, even the inanest things went viral. But even something as heart-warming as saving a homeless shelter would fade into internet oblivion once some quirky character with a snappy catchphrase caught fire.

Before walking into Ellie's condo with her overnight bag slung over her shoulder, she'd tucked all those thoughts safely away for another time. Blair was just being an alarmist, as any high-strung defense attorney was wont to be.

Yes, Lindsay had broken all the rules—again—but this time it was for an exceptionally worthy cause. Surely karma would see that and protect her from any negative blowback.

Ellie greeted her at the door and grabbed her hand. "Come in, come in. Wait till you see this." She dragged her in front of the TV as commercials aired.

Lindsay watched the ad for a second, perplexed. "Ell, I've heard of scent beads before. I just use an expensive fabric softener."

"No, no. Not this. Sit down and wait till the news comes back on."

Ellie pulled her down onto the sofa and sat stiffly at the edge, her eyes fixed on the TV screen.

"I hate dramatic anticipation. Just tell me."

"The Hope House Angel. The local news is doing a story on it tonight. They're going to show security-camera footage from the bodega across the street."

"They what?" Lindsay leapt up and felt the blood drain from her face.

"I knew this beautiful story wouldn't fade into obscurity like you said." Ellie's eyes were maniacal. "We're finally going to find out who this humble, generous soul is."

Lindsay began to stutter. "Wha…uh, no, no. That's a terrible idea."

Ellie seemed confused at her distress. "Why?"

"Babe, don't you remember our conversation the other night at the oyster house? What if this humble, generous soul doesn't want to be found out? What if they just wanted to do a good deed in secret, like Jesus would've?"

"Jesus didn't live in the age of social media. Their identity was bound to be discovered. It's not like in the thirties, when a person could've dropped off a baby in a basket on a church's doorstep and nobody would find out. Big Brother sees everything."

"You should try to put a stop to this." Lindsay began to pace.

Ellie got up and tried to calm her. "Lindsay, I don't understand you. This is the feel-good news story this city desperately needs. With crime and inflation and war all over the news, people need this to restore their faith in humankind."

"No, they don't. Nobody cares about anything but themselves nowadays."

"Oh, my God, Lindsay. That's not true. Lots of people care. They just don't know about these situations until they're brought to their attention."

Ellie pulled her down on the sofa again, but she popped back up like a buoy and continued pacing.

"This is a bad idea, Ell. This kind of notoriety could prevent other people from wanting to donate. Rich people don't want their identities known. Scammers and poor relations will come out of the woodwork and badger them for money."

When she noticed Ellie staring at her like she was a derailing train, she stopped and cooled down. "I'm just saying…"

Ellie grabbed her and forced her onto the sofa, holding her there once the commercial break was over.

This was awful. Ellie seemed more excited about this than she'd ever been about anything, and Lindsay couldn't even take the credit for it. Not that credit was what she was looking for— far from it. She was in love with Ellie and wanted to help save something that meant the world to her. It just would've been nice to see the look on her face if she could find out that Lindsay was her angel.

Not so much the look on the face of the judge, her lawyer, or her probation officer, however. This was more than just a falling-off-the-wagon moment. This was a violation of the conditions for her plea deal.

She was possibly one news story away from being the most popular new inmate in a women's white-collar prison.

"In other news," the anchorman said. "The mystery of the Hope House Angel who placed a box of cash outside a failing homeless shelter may soon be solved, thanks to a local store owner who sent in his security-camera footage to this news station."

Ellie clutched Lindsay's arm in anticipation—which was good because Lindsay felt like she was about to keel over from lack of oxygen.

The newscaster continued. "Although the footage is grainy, you can clearly make out a person approaching the side entrance of the shelter and placing a small package right outside the door."

Lindsay gently extricated herself from Ellie's grip. "I'll be right back." She hurried to the bathroom, locked the door, and whipped out her phone.

Hey, Bla… Backspace, backspace, backspace. *Hey, Attorney Maddox. Quick question…did you happen to see the local news just now?*

No. What the hell, Lindsay?

"Babe," Ellie called out from the living room. "You're missing the rest of the story."

"Be right there," Lindsay replied as she texted. *Uh, no big deal. Just a little news story on the Hope House Angel. With the security video. Is now a good time to start panicking?* She leaned against the door and braced for Blair's wrath.

Now is an excellent time. At least when you're decaying in a jail cell, I'll sleep well knowing I did all I could for you.

Awesome. Thanks, Lindsay replied. She slipped her phone into her back pocket and joined Ellie in the living room.

She was sitting on the sofa beaming her adorable light into the room and looking almost as elated as the night they both said I love you for the first time.

"Sit down with me, babe." She patted the cushion, still grinning.

Lindsay slunk over and plopped down next to her. "Were you able to make out the person's face?"

"No. You can't even tell if it was a man or a woman. But someone may recognize them."

Lindsay emitted a low grunt of agreement as she let her head fall back on the sofa. Relief was sweet if only temporary.

Ellie hugged Lindsay's arm and rested her head against her shoulder. "I stopped believing in miracles a long time ago. This is just the kind of thing to make me a believer again."

She squeezed Ellie's hand, painfully torn between the jubilance of seeing her so happy and the anxiety of knowing at any moment her illicit caper could be exposed. Security cameras. She knew the shelter didn't have any, but why hadn't she considered that neighboring cameras picked up peripheral activity? Her only saving grace was that she was cloaked in a dark hoodie and the footage from those things was usually unclear.

Still, the question loomed. Should she just come clean to Ellie right now about her gambling relapse, or should she take her chances that everything would blow over by tomorrow's news cycle?

Ellie leaned in and whispered in her ear. "Seems a shame to let all this exuberance go to waste. Follow me." She stood up and led Lindsay by the hand to her bedroom.

Lindsay offered her a sly smile and did as she was instructed. Suddenly, taking her chances seemed like an okay thing to do.

❖

After they'd made love, they lay together talking softly, Ellie on her side with an arm and leg wrapped around Lindsay like a vine. The tea-light candles had gone out, but the moon was casting its glow in through the window.

Lindsay rolled her fingertips up and down Ellie's shoulder and smiled when Ellie sighed at the gentle rhythm. She tried to recall a time when she'd felt so contented with someone that she could lie quietly soaking in her scent, her aura, and her body as it melded to hers. Maybe Stephanie? Not even Stephanie. Despite their compelling new love for each other, a wall of hiding had always remained between them.

With Ellie, no wall of defense was needed when they allowed intimacy and openness in. Despite her secret, unnamed fears, Lindsay was so ready to ride the ride with Ellie wherever it took them.

"This is perfection," she said.

Ellie kissed her shoulder. "You just read my mind."

"Hmm. It's strange to feel so in sync with someone."

"For me, I think it's because I got to know you as a friend first. I saw you being you, the good and the not-so-good, without the pressure of having to decide in a moment if you're the one, as they say. A lot of times you miss things when you view someone only in the context of being a potential partner."

"Yeah. I totally get that." Guilt began pulling Lindsay out of their secluded world. The lies were starting to stack up around the money donation. She kept telling herself that, if the shelter stayed open, the lies wouldn't matter to Ellie in the end. But as they were falling deeper in love, Lindsay had more and more to lose.

Ellie propped herself up and whispered in Lindsay's ear. "Can I tell you a secret?"

"Yes. I love secrets," Lindsay whispered back.

"I've never been happier in my entire life. I'm a little afraid to say it out loud." She buried herself into Lindsay again.

"You don't need to be superstitious about your happiness, Ellie. You deserve it as much as anyone. In fact, more than anyone I know."

She inched up to kiss Lindsay. "And it all happened when you came into my world."

Lindsay squeezed her tighter. "Aww, thank you. But you're giving me way too much credit."

"You can't deny the timing of it all. Okay, so maybe it was just a coincidence that someone saved the shelter around the same time we fell in love. But you've helped me learn to trust love again—after I'd all but given up on it."

"Oh, Ell. I love that so much." She kissed her back. "To be honest, you've helped me trust love. For the first time."

"Really? That can't be. You've had so many interesting lovers."

"But none of them made me want to stop running."

"You were with Marcella a long time, on and off."

"Why do you think it was on and off? Ell, you're just so different from anyone I've been with. You're sexy, kind, compassionate. And oh so tough when you need to be. You're intelligent, independent, and make me feel like the center of the universe when I'm with you."

"When you're with me, you are."

Lindsay's heart sank. This could all disappear if the truth were revealed. "I couldn't possibly ask for anything more in a woman. I hope you always know how much I love you."

"I hope you're always here to remind me."

Lindsay hugged her tighter. "Me, too."

After they finished their take-out sushi, Lindsay and Ellie went out onto the deck with coffees made in Ellie's espresso machine. Lindsay put her feet up on the small wicker ottoman and got comfortable.

"I'm loving this relaxing evening," she said and glanced over at Ellie, who was tapping away on her phone. "Are you working again?"

"No. I'm trying to zoom in on this surveillance screenshot to see if I can get a clearer view of the face."

So much for relaxation. "Why are you bothering with that? The news media is looking for the person."

"Not anymore. They ran that story so the person would come forward, but obviously, they didn't see it."

"Come on. Stop obsessing over it. We're supposed to be having quality time together."

"We are." She reached over and gave her a reassuring pat on her forearm, then returned to her screen. "Let me do this. It'll only take a second, and then I can post it all over social media. Somebody's gotta see it there."

Lindsay quietly surrendered to the truth. Too many people used social media as their primary news source. Once Ellie put that cropped, zoomed-in picture out there, her cover was bound to be blown. She began fidgeting in her chair as her mind raced to find a way out of this.

"If I were you, I'd just let it go and be at peace in your gratitude."

Ellie looked at her, clearly picking up on her angst. "What's the matter?"

"Nothing." Lindsay looked out on the complex grounds and sipped her coffee.

"I don't understand why you're so adamant about me not pursuing the person's identity. What's the worst that can happen? If the person says they want to remain anonymous, I'll thank them profusely and be done with it."

"That's not the worst that can happen," Lindsay muttered. "Trust me."

"You're being weird. Let me just post this and then—"

Lindsay leaned over and grabbed her hand. "Ellie, listen to me for a minute."

"What?"

"What if the person who did this could go to jail if their identity was revealed?"

"*What?*" Ellie's expression was a cross between amused and dumbfounded.

Lindsay rubbed her forehead in a moment of paralyzing indecision. The curtain on this act had to close. "Ellie, I just…"

"Lindsay, what?"

And then the words jetted out. "It was me. I'm the Hope House angel." She used air quotes to highlight the irony.

"Very funny, Linds. You don't have that kind of money. You used your retirement savings to pay for your attorney."

"Well, yes, that's true. I used all of *my* money to pay Blair, but…"

Ellie's smile melted down her face. "Lindsay, what are you saying? Did you embezzle from your clients again?"

"What? No," Lindsay shouted. "Never. The guys at the Elks Club don't have that kind of cash."

"Then how am I supposed to believe that it's you?"

"I, um, I came into some money recently, and I thought, wow, what great timing." She chuckled nervously. "I figured I would just donate it anonymously, so the shelter can stay open a few more months while Rosa works her magic."

Ellie's eye narrowed. "How does one with such a checkered past when it comes to money suddenly come into such a large sum?"

Lindsay hesitated to respond while Ellie seemed to be puzzling it out in her head.

"Oh, no. Lindsay…"

Okay. She got it.

"Lindsay, please tell me you're not gambling again."

"Well, now the word gambl*ing* suggests that it's an ongoing thing, like I'm doing it regularly, which I am absolutely not—"

"Lindsay," Ellie exclaimed. "Are you involved in some illegal underground poker ring or something?"

"No, baby. It's nothing like that. Please calm down and let me explain."

"I can't just calm down because you say so. The woman I fell in love with has been deceiving me."

"Now wait a minute," Lindsay said. "All I did was enter a poker tournament at the casino, intending to give whatever amount I won to Hope House. I just didn't know I was going to win it all."

"Why would you do that, knowing it's a violation of your probation?" Ellie paused for a second. "You won it all?"

Lindsay nodded proudly.

Back to hysteric mode. "Oh my God, Lindsay. You're gonna go to jail."

"No. No, I'm not. As long as I can make sure my identity isn't discovered."

"And how do you propose to do that? *The Independent* is coming to the shelter tomorrow to interview Rosa and me."

"Obviously, you can't talk to them."

"Fine. I won't, but how am I supposed to convince Rosa to cancel the interview? She thinks the story will catch the attention of other benefactors in the area and inspire some kind of great give."

"Fuck." Lindsay buried her face in her hands for a moment, then popped her head up. "Okay. I know. We need to find a patsy, someone to say they made the donation. Then everyone wins."

"And how do you suggest we find this patsy?"

Lindsay stared expectantly at Ellie.

"Oh, no. No fucking way."

"Your boss will be so impressed with you."

Ellie's complexion was turning a glorious shade of red.

"It was just a thought," Lindsay said.

"Well, think again."

Lindsay drummed her fingers on the table as she pondered her options. "I know. We'll get a homeless guy off the street and pay him a hundred bucks to tell the reporter that he's really a millionaire in disguise. Or, now hear me out, we can have him say a drug dealer dropped the money, and he happened to find it."

Ellie's mouth hung open as she studied her. "A homeless man? That is the dumbest, stupidest thing I've ever heard. It'll never work."

"Let's go look for that old guy who recites Shakespeare near the museum."

"I bet I know where he is," Ellie said, and off they went.

❖

After an hour roaming the streets in the humid, exhaust-filled air of downtown New Haven, Ellie stopped and leaned against a mailbox on the corner.

"I would like to restate my original claim that this is the dumbest idea you've ever had." She glared at Lindsay.

"How do you know? You haven't known me that long." She used the bottom of her T-shirt to wipe sweat off her forehead.

"Lindsay, we cannot hire a person who lives on the street to say they donated thousands of dollars to the shelter. We'll never get away with it, and I'm not going to risk losing my job over this." Ellie was trying to keep her cool, but the temperature and her frustration with Lindsay were both way above normal. "What the hell were you thinking, going to the casino to try to save the shelter?"

"I didn't actually go to the casino to save the shelter. I went because...well, because I have a gambling problem. But I'd like you to focus on the point that I saved the shelter *because* I went to the casino."

Ellie had never wanted to slap a grin off someone's face more than at that precise moment. "I think the thing I need to focus on here is that this just proves my biggest fear about you is true. I'll never be able to trust you."

That remark proved more effective than any slap.

"Ellie, of course you can trust me." She reached out for Ellie's hand. "I was going to tell you."

"No, you weren't." Ellie yanked her hand away. "You think that because you aren't addicted to drugs or alcohol that your relapses are no big deal?"

"No. I just understand that relapses are part of recovery, and that people, especially people who care about an addict, should be patient with them."

"You are unbelievable," Ellie shouted. "Don't you dare think you can get away with manipulating me. I know exactly how this works."

"I'm not trying to. I just—"

"Bullshit. You don't take your recovery seriously. You never have. You fuck up everything around you and then look for solutions to your problems in the beds of other women."

"Is that what you think this is between us?"

"I honestly don't know what to think this is with us. You talk a really good game, Lindsay, and I can see why women fall for you. I just don't know why I was so stupid to believe you'd be different with me."

"I am different with you, Ellie. I just screwed up a little. But look at the good that's come out of it."

"The good? If your parole officer finds out you went to a casino and won thousands of dollars, you could have your probation revoked. And then what am I supposed to do? Wait for you to serve out a couple of years in prison? No, thanks." Ellie stormed off around the corner onto a side street, but Lindsay was right behind her.

She caught up and grabbed her arm to stop her. "Ellie, I love you." Her eyes were pooling with uncharacteristic fear, something Ellie had never witnessed from her. "I'm not manipulating you. I'm truly, desperately in love with you."

Ellie paused, fighting with all her being against the compulsion to jump into Lindsay's arms and ignore all the red flags. The eye-pooling seemed authentic, but it was probably just a level-up in her manipulation game once she realized her smooth talking wasn't working. "I'm in love with you too, Lindsay. And it's one of the biggest mistakes I've ever made. You'll never change, and I was a fool to think you even wanted to."

"I do want to, Ell," Lindsay said as she gently held Ellie's shoulders. "I'm trying to change. I just need you to give me one more chance."

"You need therapy. That's what you need." She glanced down at Lindsay's hands still clutching her. "Let me go." Ellie couldn't hold back her emotion. "Please let me go," she said through tears.

"Ellie," Lindsay whispered as she released her gentle grip.

Ellie stormed off and left Lindsay standing on the sidewalk.

❖

By midnight Lindsay had finally placed her phone out of sight, stuffing it in her father's kitchen junk drawer. Ellie clearly wasn't going to answer her calls or texts anytime soon, and she had to break the cellphone malaise she'd been drowning in since the afternoon. How was she supposed to get any sleep? It used to be that when she created chaos for herself, it was merely collateral damage in the pursuit of self-serving fun. But this time, she'd tried to be selfless and do something that would have a lasting benefit for others. And it still ended in disaster. She lay in bed, her skin crawling with anxiety. Should she call someone? Take a drive?

She went into the kitchen and chugged a bottle of water, staring at the drawer her phone was in. Marcella. She could always call her. Marcella had made it clear that she wanted her back. It would be so easy to slip into their old routine again. Why was she fighting so hard for a woman who had such unreasonable expectations? Marcella had always been so patient with Lindsay's flaws—until her excesses eventually drove her away.

She pulled her phone from the drawer, opened her contacts, and brought up Marcella. Just call her, she thought. She'll take you back in a minute. It would be so easy…

Her thumb hovered over the number for an eternity as she stood staring numbly at her phone. Her thumb then swiped the app closed, and she dropped the phone back into the drawer.

Going backward, going back to something because it was easy—that wasn't who Lindsay was anymore. Forward was the only direction to take, whether Ellie would be there or not.

CHAPTER TWENTY-ONE

The next morning Ellie made the shelter her first stop, with a gigantic cup of dark roast for herself and a regular for Rosa. She'd hardly gotten an hour of sleep ruminating over the debacle Lindsay had caused for the shelter and for them as a couple. What was she thinking? How could someone be so disconnected from the reality of consequences?

Ellie's heart had just crashed and burned yesterday, and now she was going to have to create an excuse as to why she couldn't participate in the interview with the local online news reporter who was coming in.

"What happened to you?" Rosa stared at her as she grabbed her coffee from the tray.

Ellie touched her face. She'd seen in the mirror that morning that her eyes and face were puffy from crying and lack of sleep.

"Did you get stung attacking a hornets' nest?"

"In a manner of speaking." Ellie sat down and sipped her steaming coffee.

"Do you wanna talk about it?"

She shook her head. She'd desperately wanted to talk about it, but at that moment, it would've raised more questions than she had the strength to answer. *Damn it, Lindsay.* "Rosa, I hate to do this to you, but do you think you could handle the interview yourself today? I have to do a placement evaluation later, and it'll probably take all day."

"Sure. No problem." The look on Rosa's face gauged that she knew Ellie was lying, but she was too kind to call her on it.

"Thank you," Ellie said. "I absolutely owe you one."

"Yeah, you do. See if you can sneak in a little nap today." She gave her the once-over with a grimace.

Ellie chuckled. "Will do."

She got in her car, but before she headed to a team meeting at the office, she counted all the attempts Lindsay had made to contact her since yesterday.

The audacity.

She evidently assumed that kind, patient little Ellie would cave to her persistence and charm, but that wasn't going to happen. Their happily-ever-after was off the table. The last thing she needed in her world was to work all day in a job that depleted most of her emotional energy, only to go home to a partner who would sap the rest.

As she drove off, Gretchen's call came in on her navigation console.

"Girl, where have you been? All nice and tucked away with Lindsay?"

Ugh. "We're on a little break now, so I can hang out soon if you want."

"You're what?"

She had to think fast. She couldn't tell another soul that Lindsay was the Hope House Angel. For some odd reason, she still felt a duty to protect her. While she wasn't big on the "end justifies the means" excuse for wrongdoing, the "end" in this case was massive. So many vulnerable people were going to benefit from what she did. The least Ellie could do was not facilitate her going to jail for it.

"We, uh, we just needed a break. We were moving way too fast."

"According to who?"

"Me. The decision was mine."

"Wow. I don't know what to say. I mean, Lindsay must be so bummed."

"I think she understood. It's all good."

"Yeah. I guess if it's just a break, it's not the end of the world. Now if Kyle said he wanted a break from me, I'd end his world."

Ellie giggled. "You guys have been together forever. That would never happen."

"Well, I'm sorry it happened with you and Linds. Why don't you come over and hang out this weekend?"

"Maybe. Right now, I kinda feel like laying low."

"Okay. I get it, and I'm here if you need me. Love you."

"Thanks. Love you, too."

Ellie ended the call and drove on the highway entrance ramp amid another round of tears. Even hanging out soul-to-soul with her best friend wouldn't fix the break in her heart over Lindsay.

Lindsay sat at the kitchen table, hands on her laptop, studying the market trends of the past week and months, and made notes of the highest gainers during that timeframe. Her coffee cup was empty, and she had to pee, but her body was sluggish. Her heart, on the other hand, fluctuated worse than the market in wartime between searing pain and complete numbness.

Except now she had none of the vices she'd used to defeat her pain in the past: gambling and women. Now she didn't even want either. All she wanted was to make things right with Ellie.

The ring of her phone startled her and jolted her lethargic legs into action. It was only Gretchen.

"Hey," Lindsay said.

"Hiiii," she sang in response. "How's it going?"

"Fine. Just doing a little market research," she replied in a monotone.

"Are you okay?"

Shit. She must've talked to Ellie. "Never better."

"Cut the shit, Linds. I talked to Ellie."

Great. Now the family knew she'd fallen off the wagon in spectacular fashion and might soon be heading to prison. "It was a mistake. I learned from it, and it won't happen again."

"Don't be so hard on yourself. It can happen to anyone."

"It can?" Why was she being so nice and casual about her relapse?

"Yes. Who can blame you? It's Ellie we're talking about."

"Yeah, yeah. I did it for Ellie." Wow. Her sister-in-law was really stepping up for her. Good to know Gretchen could be called as a character witness in the future. "Thanks for understanding. I feel bad about it."

"Don't be ashamed," Gretchen said warmly. "You couldn't help that you're so into her, you came on like a psycho, obsessed fan."

"Yeah. That's right. I only—wait. I did what now?"

"She told me how she had to put the brakes on because you were moving too fast. It's understandable. I just hope you're not too upset. I'm sure it's only temporary."

"Yeah. Uh-huh. Okay. I was a little embarrassed at first, but you know…"

"Just give her some space, and I'm sure this will all work itself out."

"Oh, she's gonna get space all right."

"Don't go through this alone, Linds. Come over this weekend, and we'll have some old-fashioned, wholesome, family time. The kids love when you play with them."

"Sounds exactly like what I need. Thanks."

Lindsay ended the call, still stewing about Ellie basically telling her family that she was a stalker. But once her ego finished its tantrum, her heart sank at the notion that Ellie was telling people they were done. Making it official.

CHAPTER TWENTY-TWO

Days had gone by, and Ellie still hadn't responded to any of Lindsay's texts. She understood how hurt and disappointed Ellie was to learn that her return to gambling had saved the shelter. An unpleasant irony, to say the least. However, she couldn't understand why Ellie wouldn't at least talk to her about it now that she'd had time to cool off. They were in love. Didn't that warrant at least one more conversation so that clearer heads could prevail?

She'd contemplated showing up at work and her condo with a dozen roses and her irresistible smile, a tactic that had worked many times in the past. But in the past she wasn't a convicted felon. What could be considered a romantic gesture could now be viewed as a reason for a restraining order and a probation violation.

Instead, Lindsay opted for some words of wisdom from family. She and Gretchen sat in the backyard with a variety of White Claw flavors and a plate of crackers and sweaty cheese as the boys played in their turtle-shaped sandbox.

Gretchen placed her phone on the table between them. "Kyle wants to know if you'll work with him tomorrow. His hedge guy is on vacation this week."

"Sure. Why not?" Lindsay replied listlessly. "I know my way around a bush. Besides, Ellie still won't talk to me."

"I know. Of course she told me all about it."

"Did she say if this is going to be a permanent thing, or is she just trying to teach me a lesson?"

"You know, it would really help your cause overall if you could try to be just a smidge less flip about everything."

Lindsay threw her hands up. "I don't know how not to be me."

"Now I'm finally seeing it." Gretchen studied her, shaking her head.

"Seeing what?" She looked down at her outfit to see if something was crawling on her.

"Your smugness. Your unbelievable self-centeredness."

Lindsay almost physically lurched back in surprise.

"I always thought you were the coolest, most enviable woman in the world—smart, beautiful, stylish, kissed by the gods, if you will."

"Goddesses," Lindsay said.

"But that was because I knew you on only a superficial level. The whole time I've known Kyle, you've been clear across the country, so I never got to see who you really are behind all the glitter."

Lindsay uncrossed her legs and recrossed them. "Well, I certainly didn't anticipate the conversation taking a turn like this when I came to you all vulnerable and seeking advice."

"I'm glad you feel you can be vulnerable with me, and I am giving you advice. You just have to be willing to hear it. Ellie is one in a million, and as shy and introverted as she is, she's not gonna tolerate anyone's bullshit. You need to do some sincere, intense soul-searching if you really want to win her back."

"I have been. In the past, I wouldn't have given a meek, unblemished girl like Ellie a second look. Now I'm madly in love with her."

"You can't crowd out your demons by falling in love with Ellie. This I know as a social worker. You have to address them honestly if you want any hope of a normal, healthy relationship someday."

"In our one and only fight, Ellie said I needed to see a therapist. I thought she was just being mean."

A light laugh broke through Gretchen's sternness. "She might have been in the moment, but I know Ellie very well. She said it because she genuinely cares about you and wanted your relationship to work as much as you did."

"Then why is she being so stubborn?"

"Why are you? You came back to Connecticut with your tail between your legs. Compulsive gambling ruined your life. Then we find out you've been to the casino multiple times—"

"Twice."

Gretchen glared at her. "More than once. Multiple. How is Ellie supposed to trust you when you've shown her right up front that she can't? None of us can."

Lindsay's pride rose up her throat, practically choking her. Or was it Gretchen's words she couldn't swallow? She found no lies in anything she'd said, as fast as her brain scrambled to detect them. Worst of all, Gretchen had nothing to gain or lose in saying what she did.

She finally looked up at her sister-in-law and exhaled.

Gretchen reached over and clutched her forearm. "Are you okay? It's all right if you're not."

Lindsay nodded. "I'm just exhausted."

"Then stop fighting. Or running. Or whatever it is you're doing to avoid accepting accountability."

"Know any good therapists?"

Gretchen smiled warmly. "A bunch."

Lindsay sighed audibly, partly in defeat and part in relief. "Did I ever tell you about Stephanie?"

By early afternoon, Ellie had finished her work for the day, and rather than move on to other paperwork that needed to be pushed, she went to hang out with Rosa.

When she walked into the foyer, the sound of laughter coming from the main area greeted her. Not so unusual, as Hope House was a shelter for teens and young adults, but why hadn't Rosa told her if she had a new group of clients?

"Hey, lady," Rosa said as she got up to hug her. "Long time no see. How are you?"

"Never been better. How come none of these kids came across my desk?"

"They're not cases. They're high school students volunteering for school credit."

"They sound like they're having a party."

"That's because I don't have time to stand over them with a whip and a chair."

Ellie chuckled. "Looks like I got here just in time." She motioned toward the door, but Rosa grabbed her hand.

"Hang on. Have a seat for a minute."

Ellie plopped down and clutched the armrests in anticipation. She knew Rosa wasn't going to let her melancholy demeanor go unnoticed.

"What's going on with Lindsay?"

"Nothing. We broke up." Ellie glanced off to the side. If she'd made direct contact with Rosa's big, sympathetic eyes, she would've lost it for sure.

The chair creaked as Rosa sat back in it. "I wasn't sure if it was a done deal or just a break."

Now Ellie was ready for eye contact. "Rosa. She gambled again. Twice. And those are the times she admitted to."

Rosa nodded as though they were talking about the weather. "We know the statistics on relapse while an addict is learning to cope with their addiction. My concern is for you. How are *you* doing in all this?"

"I'm a mess. I struggle to get out of bed in the morning. I struggle to get through the day. I'm tired all the time, but I can't sleep. And I can tell by the way you're looking at me that I'm not concealing it very well."

"More or less. Have you talked to your doctor about some medication?"

Ellie shook her head. "I just miss Lindsay so much sometimes I can't breathe." She bit her lip to hold back the emotion. "I wanted so badly to believe in her. To believe we could have every dream we talked about together."

"You don't think that's possible someday?"

"Do you? You're the one who warned me about getting too involved with her from the start."

"It was a general word of advice about the risks involved with dating an addict. I was just looking out for you. As you know, addicts are individual people. You can't lump them all into the unfortunate group they happen to fit into."

"I'm confused about your messaging here, Rosie. Should I stay away from Lindsay because a lifetime of risk comes with falling in love with an addict, or should I give her another chance because, other than those two relapses that didn't even result in negative consequences, Lindsay's been doing well on her road to recovery?"

"Yes." Rosa's smile turned her round face into a cherub's.

Ellie laughed as she exhaled. "Thanks for making this situation even more complicated."

She tapped Ellie's hand. "Give yourself time to feel. I trust your instincts. Whatever you decide, it'll work out in the end."

"I don't know what to think any more, but you're right about needing time. I'm just so sad."

"Your heart is broken, *mija*. Take care of it."

"I'm trying. I just can't stop thinking about her."

"I have an idea for how you can get your mind off her for a while."

A loud shriek of laughter came from the main room. Ellie grinned. "I'm on it."

❖

Lindsay fidgeted in the waiting room for fifteen agonizing minutes before the therapist came out and led her into the office. She surveyed the attractive woman's figure in her casual, tailored outfit as she grabbed a legal pad and sat down in the chair across from her. Had she never met Ellie, Lindsay would've been plotting a way to have the woman's personal digits in her phone by the end of the session.

Had she never met Ellie, she wouldn't even be in a shrink's office.

"So where would you like to begin, Lindsay? I know in your message you mentioned relationship issues."

"Oh, there's that for sure, but my girlfriend, Ellie, well, my now ex-girlfriend, said something to me during our last fight that made me realize I might need therapy."

"Oh? What did she say?"

"You need therapy."

The therapist chuckled. "That phrase has become sort of a punch line when couples are fighting, but why do you think she said it?"

Lindsay shrugged. "I guess because my life is in shambles. I tend to go through women, I have some issues with gambling, and I think I may have some avoidant-attachment disorder."

"Okay then. Since points one and three are closely related, we can start there."

"Sure." Lindsay made herself comfortable in the chair. "What do you need to know?"

"Well, you said Ellie suggested that you need therapy. Are you here for her or because you agree with her?"

"I guess it wouldn't hurt to take a look under the hood. You know what I mean?"

"It never does, but you can't embark on a journey of self-discovery just to get a girl back."

"I can't?"

"You can, but ultimately, it's a waste of everyone's time. If you're going to see any benefit from it, you have to be open to the process outside of anyone's influence."

Lindsay sighed, frustrated with herself.

"Have you had many relationships?"

"Lots."

"And who usually ended them?"

"Me."

"I'll assume you had your reasons."

"Of course. Mostly because I'd become restless and want new experiences. I didn't want to settle into something that wouldn't fulfill me long term."

"What is it about this particular ex that made you want to try therapy?"

"She's just incredible." She smiled in the warm memory of Ellie's presence. "I've never felt like this with anyone before. Except maybe Stephanie." *Wait. Where did that come from?*

"Who's Stephanie?"

"A former girlfriend from a dozen years ago."

"Do you remember why you broke up?"

"Aside from Ellie, she's the one girl I didn't break up with. She died."

"Oh. I'm sorry." The therapist seemed to settle into her chair as she adjusted her grip on her pen. "Perhaps we should start there."

"I've never talked about this to anyone before. I mean, a few friends in LA knew about us, but by the time I could afford to start traveling back and forth between coasts, Stephanie had already gotten sick. Then, when she passed, I couldn't even bring myself to talk about it with my family back home."

"This certainly informs your lack of desire or ability to give yourself fully to someone again."

"Really?"

"You didn't just lose Stephanie because you outgrew her. She died; she was taken from you. That's a whole different animal when it comes to processing loss. Had you sought any counseling when it happened?"

Lindsay shook her head. "I was in my late twenties. I had the 'that's life' mentality about it and forged on. It's not like anyone in her life knew we were anything more than friends."

"She was in the closet?"

Lindsay nodded. "The youngest in a big Italian Catholic family. I'm surprised she never moved away so she could live freely."

"You can move to the other side of the world, but if you can't give yourself permission to be who you are, you'll never live freely. Is that why you moved to California?"

"No. I got into UCLA. It was like, hey, a four-year paid vacation. I'm in. I stayed because the small hedge-fund firm I interned at offered me a job when I graduated. A year later they hired Stephanie, and our friendship slowly turned into a magical romance." Lindsay's fingers trembled on the arms of the chair as she began to pull memories out of her vault.

The therapist also noticed. "Do you need a moment?"

Lindsay exhaled. "No. It's just a little unsettling going back there. It's been a long time."

The therapist nodded. "You're ready to. Otherwise, you wouldn't be here. But let's take it at your pace."

"Being here is also making me understand why I didn't go to therapy back then. My insides are quivering."

She smiled. "That's a common physiological response when you start unpacking painful memories. If this were easy, everyone would see a therapist, and we'd live in a world with zero emotional instability."

"Imagine that," Lindsay said dryly.

"So not only did you not get professional help, but you didn't get much emotional support from anyone outside your small friend circle."

"Our group became really tight when she was diagnosed. The four of us were a team all through her treatment. I mean, I was never alone."

"But you also weren't acknowledged as her partner by family, co-workers, others in your lives. Your love, the bond you shared, wasn't validated because you had to keep it hidden."

Lindsay flinched as though gouged with a sharp object. "I never even came clean about it after she passed. I wanted to honor her wishes."

"To keep you and what you both shared a secret. That had to be difficult."

"I understood. She was several years older than me, and her parents were a lot older and had a very different mindset from my parents."

"So she was laid to rest, and then you soldiered on."

"What else was I supposed to do?"

"Is that when your gambling became a problem?"

"I wasn't even gambling then. Through a series of random occurrences, I met the people who would introduce me to cards. I'd also started making really good money, so that's when the excess started, too. I gained a few celebrity clients, started hanging out with gay ones, and even began a relationship with an actress."

"No kidding? Which one?"

"Marcella Hughes."

The therapist paused. "Oh, yes. I remember her. Stunning woman."

"And then I was off and running. And running. Anything to keep my mind off Stephanie and all the things I didn't or couldn't face during my time with her."

"Were you and Stephanie serious before she became sick?"

"I thought she was the one. I knew she was. We loved traveling, any kind of adventure. We talked about buying a place together, all that. And then her diagnosis. We had to shelve all the plans we were making so she could go through treatment." Lindsay trailed off. "I really believed she was going to beat it."

"And when she didn't, your life ended up on the trajectory that led you back here."

"Well, you skipped the part where I embezzle money from my employer, get arrested, lose my townhouse in Santa Monica..."

"I figured you wouldn't mind if I did at this point." The therapist smiled. "We're here to help you unpack the issues that caused your downfall, not dwell on them."

"I'm glad I came here," Lindsay said, feeling humbler than she'd ever imagined possible.

"Are you regularly attending GA meetings?"

Lindsay resisted the temptation to gloss over the truth. "I think it's like you said. I need to unpack the baggage that led to the gambling first. I mean, what good does it do drilling 'I can't gamble, I can't gamble' into my head without digging up and examining what was causing the behavior?"

The therapist smiled. "You've done very well this session. Same time next week?"

Lindsay left her first foray into therapy feeling somewhat lighter. She'd been carrying Stephanie's complicated memory around for so long, she hadn't even thought about the weight of it. Or the repercussions.

Maybe it wouldn't get Ellie back, but it was time to lay the memory of Stephanie and what could've been to rest. Before she ended up losing another woman to it down the road.

CHAPTER TWENTY-THREE

Lindsay sat down at their table toward the back of the posh bistro. Marcella always insisted on sitting away from the bustle in restaurants, even though most times she came and went unnoticed, especially in ritzy little Connecticut towns. For Marcella's sake, Lindsay hoped that would change once she made her triumphant return to acting in the new Broadway production she'd just begun rehearsals for.

"Have you started scenes with Viola Davis yet?" Lindsay asked.

"Yes, and she's a pleasure to work with. Let me guess. You want me to arrange it so you can meet her."

"Uh, no. Just making conversation."

"Oh. Is that where we are now? You have to 'make' conversation with me?"

Lindsay smiled patiently. "Why are you doing this the minute we sit down together?"

Marcella's hard expression softened. "I'm just cranky because you're in love with someone who isn't me."

"Thank you for your candor. And for finding the time to have lunch with me now that you're busy with the play."

"You sounded so down on the phone; it was making me depressed. Think of this as a welfare check."

"I'm okay, Marcella. I just screwed up something very meaningful, and it hurts."

"Ellie?"

Lindsay nodded.

"You're not together anymore?" Her eyes sparkled with possibility.

She shook her head, the mere thought almost bringing her to tears.

"That's too bad. She must be something extraordinary for her to do this to you."

"She is."

"Aww. I'm sorry. What did you do, cheat?"

"Absolutely not. I'm in love with her. I don't want anyone else. The problem is I did a bad deed trying to do a good one."

Marcella rolled her eyes as she raised her glass to her lips. "It all sounds rather dull."

"It's not. I gambled. I played in a poker tournament and won. Then I secretly donated the winnings to save the shelter where Ellie works."

"How disgustingly romantic. But I'm sorry. I don't see a problem in that."

"According to her, it shows her that I'm a liar and can't be trusted."

Marcella's nostrils flared in disdain. "Yuck. It's clearly time for you to move on from Little Mary Sunshine."

"Mar, I'm kind of a gambling addict. It was a big relapse, and I lied about it. I can understand why Ellie would see it as a major red flag."

"Are you a true gambling addict or just a self-indulgent little brat that needs to grow up?"

"I guess the jury's still out on that one. But thanks for the new perspective." She winked, clicked her tongue, and shot her with a finger gun.

Marcella gazed at the stunning gardens outside the window. "Hmm. I hate to see you so dreary, darling. A situation like this requires something big, some grand gesture that shows Ellen—"

"Ellie."

"That shows *Ellie* that you are worthy of her trust and that your feelings for her are real."

"If donating a shit ton of money that I could've used myself to her floundering shelter isn't grand enough, then I'm out of ideas."

Marcella fished the cherry out of her Manhattan with a stirrer and popped it into her mouth. "Let me run this scenario by my PR guy. You're not letting your epic Robin Hood moment go to waste."

Lindsay smiled, remembering why she'd always run back to Marcella. "I'm glad you're going to be on this coast for a while."

"Somebody has to spank you into shape." Marcella flashed her a racy smirk. "You're gonna owe me for this one."

"Fine. At this point, who don't I owe?"

The day came for Marcella's live Zoom interview with TMZ, in which Lindsay would join her as well. Marcella's PR man had to be an evil genius for the story he concocted about the charitable donation Marcella had made that saved an inner-city shelter for unhoused LGBTQ teens and young adults in Connecticut.

Lindsay sat in the prettiest corner of her father's apartment she could find with the midday sun stretching across her from the window. She'd set up her laptop on a TV stand and hoped her father wouldn't come home earlier than he'd planned. Her teeth were practically chattering as she waited for the host to connect them on the call.

After a couple of tips from the TMZ interview prepper, they went live.

"Joining us now is eighties screen siren Marcella Hughes, who's currently in rehearsals for her Broadway debut happening early next year. Marcella, thank you for being here."

"Thank you for having me, Harvey." Her tone was pure sensuality, not an ounce of which had been diluted over the decades.

"First, tell us about the production."

"I'm so excited to be making my stage debut with the stunning Viola Davis by my side in a brand-new play, *Still I Rise.* It's an adaption of Maya Angelou's famous poem, and its director, Maddy Vincent, is the hottest young Black female theater director on Broadway."

Lindsay grinned as she watched the banter volley between Marcella and Harvey, wondering when the hell the interview was going to turn to the shelter donation.

"It sounds like just what Broadway needs," Harvey said, gushing. "I can't wait to see you at the premiere."

"Thank you, honey."

"But that's not the only reason you're here with us today."

"Oh, no, no." Marcella obviously attempted to sound modest. "The shelter thing."

"Also joining us is Hope House shelter advocate, Lindsay Chase. Welcome, Lindsay. Tell us about Hope House and Marcella's role in saving it."

Lindsay glanced at Marcella's screen as she beamed like the hero she was pretending to be. "Well, Harvey, Hope House is located in downtown New Haven, Connecticut and has been serving the needs of unhoused and at-risk LGBTQ teens and young adults for over fifteen years. But when its talented, compassionate social worker, Ellie Tuttle, told me that it was about to shut down this fall due to lack of funding, I shared its plight with Marcella Hughes, and she immediately showed up for the youth with a sizable donation that will keep Hope House's doors open for the foreseeable future."

"That is wonderful and truly inspirational, Marcella," Harvey said. "With so many worthy causes vying for donations, what made you choose this one?"

"Well, being a member of the LGBTQ community myself, when my ex-lover, Lindsay Chase, told me what was happening, I just knew I had to step in and put my money where my mouth had been." Her smirk was priceless.

Lindsay's jaw fell open at the revelation as she remembered that thousands, if not millions, would see the interview.

"Marcella, did you just come out live on TMZ?"

"Oh, Harvey, does anyone really have to come out anymore?"

"Yes, they do, especially an actress with your cult following who's about to be reborn as a Broadway star."

"Harvey, dear. Aren't you charming."

He grinned. "Any chance you and the lovely Ms. Chase here will get back together as result of this joint goodwill venture?"

Lindsay widened her eyes in disbelief.

Marcella offered him a sassy grin in return. "Ms. Chase is in love with Ellie, the social worker, so, alas, she and I will continue to remain good, good friends."

"You heard it here first, folks," Harvey said. "I'd like to thank Lindsay Chase and the inimitable Marcella Hughes for joining us. Good luck with the Hope House shelter, and Lindsay, good luck with Ellie. And don't forget to catch Marcella Hughes's Broadway stage debut in *Still I Rise* in early February."

Once the host ended the call, Lindsay picked up her phone and dialed Marcella.

"Yeeeees?" Marcella drawled playfully.

"You are incredible, and so is your PR guy. I can't believe he cooked this up."

"He's worth every penny I pay him. He nearly passed out at the perfect timing of this chance to promote the play just as rehearsals are starting."

"The whole thing was flawless, Marcella. I can't thank him and you enough."

"He doesn't deserve all the credit. I'm the one who decided to throw in the shout-out to Ellie and your undying love for her."

"Yeah, about that. She happens to hate my guts and knows the whole truth about the donation. I can only pray she doesn't come forward and blow up our spot."

"I don't know the woman, but I can't imagine her doing anything that would destroy all the positive press this interview will generate for her shelter."

"True. As much as she hates me, she'd never do anything negative against the Hope House. Besides, her refusing to speak to me is the worst revenge she could take anyway."

"I'm sorry, honey. I do hate knowing you're upset. But maybe this is the time you need to work on yourself."

"That's what everyone keeps telling me." And frankly, she was tired of hearing it.

"I hope you're doing it. As virtuous as your decision was to give your winnings to the shelter, it troubles me that you're still doing what led you to your downfall. And I won't be there to pay off your restitution next time you need it."

"I know that, Marcella. I wouldn't even think to ask."

"Let's not end this joyous call on a sour note. We'll do lunch again soon."

"Yes. And thank you for coming through for me yet again."

"Of course. Be a good girl." She made a kiss sound and ended the call.

Lindsay leaned back in her chair, looked around her father's quiet apartment, and sighed. Since her seventy-year-old father had met the widow Gloria at the Elks Club, even he had a more interesting life than she did. With no legit job prospects, no place to call home, and, most importantly, no Ellie, she'd begun to feel every beat of the phrase "no good deed goes unpunished." If she hadn't tried to be a hero in Ellie's eyes, she'd still have her in her life.

What a tradeoff.

Ellie had missed Rosa's phone call that morning while she was in staff meetings, so she decided to swing by the shelter instead of calling her back. When she walked in, she heard talking coming from Rosa's office, but Rosa was just sitting there in front of a laptop.

"Are you on a virtual call?"

Rose shook her head as she waved Ellie into the office. "Have you seen this? Any of this on social media?"

"You know I don't go on till later in the day. What's up?"

Rosa turned her laptop toward Ellie.

She knew what she was seeing but couldn't actually believe it. "Is that Marcella Hughes…Oh, my God, and Lindsay?"

"Marcella Hughes is the Hope House Angel. Did you know that?"

"Uh…No. What's Lindsay doing there?"

"She told her about the shelter closing. How else would Marcella have known? I guess she wanted to donate anonymously, but with all the buzz on social media about finding out, Lindsay got her to agree to come forward."

"I'll bet she did," Ellie said, her tone laced with suspicion.

"Damn, girl. You got some friends in high places."

"That's news to me." Ellie sat down and watched the entire interview. Afterward, she searched the hashtag *hope house angel* and *Marcella Hughes* to see what came up. What if Lindsay had taken a fall to protect Marcella's privacy, telling Ellie she'd won the money at the casino? If the story they told on national TV was true, then she'd broken up with her and been miserable without her all this time for nothing.

Or, more likely, Lindsay had contacted Marcella for help getting out of this latest jam she'd gotten herself into.

But how could she find out for sure?

With nobody knowing the "secret" Lindsay had told Ellie, she'd have to take a leap of faith if she was going to believe in Lindsay again.

But that was a big "if."

CHAPTER TWENTY-FOUR

Within a day of their interview airing on TMZ's various platforms, Lindsay's social-media followers ballooned to over a thousand. And Marcella Hughes was trending again. Mission accomplished for Marcella, but other than the followers and several marriage proposals from men, women, and children, all Lindsay got was a lukewarm "nice interview" text from Ellie. No thank you, no extending an olive branch. Not even a hint of a gush over Marcella spilling the tea that she was still in love with Ellie. Just a pert little *nice interview* she probably had to force herself to send.

C'est la vie. Lindsay Chase chased no one.

She met up with her father and his buddies at the Elks Club for happy hour after another frustrating afternoon of searching for a job that would pay her enough to afford a small apartment of her own.

After a glass of warm beer and a few cold buffalo wings, Wally suggested they all head into the back room for some poker.

"I'm going to have to respectfully decline, Wally. I'm saving my pennies so I can get out on my own and give this guy back his privacy." She pointed her thumb at her father sitting on her left.

Her father's lady friend, Gloria, smiled at her. "No rush, honey. I've got plenty of room for him at my place."

The group of guys hooted and whistled at her father, who sat quietly grinning and blushing.

"All the same," Lindsay said. She buried her face in a fresh beer, seized by an odd conflation of ick and happiness that her father had finally found someone he wanted to spend time with.

He leaned toward her and said quietly, "You can stay as long as you want. I like having you around."

"Thanks, Dad. And don't worry. When I do leave, I won't be going far."

He smiled with what she could've only interpreted as relief.

She excused herself and stepped outside to answer a call from a number she didn't recognize. She usually ignored those, but what if it was Ellie calling her from another line?

"Lindsay Chase?"

"Who wants to know," she replied to the unfamiliar voice.

"You probably don't remember me," the woman said, "but I'm a former client of yours—"

"I'm sorry, but all the restitution money's been disbursed."

"No, Lindsay. I wasn't involved in that. I was the president of Quest-Centrics, the bio-medical software company."

"Oh, yes." Her tone was instantly brighter. "I remember. Delfine Newton, right?"

"Yes, yes," she replied. "Wow. You've got some memory."

"It's one of the things I still have going for me."

"Oh, I'm sure you still have a lot going for you."

That sounded rather flirty. Delfine, Delfine. Did she sleep with her once? "So, what can I do for you?"

"Well, I've started my own biomed software company on the East Coast, and I need a strong, savvy financial wiz on my team."

"Wow. Congrats. And you'd like me to recommend someone for you?"

Delfine chuckled. "Several people have already recommended someone. You."

"Me? You must've gone deep into the vaults to find someone in the biz who'd recommend me. Have you heard about my recent…" throat-clear…"troubles?"

"I have. From your former boss at the LA Group. He's a friend of mine and spoke highly of you, despite your stumble."

"I have nothing to back it up, but I'm honestly not that person anymore, the one that *stumbled* into grand larceny."

"I know that, too. Jake said you were one of the best hedge-fund managers he ever knew, and he liked you as a person as well. He was really upset the way things turned out."

"Likewise."

"But what really put you on my radar was the interview you did with Marcella Hughes. For you to have that much cash at your disposal and choose to give it away to a charitable organization basically showed me what I needed to know about you."

Lindsay smiled. It was the first time in a long time she'd genuinely felt good about herself. "I'm so grateful for your offer, but you know, I lost my SEC license."

"You don't need one. I'm a private corporation, and I'd like you to be my CFO. You'd have no connection to private investors. The salary starts at one-fifty K, with health benefits and stock options. You'd work from home four days and come into the office in Manhattan one day a week. Sound like something you'd be interested in?"

Through all her stammering, Lindsay managed to get out a yes.

"Awesome. Why don't you come into the City next week, meet the staff, and see the office. We'll go to lunch and call it an official interview."

"Uh, yeah, um. Wow. I seem to have lost the ability to speak in complete sentences. An opportunity like this was not at all on my radar."

"I respect the people who still respect you, Lindsay. That's a great place to start."

They ended the call, and Lindsay immediately thought to text Ellie with the unbelievable news. Then she stopped. She had to start getting used to the fact that Ellie wasn't her girlfriend anymore. Wasn't even her friend at this point, and who knew if down the road she'd want to be friends with an ex who'd broken her heart. For now, she just needed to take the win and move forward.

She forced the smile back onto her face and returned to the table. "Wake up, Wally," she shouted. "What were you saying about playing a few hands?"

"Hell, yeah," Gloria said, and one by one, all the Elks at her father's table rose from their chairs and migrated toward the back room.

At least these people knew how to have a good time.

❖

After losing count of how many times she'd watched the now-viral Lindsay-Marcella interview, Ellie knew she wouldn't be able to let go until she and Lindsay had a conversation about where the money really came from. A phone call or text wouldn't cut it. She needed to see her face, read her body language to feel satisfied with her answer.

This latest explanation for the money made Ellie feel better that Lindsay hadn't gotten it from gambling. But regardless of the scenario, the woman she loved and trusted had looked right at her and lied in her face. Quite convincingly.

Now, sitting across from her with her fingers clasped together and resting on the table, Ellie studied Lindsay like she was interviewing her for security clearance at the Pentagon.

After an awkward smile that Ellie hadn't returned, Lindsay finally broke the silence. "I can't tell you how happy I was to get your text." Her eyes exuded a hopefulness Ellie felt bad about squashing.

"Don't get excited. I only wanted to meet you to ask you one question. And I want the truth. No more fabrications or clever maneuvers with words. Just the truth." She sucked on her iced-coffee straw and, with her eyes, dared her to lie.

Lindsay raised her hand as if about to testify in court. "That's all you'll get. I swear."

Ellie bobbed her head, unmoved by the theatrics. "Which story about the money is true: the one you told me or the one you had Marcella go on TV and tell?"

Lindsay's gaze was down as she fingered the bottom of her cup of iced green tea.

Here it comes, Ellie thought, the version she so wanted to be true. Lindsay hadn't gambled, and Marcella really was the generous philanthropist who'd intended to remain anonymous. At last, their painful separation could finally end.

"The one I told you," Lindsay said, still looking down. "I really did win it at the casino." She finally looked up and directly into Ellie's eyes.

"So you're not just a liar. You're a con artist, too." Ellie shook her head against the disappointment starting to break down her reserve. "How long did it take you to come up with that farce you and Marcella performed for TMZ?"

"I had nothing to do with that idea. I only went to Marcella in desperation and told her I was about to be outed as the Hope House Angel and explained the legal consequences. Her PR man decided to turn it into the start of a publicity tour for her upcoming play, and I just went along with it."

Ellie sneered. "And why wouldn't you? Anything to save your own ass." She sighed and gazed off at the colorful Southwestern wall art.

"Wow. That is so unfair. I didn't have to do the interview with Marcella. I showed up to make sure the shelter's story was told and wasn't swallowed up by the altruistic Marcella Hughes and her Broadway-debut angle. That's exactly what would've happened if I hadn't been there to put a face on Hope House. I did it for you, Ellie, whether you want to believe it or not." Lindsay leaned back in her chair and stared out the window, clearly spent with frustration.

Ellie pulled her drink to her face as shame began to undermine her anger. "I guess you must be telling the truth," she said softly. "This was your chance to pick the story that would've exonerated you for gambling."

"I'm through finagling with the truth, Ell. It's cost me too much. I mean, I can get another house and another job someday, but I'll never get another you."

Ellie knew her eyes were pooling, but she hadn't expected the little lovelorn whimper that escaped.

"I don't expect you to believe any of this," Lindsay said. "But that's where I am these days."

"Thank you for being honest about this. And thank you for what you said about me on TV."

"I meant every word of it."

Ellie nodded. If she'd opened her mouth to speak, she would've been deluged by emotion.

Lindsay's fingertips drummed out a beat on the table. She seemed to be holding back a sort of deluge of her own. Then her gaze finally met Ellie's. "So where does this leave us? I mean, if there even is an 'us' anymore."

"I want there to be, but my head is still spinning. I don't know who the real Lindsay Chase is."

"Maybe if you give me another chance to show you—"

"I don't need any more heroic acts, Lindsay. I just want to be able to trust you. And that's going to take more time."

Lindsay seemed to be choking back a reaction as she stood up. "I understand. It was nice seeing you again." She lingered for a moment, and Ellie knew why.

"You too." She got up and leaned into Lindsay's open arms. The hug felt amazing, familiar, and all too tempting. "You take care of yourself," she said as she wriggled out of the embrace.

At that, Lindsay slipped out the door of the coffeehouse without looking back.

Ellie watched her go. Despite all her angry bravado, she needed to lean against the wall to stop herself from crumpling to the ground like an old coat flung off by an uncaring human.

Was that the outcome she'd hoped for? In any event, it was the outcome she got.

CHAPTER TWENTY-FIVE

By the time the trees began shedding their colorful leaves, Lindsay had enough money for an apartment in a new building within walking distance to the center of town. She treasured having her own space for meditation and quiet contemplation on her deck overlooking a river. Said deck also served as her office on sunny days, from where she telecommuted for Biometrics and occasionally googled Hope House, hoping to glimpse Ellie's name.

It had been weeks since she'd seen or spoken with her, and she was learning how to live each day staying laser-focused on the few things within her control. Although she'd been fully aware that falling in love with Ellie at that time had been an invitation to ruin, she'd gone for it anyway—in true Lindsay Chase fashion.

Another hard lesson in consequences. The hardest of all. She'd missed Ellie desperately. Each day was a marathon struggle not to contact her. She vowed to herself not to disrespect Ellie's wishes, but more importantly, she needed to take care of herself. She needed this time to get to know and understand her true self through her therapy sessions, to reconstruct a life of independence, and maybe, just maybe, regain her reputation as someone worthy of trust.

She'd read an article last week about how Hope House had received so many additional donations from the publicity her and

Marcella's interview generated, they were able to buy outright a nearby historic home that was being renovated into a full-service shelter facility. Now they'd never have to worry about closing their doors again. Awesome.

When she found herself on the doorstep of the temporary shelter, no one was more surprised than she was. Except maybe Rosa.

"Mamacita." She embraced her tightly. "I'm so glad to see you."

"Same, Rosa."

She released her hold on Lindsay and studied her. "You look so well. I won't lie and say I hadn't worried that you'd gone down a bad path since you…you know."

"I won't lie and say I hadn't thought about it every day for a solid month. But I didn't. I'm okay."

Rosa was beaming. "I can see that. What brings you back?"

"I want to volunteer."

"Oh, no. Not through another court order?"

She knew Rosa was teasing, but her expression could've won her an Academy Award. "No. I want to give back. Sounds clichéd, but here I am."

"I'll take you, cliché and all. What do you have in mind?"

"Kinda like what Ellie had suggested months ago: a weekly support group for the kids. Talk about addiction and the piled-on shit that goes with growing up being LGBTQ plus in this country."

Rosa nodded. "The *free* country where these kids only have rights depending on who's in office."

"I figure they might appreciate speaking with someone like them who's lived through both types of administrations."

"That sounds perfect, my dear." She glanced around as if planning a conspiracy. "Do you want to do it on a day Ellie's here?"

Lindsay chuckled. "No. That's okay. Any day but Wednesday and Friday. That's when I go into the City for work."

"How does Thursday at four thirty sound?"

"Sounds great. Thanks." She lingered with her hands in her pockets as she swiveled side-to-side on her heels. "So. How is Ellie?"

"Same old workaholic Ellie." Rosa's eyes brightened as if she were speaking about her own daughter. "A lobby group tried to recruit her for a hell of a lot more money than she's making now, but she turned them down. Doesn't want to leave her job with the kids."

"The kids that make her cry at least three times a week."

They both laughed, but inside Lindsay felt like she took a punch. Clearly, Ellie wasn't struggling as much as Lindsay was to move on. Seemed like she already had.

"Good for her. These kids are so lucky to have her."

"They're lucky to have you, too. See you Thursday?"

Lindsay nodded and left, waffling between enthusiasm for her new volunteer opportunity and the ache of still loving and missing Ellie.

❖

Rosa had texted Ellie and asked if she could stop in at the State Street shelter after the hearing that she had to attend at the courthouse around the corner. That always meant that Rosa wanted an afternoon caffeine boost from something more appetizing than the shelter coffee pot.

When she read in the text that Rosa wanted an iced pumpkin-spice latte, a sudden memory tugged at her heart. Lindsay loved everything pumpkin and had mentioned over the summer that she couldn't wait for fall so she could start indulging in all the tasty goodness of the season.

One morning in July, Ellie had surprised her by making pumpkin scones for breakfast. Ellie grinned at the memory of Lindsay's sleepy face as she danced at Ellie's kitchen table while she devoured one with her coffee. So many memories of her time with Linday still randomly took her by surprise.

She exhaled and shook off the tender, fleeting thought. Would she ever be able to think of Lindsay without being pushed to the precipice of tears?

When she walked into the shelter, she heard voices beyond the partition that separated Rosa's work area from the main room. Before she could peek around it, Rosa came out and intercepted her. Ellie handed her the drink, and Rosa inspected the sticker on it.

"You said pumpkin spice in the text."

"I know. Wait here a second." Rosa disappeared around the partition with the drink.

Ellie immediately crept up and peeked into the room. Four teens sat in a circle with a woman whose hair was up and her back to Ellie. When Rosa handed her the drink, Ellie knew that, before she even saw Lindsay's profile, it was her.

Her gasp was almost loud enough for everyone to hear. She rolled herself around the corner of the partition and leaned against it, taking in a gulp of air.

When Rosa came back, she'd clearly noticed Ellie's expression. "What are you doing here? I told you to wait over there."

"You also could've told me that drink was for Lindsay," Ellie said in a scratchy whisper. "Why is she here?"

"What does it look like? She's running the program that you suggested to her back in the spring."

"Oh, how lovely," Ellie said. "Well, if she thinks this is going to—"

Rosa held up her hand. "She doesn't think anything, Ellie. She didn't say to tell you she was doing this, didn't ask for a day she knew you'd be here. She just said she wants to give back. And I'm letting her."

Ellie rubbed her forehead as she took a minute to regroup. "Oh, yeah. Of course. It's commendable that she wants to volunteer."

Rosa nodded. "So if you want to avoid running into her, she'll be here every Thursday from four thirty to six."

Ellie sighed. As much as she wanted to avoid Lindsay, seeing her face or hearing her name still had the power to spin her into an alternate reality. One where she could believe that the Lindsay beyond that partition, giving of herself and expecting nothing in return, was the version Ellie could trust she'd always be.

"Or you can go in there and co-mentor the group with her," Rosa said with a shrug.

She smiled. Rosa was so slick, Ellie could almost believe she hadn't orchestrated this whole thing. "Maybe another time. Lindsay seems to have a handle on it today."

"Ellie. Hi."

She turned and caught her breath at Lindsay standing at the corner of the partition, looking as stunned as she felt.

"I guess I have you to thank for this?" She shook the ice in the pumpkin-latte cup.

"Hi, uh, yeah. You're welcome."

"I have to go answer the phone."

Ellie's voice escalated to a manic pitch as Rosa scurried off. "The phone that's not ringing? Rosa?" She calmly brushed an errant curl from her face as she turned back to Lindsay.

"Well, I won't keep you," Lindsay said. "The kids are on a quick pee break, and I just wanted to thank whoever brought me this."

"You're welcome," Ellie said. "And congrats on your new mentoring gig. How many weeks is it?"

Lindsay seemed puzzled. "I'll be here for as long as there are kids who need this."

"That's awesome. They're lucky to have such a strong role model show up for them."

Lindsay shrugged. "Not to sound like my old selfish self, but I think I'm getting more out of this than they are."

Ellie chuckled. "Sometimes it works that way. And that's okay, too."

Lindsay seemed attuned to the room behind them as it began to fill with chatter. "I better get back. Thanks again for this, and, uh, it was nice seeing you again."

"Yeah. Nice seeing you, too."

For a blip of a moment, neither of them moved. It was as if some vestige of their past love affair held them in place, waiting to see if an old flame would reignite under the embers.

Ellie let out a deep sigh before about-facing and hurrying out the door. Her whole being was ablaze from the spark of Lindsay's allure. This new picture of her was going to linger in Ellie's mind for some time.

❖

The next morning, Lindsay sat in the quiet car of Metro North heading into the City. A palette of colors flickered past her as the train rolled through the affluent suburbs of southwestern Connecticut. Her brain was still processing the particulars of her unexpected encounter with Ellie and tormenting her with all the things she could've and should've said. Was there a word or a gesture that could've changed things between them in a beautiful flash instead of the stream of lame pleasantries they'd exchanged?

Ellie looked more breathtaking than she'd ever seen her. Was the long absence just playing with her head? Or was it that without all of Lindsay's bullshit stressing her out, her pure, natural glow had been able to return and flourish.

She sipped coffee from her travel thermos and flipped open her laptop. Obviously, the encounter was the universe's way to show Lindsay that Ellie was better off without her and that she needed to let go of the string of hope she'd had wrapped so tightly around her finger it was cutting off her circulation.

Once the tears of acceptance stopped clouding her eyesight, she resumed prepping for the staff meeting scheduled for later that morning.

Shortly before arriving at Grand Central Station, Marcella's number came up on her phone.

"Hi, Marcella."

"I need a date next Saturday," she blurted.

"I hear Sharon Stone is free these days."

"I'm assuming you are, too, since you never leave your apartment except to go to work twice a week."

"Where are you taking me?"

"The Hope House reopening gala." Marcella said it like they'd been talking about it for weeks.

"How lovely that you got an invitation. I didn't." Lindsay couldn't disguise the hurt in her voice. Did Ellie despise her so much that she couldn't even invite her to the event herself? Like when she was standing right in front of her yesterday?

"Is that a yes?"

"Well, I don't know. Will I be welcome there?"

"Don't be silly. You're coming as my escort."

"Uh, not to mention the fact that I'm the reason Hope House still exists. You'd think Ellie or Rosa would've had me first on the guest list."

"Don't be a diva. That's my job. Now get yourself something spicy to wear by next week. We'll be arriving by limo. And none of this shabby-chic business. Got it?"

"I figured I'd go with a modern crunchy-granola look. Does that work?"

"Don't you even joke about a thing like that. I need you to look hot for the photo ops."

"If you're interviewed, you better not tantalize the press by telling them we're an item again."

"You wish."

She ended the call before Lindsay had a chance to reconsider the invite. Not that she would. And pass up another chance to see Ellie?

❖

Ellie was reveling in happy hour with Rosa on Friday. Rosa's timing in asking was impeccable. Her invitation must've come from concern or pity because, since she'd shut Lindsay out of her life, she'd returned to her introverted, almost brooding ways. In a way it was a relief. Loving Lindsay had been all-consuming. With all the upheaval in her professional life surrounding the shelter, the last thing she'd had room for was the emotional turmoil of falling head over heels for a woman with a rather dubious moral compass.

When their second round of margaritas arrived, Rosa apparently felt safe going in for the deeper dive. "So how do you think you'll be if Lindsay comes to the Hope House gala?"

The thought had been on her mind more and more as the event drew closer, and the building anticipation had her feeling like she was on a permanent caffeine buzz.

"If I see her first, it won't be an issue." Ellie busied herself piling pico de gallo on a warm tortilla chip.

"You can't spend the evening trying to avoid her. It'll be physically impossible, especially if Marcella shows up."

"Marcella's already committed to show. It'll be great press for her upcoming play."

"Then it's very possible Lindsay will come with her."

"She might not. Lindsay's probably already found a new girlfriend and has put this sordid business of social work behind her."

"I highly doubt that. She seems very focused on running her support group. In any event, you should prepare yourself in case she's there."

"My honest answer to your question is that I think I'll be a nervous wreck. But kind of in a good way. I still miss her."

"Well, that's no revelation. I know you're still struggling." Rosa licked a bit of salt from the rim of her glass and then dropped this bomb. "Have you thought about giving it another go with her?"

"You mean giving myself another opportunity to have my heart shattered? Gee. I don't know. Let me think about that one." She jerked her head away and then back again. "How about no?"

Rosa was undeterred. "Or you can try taking things slowly this time and see if she's changed."

Ellie respected Rosa's opinion. She never would've suggested Ellie do anything if she personally believed it was a bad idea.

"From what Gretchen tells me, she's living a quiet life in her own apartment, still working for that same finance company."

"Consistency. That's a clear indication of a changed woman."

"That's the version she shows Gretchen. Who knows what she's up to the rest of the time. She may even be back with Marcella for all I know."

"That's an awful lot of speculation when all you have to do is reach out to her and have a conversation."

Ellie sighed and sipped her margarita, savoring the pinch in her throat as it rolled down. "God, this is good."

"Is that a 'no' on the reaching out to have a conversation?"

"I'm scared, Rosa. And still so conflicted. I love her so much, but I don't trust her. And I'm just not ready to find out if I can trust her again if it means putting my heart on the line."

"I get it. Having a relationship with someone you feel you need to make excuses for is risky business."

"I just feel that she'd have eventually outgrown me anyway. She always seemed to be moving on from one dopamine rush to the next."

"Now that's where I'll stop you. No way will I let you think you aren't enough—for Lindsay or anyone else. I think you're doing the right thing, though, by giving yourself more time."

"You just said I should give it another go with her."

"No, no. I asked if you'd thought about it. Evidently you have, but you're not ready. Maybe you never will be, and that's okay."

Ellie swirled a chip in the salsa verde. What if Rosa was right? What if she never felt ready to try again with Lindsay? Through all her angry bluster about "never again," her heart secretly kept a tiny toe in the door for "maybe someday."

"It makes me unspeakably sad to think of my life without Lindsay in it. Or maybe it's just that I sucked down this second marg too fast."

"It is equal parts both. What's sadder is that we should've ordered a pitcher."

"That's one problem in our lives that's easy to resolve," Ellie said as she waved over their server.

❖

On Friday, Lindsay spent her lunch hour in a midtown Manhattan boutique shopping for the perfect outfit. Gretchen and Kyle were in town for the day, and the three of them had tickets to a play that evening. While Kyle sat in an Irish pub down the block, Gretchen helped her pick out things to try on for the gala.

"You can't go business-pantsuit to an event like this," she said. She also held up shredded, bejeweled jeans and a top full of slits. "Or dress like a rock star."

Lindsay huffed. "I don't see the problem. These are both hot looks."

"Not for an evening soirée. You're not handling a hostile takeover or playing in Aerosmith. How about this?" She held up a sleek, low-cut dress.

Lindsay wrinkled her nose. "It's silver."

"It's gray. The fabric has a sheen to it." Gretchen smiled lasciviously. "Imagine this with a pair of hot heels."

"I'm going to a gala, not trying to seduce a ninety-year-old billionaire. I'll go with the first one I tried on."

"Think hard on that. This ensemble will also be effective for seducing a thirty-something social worker, especially with this plunging neckline."

"Fair point." Lindsay deliberated over which outfit would grab Ellie's attention more. "But then I don't want it to be obvious that I'm trying to seduce a woman who made it clear she didn't want me anymore. I'm not that pathetic." She turned pensive. "Hmm. I've never had a woman not want me anymore."

Gretchen stared at her in what appeared to be disgust. "That's not true. Marcella dumped you."

"Not without my help. And we always hooked up between getting back together anyway. But Ellie is so different from what I'm used to."

"She's the classiest chick you'll ever get, dear sister-in-law. If I were you, I'd take full advantage of this reception. Make a detailed plan to get her back—if that's what you still want. I mean, are you and Marcella attending as a couple?"

"No," Lindsay said with more gusto than necessary. "I've made too much progress in therapy to go back to a codependent, chaos-chasing relationship like that."

Gretchen smiled. "Good for you. Kyle and I were saying the other day we couldn't believe you weren't working a new woman yet."

Lindsay paused from gathering up the unchosen outfits. "That's really the perception everyone has of me?"

Gretchen sucked in her cheek. "From what I've heard over the years, it's well-earned."

"Well, I hope what I've been doing over the last six months is helping me unearn it."

Gretchen looked at her watch and then at the outfit Lindsay had selected as they walked up to the register. "We could've spent this last hour at the bar drinking with Kyle."

"Except I have to get back to work now. Go get yourself buzzed, and I'll meet you at the restaurant at six."

"I'm on it." She gave Lindsay a peck on the cheek and was out the door.

As Lindsay walked back to the office, she reflected on Gretchen's comment about how she and Kyle were "surprised" she wasn't "working a new woman" already. It sounded so sleazy. Is that really the image of herself she'd projected for so long?

What a contrast to the side of her Ellie had helped bring out—if that side ever existed before Ellie came into her world. It might have before Stephanie died. She was there for her through her diagnosis, treatment, and when she'd decided to stop treatment because it had quit working. Being self-centered simply hadn't occurred to her during Stephanie's battle.

After her passing, however, Lindsay's focus had seemed to devolve into the pursuit of anything she thought would fill the colossal void Stephanie's absence created. Sex, drinking, gambling, any kind of self-indulgence that would deaden the sense of loss that would've consumed her if she hadn't railed against it.

Losing Ellie mimicked that darkness, but this time she hadn't felt compelled to pursue destructive behaviors to cancel it out. She was allowing herself to feel it. The feeling was sad and awful but also empowering once she'd realized she could still get out of bed and discover purpose to her day. And that was because of Ellie.

Maybe it was time she allowed herself one last indulgence, one moment totally without inhibition to go for what she wanted regardless of consequences.

And the gala would be the place.

CHAPTER TWENTY-SIX

The night of the Hope House gala, Lindsay gladly accepted a second glass of champagne as she and Marcella traveled there in a limo. While she was quite proud of the way she'd transformed her life both professionally and emotionally, she wasn't fond of this new humble-servant thing. When she'd finally dumped her bad habits and even badder attitude, her swagger seemed to have gone with them. Now she was experiencing ordinary things like nervousness and insecurity. All the unpleasantries mortals felt in their daily lives.

She belched and placed her empty flute glass in the holder. "What if she won't talk to me?"

"Of course she'll talk to you," Marcella said, looking down at her phone. "From what you've said about her, she's anything but petty."

Lindsay smiled with relief. "That's true. She's gracious and warm and...Oh, God. I just had a sickening thought. What if she's there with her new girlfriend?" She choked back another burp.

Marcella looked up. "She has a new girlfriend?"

"She does?"

"I don't know. That's what I'm asking you."

Lindsay grabbed the bottle of champagne and refilled her flute. "I'm sure she does by now. She got so much attention from our interview, some opportunist probably came along and scooped her up. Who would blame them? She checks everyone's boxes." Suddenly, the knife twisted. "She didn't invite me personally because she forgot about me."

Marcella reached over and plucked the champagne bottle away from her. "Stop getting worked up over Ellie. Nobody needs you sloshed before you even stroll into this shindig."

"That's easy for you to say. You weren't slighted. They're treating you like the Woman of the Hour, and you didn't do a thing except promote your play."

"Is that so? I gave an Emmy award-winning performance in that interview for you. And I guess saving your ass from jail a second time and giving the shelter national attention is also your idea of doing nothing."

Lindsay chugged the last of the champagne in her glass. As the bubbles stung all the way down, she stewed in her shame. Marcella sat like a statue, staring straight ahead.

"I'm sorry," Lindsay said after a long silence. "I don't know what I'm saying."

"I know you're hurting, but that's no excuse to shit all over my parade."

"You're right, and I didn't mean any of it. You've done so much to make this event happen. You deserve to be treated like royalty tonight."

"Yes, I do. But how am I supposed to savor it all if I know you're miserable? Why can't you at least wait and see what happens with Ellie before you go all doomsday on me?"

"Okay. Yes. I'm clearly overthinking."

"What an understatement. I've never seen you this neurotic before. It must be love."

"Yeah, love." Lindsay writhed at the suggestion and then quickly regrouped. "I'm sorry for tarnishing our fun night out."

"Apology accepted." Marcella drew the champagne bottle out, ready to pour. "Now let's have the fucking time of our lives tonight."

❖

With an eye on the entrance, Ellie paced the receiving room in the old Victorian home that Hope House had been able to purchase outright with the flood of donations pouring in after the famous interview. When she'd invited Marcella as the guest of honor, she'd suggested that she bring Lindsay as her plus-one but requested that she not let Lindsay know she'd mentioned it. Hopefully, she'd kept her word.

When Marcella made her grand entrance, all eyes were naturally on her. But Ellie bobbed around the heads converging around her and trained her eyes on Lindsay, floating in Marcella's wake. In a tailored black pinstripe suit with sparkly silver camisole, Lindsay dazzled. Ellie swallowed hard as she processed the breathtaking image. God, she'd missed her. Why had she been so stubborn in refusing to give her another chance?

Tonight could be their second chance—if Lindsay hadn't already moved on.

Ellie waited patiently for the crowd surrounding them to dissipate, trying not to let her eagerness show. The moment she and Lindsay made eye contact, she whirled around in a panic and headed toward the makeshift bar in the living room. She went up behind Rosa, who was talking with guests, and clutched her arm.

Rosa swung around. "What's the matter?"

"Marcella and Lindsay are here."

"Fantastic." She politely excused herself from the group and tugged Ellie's arm. "Let's go see them."

"Now?"

"No. Next Thursday. Of course now."

"I need a minute to collect myself."

"Well, don't take too long. We can't keep our savior waiting."

Ellie ran into the ladies' room and studied her reflection in the mirror. "Oh, no. No. Not now," she said to the red blotches breaking out on her neck. "This is the biggest night of your life, and you're going to go out there looking like you got clotheslined by a linebacker." Breathe. Just breathe.

After she splashed some cold water on her neck, she took a deep breath and went to greet their honored guests.

Luckily, Rosa was still chatting with them, so she could casually slide into the conversation. As she approached, all three heads turned toward her in unison. She headed directly toward Marcella with hand extended.

"Marcella, it is so wonderful to finally meet you in person." Their handshake morphed into a hug.

"Darling, likewise. Thank you for having us here on this fabulous occasion."

"Well, you made it all happen." Ellie glanced quickly at Lindsay with a sheepish smile. "Nice to see you, too, Lindsay."

"Same," she replied with a curt smile and turned to Rosa. "You have a great place here for the shelter. It really looks and feels like a home."

"With the eight new bunk beds Furniture City donated, it's going to feel like one, too, for up to sixteen unhoused youth." Rosa took Marcella's hand in hers. "And I'll never be able to show the gratitude in my heart for you for making this happen. And Lindsay, too."

Ellie noticed Lindsay's uncomfortable grin and felt bad about Rosa adding her as an afterthought. Lindsay deserved ninety-nine percent of the credit, and everyone was pouring it all over Marcella.

"Yes," Ellie said, looking at Lindsay. "We're eternally grateful to both of you."

"Let's get you ladies a drink, and then I'll show you around the house," Rosa said.

The three of them walked toward the bar, but Ellie trailed behind, nursing her disappointment. So much for the Hollywood ending where she and Lindsay laid eyes on each other, ran into each other's arms, and lived happily ever after. Had Marcella told her about her special request or kept it a secret?

She exited the tour early and went down to the living room to listen to the acoustic guitarist perform while nursing her new wounds. Okay, if Lindsay wanted to be done with her, fine. She'd have to accept that fact, but not before she'd said the words directly to her face. She casually glanced over her shoulder and noticed Lindsay standing like an outsider watching the performance from the hall.

Ellie got up before her nerve vanished and made her way over. "Hi."

"Hello." After a blip of a forced smile, Lindsay returned her attention to the music.

"So, I can tell by the temperature in the room that you've gotten over me. Or us."

"You sound disappointed," Lindsay replied, her attention evidently still on the performer.

"Is it true?"

She finally turned and faced her. "Why do you care, Ellie? I haven't heard from you in weeks after your coffeehouse sendoff, so don't tell me you're surprised if I've moved on."

If. Hmm. "Did Marcella not tell you?"

"Not tell me what? That there was a little party going on tonight? Ha. The joke's on you. Obviously, she did."

Ellie smiled, patient with Lindsay's attitude. "Lindsay, I asked her, well, suggested, that she bring you tonight as her plus-one but not tell you."

Lindsay shifted her weight to her other hip and crossed her arms. "Odd. And the point of that?"

"Sort of an insurance policy. I was afraid if I invited you myself, it might sway your decision to come because you're still mad at me or something."

"Like you'd care if I didn't show."

Lindsay's abrasive edge was starting to irritate her. "I'd care very much. I've missed you terribly, Linds. Believe it or not."

"So terribly that you never called or texted?"

"For a while I wasn't sure what to do. I just knew we needed this time apart. You can't tell me you haven't used it wisely. Congratulations on your new position, by the way."

"Thanks. It keeps me out of trouble. As an added bonus, I get to leave the state twice a week because it's work-related."

"Wow. Good for you. You're living the dream again."

"In some ways." She shrugged. "You are, too." She brightened as she indicated their surroundings.

"Professionally, yes," Ellie said. "I've never been more satisfied with or optimistic about my career choice. Personally, though. That's a different story." She mimicked Lindsay's shrug.

"I don't gamble anymore. At all. Not even with my dad's buddies."

Ellie's feelings for Lindsay were dangerously close to bubbling to the surface. "That's good. I'm happy for you."

"Therapy really helped me see how and why gambling took over my life. But I'm doing well, learning new stuff about myself all the time."

"That's funny. Me, too. And it's mostly because of you."

"I'm so sorry for hurting you, Ell. I never meant—"

"No, no. What I mean is that I've come to realize where I was wrong. I shouldn't have expected perfection from anything. Or anyone. We're all supposed to be evolving and learning from mistakes. And what I learned from mine is that there isn't any imperfect person on earth I want to be with more than you."

"Really?"

Ellie's nod released her pooled tears, and they crawled down her cheeks. "But I was afraid I'd learn that you didn't want me anymore. I couldn't face it in a call or a text."

"So you had Marcella be your mediator."

"Doesn't everyone?" She wiped the tears from her face.

They shared a giggle, and then Lindsay touched her hand. "Would you like to have dinner this week and catch up? It seems we have a lot to talk about."

"I'd love to." The heaviness lifted from Ellie's heart like morning fog on a beach day. "But on one condition."

Lindsay's brows seemed to furrow with concern. "Okay…"

"That I don't have to wait until then for a good-night kiss."

Lindsay grinned. "Really? After all this time, you can't wait just a few more days?"

Ellie shook her head with a cheeky look.

"Well…" Lindsay swiveled in place like a shy schoolgirl. "How about I give you one on loan for now?"

Lindsay smiled, then Ellie smiled, and their lips met in the middle for a tender, sensuous kiss.

With her lips still smoldering, Lindsay wandered around the gathering until she finally located Marcella, who was indulging some local dignitaries who had been gushing over her. She clearly needed a lifeline, so when Lindsay caught her eye, she waved her over.

"Not a moment too soon," Marcella said as she fanned her glistening skin with a folded program.

"It's getting late," Lindsay said. "We have to get you back to the City."

Marcella looked to her right, then her left, as though she were being followed. "Listen. I don't know how to tell you this, so I'm just gonna say it. Ellie was seen kissing someone earlier."

"Oh my gosh, no," Lindsay said.

"Probably some obsequious little whore looking to cash in on Ellie's fifteen minutes of fame."

Lindsay squeezed back a smile. "Was the slut wearing a pin-striped jacket with a silver top underneath?"

"My mole didn't say what she was wearing. He just—" Marcella looked down at Lindsay's camisole. "You asshole." She gave her a playful yet hard palm to the shoulder.

Lindsay covered her mouth as she laughed. "I'm sorry. You were so theatrical about it. I didn't wanna stop you mid delivery."

"You and Ellie made out? Was she drunk? Are you back together?"

"Sort of. No. And maybe."

"What do you mean by *maybe*? Stop toying with me."

"We're having dinner this week. We have a lot to talk about. But if her kiss was any indication of how she feels, then only a sucker would bet against us."

Marcella's whole face smiled, her eyes gleaming with sincerity. "I'm happy for you, kid. Not so happy for me, but I can see you're truly in love. And other than me, you couldn't have picked a better woman to fall for."

Lindsay held out her arm for Marcella to hold as they headed toward the limo. "You're not going to ditch me once you become a huge Broadway star, are you?"

"I don't know. Probably."

Lindsay laughed. "Not on your life, toots. Good friends are hard to come by."

❖

As Ellie poured their wine, Lindsay glanced around the restaurant at the walls covered in theater-legend caricatures. She could've taken Ellie to any other trendy place for a pre-show dinner near the theater district, but this night called for an immersive experience.

"Happy three months, babe," Ellie said. "Or is it five? Do we count the first two?"

Lindsay smiled and clinked her wineglass against Ellie's. "I'm going with eight. I'm counting the three months we were technically broken up."

Ellie giggled. "It wasn't technically. We were actually broken up."

"Okay, but if I didn't date anyone else, and you didn't, then it's allowable to count that time in the grand total."

"I like your math." Ellie reached across the table, and Lindsay met her for a kiss. "And I love this restaurant. It's the perfect level of kitsch before a Broadway play."

"And a premiere no less," Lindsay said. "I'm so nervous for Marcella."

"Why are you nervous? She's a bona-fide star."

"She hasn't done theater since she got to LA in the late seventies. And it wasn't even for that long because she got her first part in a movie soon after."

Ellie shivered all over. "This is the most exciting night of my life. A weekend in New York City with the love of my life, a real Broadway-opening night, and then an after-party with the stars."

Lindsay smiled at Ellie's animated enthusiasm. And then she flashed back to that raw, gray day in April when she had landed at Bradley International with nothing left of the world she'd known except a few overstuffed suitcases.

It had been the darkest hour of her life, aside from losing Stephanie. And then came Ellie, who had turned it all around—around, upside down, and inside out.

Even at the height of the high times in LA, she couldn't remember feeling a sense of safety, warmth, and contentment like Ellie brought to her.

"Stop worrying about Marcella. She's gonna kill it."

Ellie's words jolted her back into the present. "I know she is."

"Then why do you look so intense?"

Lindsay breathed in Ellie's loving blue eyes and hope-filled aura. "I'm just thinking of how lucky I am and how grateful I am for the life lessons that brought me to you."

"Lindsay." She grabbed both of Lindsay's hands with a big, pouty smile.

The sentiment seemed to surprise Lindsay more as she choked down the emotion that had risen in her voice. She sat back in her seat and sipped her wine. "Anyway, who's ready for some food?"

Ellie stared almost directly into her soul. "I'm ready for anything with you."

Lindsay exhaled. Tonight was the beginning of more than just Marcella's Broadway career.

❖

After the show, Lindsay and Ellie joined the cast for the private party at a cocktail lounge a few doors down from the theater. On her way back from the ladies' room, Lindsay stopped for a moment at the sight of Ellie and Marcella standing at a tall table engrossed in conversation. Ellie was so clearly enthralled by whatever story Marcella was regaling her with that she almost didn't want to return to the table until she'd finished, for fear of interrupting.

But knowing Marcella, it would be a long wait.

As Ellie listened, she reached her arm around Lindsay's waist when she returned to the table. "Marcella was just telling me about the Hollywood casting couch in the early eighties."

Marcella scowled. "The things that creeps like Weinstein got away with back then. Men who never stood a chance of getting laid without that studio power behind them were sleeping with the most beautiful women the universe had ever seen."

"Thank God they don't get away with it today," Ellie said.

Marcella's smile was warm, yet cynical. "What makes you so sure they don't?"

"But today actors can speak up about it."

"Hmm. They did back then, too, but with very different outcomes. Why do you think I stopped being a 'movie star' in the nineties?"

Ellie gasped. "No way. The story was you decided to retire on a high note." She glanced at Lindsay, who gave a confirming nod.

"I guess you could say that. By my early thirties I'd had enough, especially after I'd realized I wasn't even into men in general, let alone some slobbering, pock-faced swine who wanted to crawl all over me in exchange for a mediocre film role."

Lindsay's stomach plummeted. "Jeez, Marcella. You never even told me that."

"That's how long it's taken me to be able to talk about it. I'll be putting it all out on full display next year when I'm home in LA and begin writing my memoir."

Lindsay and Ellie exchanged looks. "You're moving back to California next year?" Lindsay couldn't disguise her disappointment even in such an electrifying atmosphere.

"Sooner if the play's a flop."

"That's impossible," Ellie said. "The play is sold out for the next three months."

Marcella nodded. "Viola Davis's star power. Totally expected. It could wind up being a huge hit, or ticket sales could very well wane after that."

"I hope not," Ellie said.

"Yeah. I'm loving our Friday lunch dates."

Marcella cupped Lindsay's cheek. "Aww, aren't you a delight, both of you. Well, you know where I'll be once your probation's over."

Ellie smiled at Marcella and squeezed Lindsay's hand. "Then I guess we better make the most of the time you're here."

Marcella nodded. "I'll expect both of you at Chez Rolande's next Friday at one sharp."

"I'll see if I can put in for a vacation day then," Ellie said.

"You simply must," Marcella said.

"She's busier than usual these days," Lindsay said. "She started working with the State on developing her foster-care transition program. What she's been doing in New Haven is about to become a pilot program for the state."

Ellie was now in full blush, but Lindsay couldn't help bragging about her.

"Fabulous," Marcella said. "If you need me to do another fabricated interview with TMZ to promote it, I'll call my old pal, Harvey."

Ellie almost spit out her drink. "Thank you, Marcella, but I hope we never need to invite you in for such razzle-dazzle again."

Marcella shrugged. "I thought it was fun. Didn't you, Linds?"

"I don't know if 'fun' is the word I would use. After all, my freedom depended on the outcome."

"Well, as Bill Shakespeare said, 'All's well that ends well.'" Marcella crinkled her nose and sipped her cocktail.

The play's producer approached. "Marcella, the press is here. Would you like to join us?"

Marcella sucked in her cheeks and offered them a sassy grin before being led away.

"Wow," Ellie said as she and Lindsay watched her go. "Just wow."

Lindsay sighed in agreement. "Marcella."

Ellie turned to her. "I get it now. I get it all. If I were you back then, I would've dived headfirst into anything with her and never looked back, too."

Lindsay patted her heart. "I feel so seen."

She wrapped her arms around Lindsay's waist. "I've had the best night of my life, babe. My life in general is the best it's ever been. When I think of how I almost robbed myself of this by being so pessimistic and losing faith in you..." She shuddered.

Lindsay caressed Ellie's shoulders. "Hey. In the beginning, I gave you plenty of reasons to."

Ellie seemed to appreciate the acknowledgment as she gazed into her eyes. "I love where we are now. If everything we went through got us here, then I'm grateful for it all."

Lindsay sighed as she returned her gaze. "You know, during my community service, I'd watch you interact with the kids, and I'd think how fortunate they are to have such a strong advocate on their side. You did anything you could to help them learn to become the best versions of themselves despite their adversity. While we were apart, I realized you did the same for me. And thank you for sending me to Margo."

"You couldn't find a better therapist. Thank you for sharing your story about Stephanie with me."

"As Margo says, keeping secrets doesn't keep the peace. It only keeps us from moving forward and finding it."

Ellie laced her fingers through Lindsay's. "We have so much to look forward to."

"Whatever lies ahead, I'm ready to embrace it with you."

THE END

About the Author

Jean Copeland is an author, blogger, and educator from southern Connecticut. She won the Alice B Lavender Award and the "Goldie" for debut author for *The Revelation of Beatrice Darby*. Since then, she's penned nine more novels with Bold Stokes Books on her own and with friends and co-authors, Jackie D and Erin Zak. She's also published numerous essays and short stories in a variety of print and online publications. *Charity Case* is her tenth novel.

Books Available from Bold Strokes Books

A Conflict of Interest by Morgan Adams. Tensions rise when a one-night stand becomes a major conflict of interest between an up-and-coming senior associate and a dedicated cardiac surgeon. (978-1-63679-870-7)

A Magnificent Disturbance by Lee Lynch. These everyday dykes and their friends will stop at nothing to see the women's clinic thrive and, in the process, their ideals, their wounds, and a steadfast allegiance to one another make them heroes. (978-1-63679-031-2)

A Marvelous Murder by David S. Pederson. When a hated director is found dead in his locked study, movie star Victor Marvel, his boyfriend Griff, and friend Eve seek to uncover what really happened to Orland Orcott. (978-1-63679-798-4)

Big Corpse on Campus by Karis Walsh. When University Police Officer Cappy Flannery investigates what looks like a clear-cut suicide, she discovers that the case—and her feelings for librarian Jazz—are more complicated than she expected. (978-1-63679-852-3)

Charity Case by Jean Copeland. Bad girl Lindsay Chase came home to Connecticut for a fresh start, but an old, risky habit provides the chance to save the day for her new love, Ellie. (978-1-63679-593-5)

Moments to Treasure by Ali Vali. Levi Montbard and Yasmine Hassani have found a vast Templar treasure, but there is much more to the story—and what is left to be found. (978-1-63679-473-0)

The Stolen Girl by Cari Hunter. Detective Inspector Jo Shaw is determined to prove she's fit for work after an injury that almost killed her, but a new case brings her up against people who will do anything to preserve their own interests, putting Jo—and those closest to her—directly in the line of fire. (978-1-63679-822-6)

Discovering Gold by Sam Ledel. In 1920s Colorado, a single mother and a rowdy cowgirl must set aside their fears and initial reservations about one another if they want to find love in the mining town each of them calls home. (978-1-63679-786-1)

Dream a Little Dream by Melissa Brayden. Savanna can't believe it when Dr. Kyle Remington, the woman who left her feeling like a fool, shows up in Dreamer's Bay. Life is too complicated for second chances. Or is it? (978-1-63679-839-4)

Emma by the Sea by Sarah G. Levine. A delightful modern-day romance inspired by Emma, one of Jane Austen's most beloved novels. (978-1-63679-879-0)

Goodbye, Hello by Heather K O'Malley. With so much time apart and the challenges of a long-distance relationship, Kelly and Teresa's second chance at love may end just as awkwardly as the first. (978-1-63679-790-8)

One Measure of Love by Annie McDonald. Vancouver's hit competitive cooking show Recipe for Success has begun filming its second season and two talented young chefs are desperate for more than a winning dish. (978-1-63679-827-1)

The Smallest Day by J.M. Redmann. The first bullet missed— can Micky Knight stop the second bullet from finding its target? (978-1-63679-854-7)

To Please Her by Elena Abbott. A spilled coffee leads Sabrina into a world of erotic BDSM that may just land her the love of her life. (978-1-63679-849-3)

Two Weddings and a Funeral by Claudia Parr. Stella and Theo have spent the last thirteen years pretending they can be just friends, but surely "just friends" don't make out every chance they get. (978-1-63679-820-2)

Coming Up Clutch by Anna Gram. College softball star Kelly "Razor" Mitchell hung up her cleats early, but when former crush, now coach Ashton Sharpe shows up on her doorstep seven years later, beautiful as ever, Razor hopes the longing in her gaze has nothing to do with softball. (978-1-63679-817-2)

Firecamp by Jaycie Morrison. Going their separate ways seemed inevitable for two people as different as Fallon and Nora, while meeting up again is strictly coincidental. (978-1-63679-753-3)

Fixed Up by Aurora Rey. When electrician Jack Barrow and artist Ellie Lancaster get stuck on a job site during a blizzard, close quarters send all sorts of sparks flying. (978-1-63679-788-5)

Stranded by Ronica Black. Can Abigail and Whitley overcome their personal hang-ups and stubbornness to survive not only Alaska, but a dangerous stalker as well? (978-1-63679-761-8)

Whisk Me Away by Georgia Beers. Regan's a gorgeous flake. Ava, a beautiful untouchable ice queen. When they meet again at a retreat for up-and-coming pastry chefs, the competition, and the ovens, heat up. (978-1-63679-796-0)

Across the Enchanted Border by Crin Claxton. Magic, telepathy, swordsmanship, tyranny, and tenderness abound in a tale of two lands separated by the enchanted border. (978-1-63679-804-2)

Deep Cover by Kara A. McLeod. Running from your problems by pretending to be someone else only works if the person you're pretending to be doesn't have even bigger problems. (978-1-63679-808-0)

Good Game by Suzanne Lenoir. Even though Lauren has sworn off dating gamers, it's becoming hard to resist the multifaceted Sam. An opposites attract lesbian romance. (978-1-63679-764-9)

Innocence of the Maiden by Ileandra Young. Three powerful women. Two covens at war. One horrifying murder. When mighty and powerful witches begin to butt heads, who out there is strong enough to mediate? (978-1-63679-765-6)

Protection in Paradise by Julia Underwood. When arson forces them together, the flames between chief of police Eve Maguire and librarian Shaye Hayden aren't that easy to extinguish. (978-1-63679-847-9)

Too Forward by Krystina Rivers. Just as professional basketball player Jane May's career finally starts heating up, a new relationship with her team's brand consultant could derail the success and happiness she's struggled so long to find. (978-1-63679-717-5)

Worth Waiting For by Kristin Keppler. For Peyton and Hanna, reliving the past is painful, but looking back might be the only way to move forward. (978-1-63679-773-1)